The Colloghi Conspiracy

The Colloghi Conspiracy

Douglas Hill

LONDON
VICTOR GOLLANCZ LTD
1990

First published in Great Britain 1990
by Victor Gollancz Ltd,
14 Henrietta Street, London WC2E 8QJ

Copyright © Douglas Hill 1990

The right of Douglas Hill to be identified as author of this work has
been asserted by him in accordance with the Copyright Designs
and Patents Act 1988.

British Library Cataloguing in Publication Data
Hill Douglas
   The colloghi conspiracy
   I. Title
   813'.54[F]

   ISBN 0-575-04579-5
   ISBN 0-575-04779-8 Pbk

Typeset by CentraCet, Cambridge
Printed and bound in Finland by
Werner Södeström Oy

Just for Elizabeth

just for fun

Part One

The Time Traveller

Chapter 1

There is a saying that if you stand around long enough on Bumstead Concourse, at the centre of Alph City on the planet ClustAlph, you'll run into everyone you've ever known.

It's a myth, of course. A story put about by the traders and tricksters who ply their professions around the Concourse. Not even a very clever story, either. Who would want to run into everyone they've ever known? For me, as for most folk, that list would include a lot of total undesirables, not to mention enemies.

The truth is that the Concourse is simply the only place in Alph City where anything interesting ever happens.

The city is the primary metropolis on ClustAlph, the largest world of the planetary cluster that forms SenFed Central – the executive and admin centre of the Federation of Sentient Worlds. The whole of the cluster is populated mainly by SenFed politicians, emissaries, diplomats and so on, with supporting armies of public servants who are themselves supported by Intelloids, mandroids and other artificial intelligences. In short, it is not a fun place. Except for a few designated spots of liveliness, particularly Bumstead Concourse in Alph City.

So I always wander over there, on the rare occasions when I have to visit SenFed Central. This last time, I'd brought in a few kilos of plastifilm print-out from a backward little planet called Vigne Rux, which doesn't trust intersystem comm-link technology. Probably their forms of it are out of date, or out of order. The print-outs had to do with SenFed taxation, and had to be delivered to an Administrator in Alph City. At least he called himself an Administrator. On the payroll he was probably an assistant to a deputy to a junior Vice-Administrator of one sub-sub-department of the SenFed Taxation Office.

I'll admit that I don't care for tax people. They always seem to be more extremely infected than anyone by the public-servant contradiction syndrome. That's the one that causes public servants, when they want something from you, like some small tax payment or other, to move with the eye-baffling speed of a Sisythica ghost-viper. Often just as poisonously. But when *you* want something from *them* – when, that is, public servants actually get asked to serve the public – they reverse themselves, reflexively, and become secretive, obstructive and slow.

I'd been fairly sure my Administrator would react the latter way to my bill, and I was right. So I decided to stay in Alph City awhile, in the hope that my actual presence might urge him to come out of what seemed to be a non-stop meeting and start processing my payment. Anyway, I had nowhere else to go. No other job demanded my attention at that moment – and I had no wish to waste time and fuel going somewhere else to hang around, when I could just as well hang around Alph City. To be precise, around Bumstead Concourse.

The Concourse is a combination of park, playground and plaza, named after the human who first developed the visionary idea of Sentient Unity in the galaxy. He was probably a tax man, too. If he was around to see it now he'd be delighted, because the Concourse is always thronged with sentient unity. Except for the frequent occasions of *dis*unity, when jostling crowds, grasping traders and light-fingered thieves get too much for visitors' tempers.

On the third day of my hanging around, I made my way to the Concourse about mid-afternoon. As usual, it was packed with humans and exters (extraterrestrials, as humans have always tended to call non-humans) in just about every conceivable form. And some that seemed *in*conceivable, even while you were looking at them. I was idly wondering, as I often do, whether any of those folk were there looking for everyone they'd ever known, on the lines of the old myth. And whether anyone has ever found them.

That day, though, was the only time that I ever met anyone I knew on the Concourse. But I didn't know him well, and he was a long way from being on my list of people I'd *like* to meet there.

My feeling for him was not at all improved when he told me some news that meant that someone was going to start actively trying to kill me.

I'd been heading for a sleazily interesting bar that I liked, on one side of the Concourse. Just outside its door, a hand fell heavily on my shoulder and a loud, confident voice cried, "Del! Del Curb!"

I could hardly pretend that I wasn't me, even though I'd recognized the voice. So I turned glumly and looked at him. His name was Chertro, he was tall and lanky with a leathery, grinning face, and he wore the uniform and insignia of a middle-ranker in the Federation Police.

"Garishly dressed as ever, Curb!" he said with a laugh, clapping me on the shoulder over-familiarly.

I don't know why he should have said that. My tunic and trousers were a very modest rose-pink, over a charcoal shirt. My belt, boots and other accessories were plain white with fine pink stripes. And my short cloak's coloration – ranging from violet to deep purple depending on the angle of the light – seemed to me to set the whole ensemble off very tastefully. I'd worn it, after all, in case I had to visit a tax official in his office. Hardly garish.

Besides, Chertro's greenish-brown FedPol uniform with its grape-and-cherry insignia wasn't the soberest outfit on the Concourse by a long way.

But he didn't seem to notice that I wasn't pleased with either his comments or his company. He marched into the bar with me, ordered drinks, and launched into a monologue as if I was a long-lost relative aching to be brought up to date with family gossip. I didn't listen to much of it, at first – but my attention became riveted when he started rambling on with his really big and important piece of news.

"So that'll be it for me," he finally wound up. "Out of the FedPol at last, and on my own, freelance, with Mala. Same as you, once, Curb. Only with all our contacts and know-how, she and I ought to make a good job of it."

He was chortling as he said the last part, so I imagined it was his idea of good-natured chaffing. I ignored it. I don't think I even heard it properly. Just as Chertro didn't seem to have noticed how my eyes were staring and my hairline was suddenly damp with sweat.

He'd said he was leaving the FedPol. And that simple fact meant that before long I could be in serious danger of leaving this life.

He didn't know that, of course. He clearly thought that I'd be interested in his news. And in other circumstances I might have been. Because he'd said that he was going to start up as an interplanetary investigator, which had been my profession once. And that he'd be partnered by Mala, as I'd been once.

Mala Yorder, small, decorative and strong-minded. She had come to join me in the courier business, when I was getting it organized – but had stamped away, out of my life, after some mishaps and misunderstandings on a planet called Fraxilly. She'd then gone to set up house with Chertro, whom she'd known before when she, too, had been in the FedPol. And I'll admit that I'd been hurt by her defection.

Not that she and I were ever anything more than business partners. But I'd always reckoned that we would be. I'd felt sure that she was deeply, perhaps subliminally, drawn to me. And that all she had to do was let herself admit it.

Instead, she'd left. And it took me a long while to get over it. Weeks. In the end, though, I saw the sad truth about her departure. Chertro was an ex-lover of hers, and was also tall and rangy with those craggy good looks that so many women seem slavishly affected by. Mala was not the first woman I've known whose better judgement could be at the mercy of her hormones.

Still, since I'm fairly resilient emotionally, I had put my feelings for Mala firmly behind me by the time I met Chertro that day. Anyway, sitting in the bar with him, I wasn't concerned about Chertro's continuing alliance with Mala. I was concerned with the fact that his imminent departure from the FedPol was going to get me killed.

With a slightly shaking hand I pushed away my mug of herbi-ale and ordered a double steamer. It's the kind of drink that loosens the anchor-chains of your brain and de-scales your teeth at the same time. Chertro, who is never going to win prizes for depth of perception, frowned craggily at me.

"You hitting the booze hard these days, Curb? Better ease up. You look like a man who's gonna be sick."

Sick? I looked like a man who was going to be *dead*.

Because Chertro, unknowingly, had for some time been just about my only protection against the most lethally dangerous enemy I'd ever made.

Those little mishaps that I'd experienced on the planet Fraxilly hadn't just provoked Mala into walking out on me. They had also totally enraged a man named Pulvidon. He was a highly placed executive – and executioner – in one of the galaxy's most powerful criminal organizations, known as Famlio. I'd thwarted some of Pulvidon's plans on Fraxilly – and he had sworn an oath to put an end to me.

At the time, though, he had been restrained. Partly because I'd paid Famlio a cripplingly large sum by way of damages. But partly also because Famlio's upper echelons saw that I had a connection (through Mala) with the FedPol (through Chertro). I came to realize, after Mala left me, that neither she nor Chertro would really have cared much if Pulvidon had turned me inside out and sold me for spare parts. But the Famlio upper echelons didn't know that. They just saw potential trouble in the FedPol link.

Now, however, Chertro was going freelance. The link would be gone. The money I'd paid to Famlio was no doubt also gone, and forgotten. Just a tiny entry in their ledger of extortion, which was hardly their biggest source of income. So no one in Famlio would raise an eyebrow if – *when* – Pulvidon decided to remember his oath and come after me.

Chertro was still rambling, some unlikely anecdote about his latest case, when I muttered a half-excuse and left him sitting there in mid-sentence. I may have spilled the rest of my steamer, since I have a vague memory-image of what it did to the polished surface of the bar. Outside on the Concourse, I couldn't help hunching a bit inside my cloak, twisting around and around to check the throng, watching for a glimpse of the Famlio colours.

Famlio people wear a distinctive uniform – black over-tunic and trousers with a white chalk-stripe, black shirt with broad white necktie. It's supposed to be symbolic, representing the garb of a legendary criminal group that thrived back in the ancient times on Old Earth, before the End. For perhaps the same reason, Famlio is also exter-phobic, recruiting only humans to its ranks.

Anyway, I saw no humans in black and white around me on the Concourse. But I hadn't really thought I would. By then my well-developed survival instinct had kicked in, and I was remembering that I still had a few useful things going for me.

One of them was time. Pulvidon surely wasn't going to start coming after me, I reassured myself, until Chertro had actually hung up that tasteless uniform for the last time. For another thing, Pulvidon would never send others after me. He'd sworn an oath, and that peculiar contradiction called Famlio honour would oblige him to fulfil it – to finish me – on his own.

"You won't find *that* so easy, chum," I muttered aloud, earning a surprised look from a nearby exter who resembled a clutch of large hairy squares held together by string.

My survival instinct was telling me to get off-planet and do some constructive thinking. Or at least to get off-planet – because you can't be found in deep space if you don't want to be. Often even if you do. And I knew that I could manage for years if I had to, staying out in space except for brief random touchdowns for work purposes or re-equipping.

So I pushed my way through the crowds, hailed a skim-cab and headed for my well-protected ship in Alph City's spaceport. The skim was operated by a built-in artificial intelligence, a low-level of limited capability which seemed to be running a private race or maybe just showing off its mechanized reflexes. We reached the port without hitting anything, though, and I would have bet my whole Fedbank account that nothing could have followed us.

Outside my ship I checked carefully around me, then triggered the remotes that lower the ladderamp and unseal the airlock. Inside, I headed straight for my own cabin, ignoring the typically cheery greeting from the Posi who runs the ship. She seemed to want to chat, as she often does, and I shut her up, as I often do. The cabin looked like a small, cosy haven of security, leading me to soothing thoughts of hot showers and cold drinks. So I flung my cloak aside and began peeling off my clothes.

I was in the tangled position of one boot on and one boot off, with unfastened trousers slipping down to my knees, when I got that familiar clammy feeling between the shoulderblades.

I whirled, feeling my balance go as the trousers dropped the rest of the way to my ankles. And feeling raw squalling terror claw at my intestines as I tripped and fell.

Across the room, with a carnivorous grin showing teeth as white as his tie, stood Pulvidon.

Then all the lights of my consciousness were suddenly switched off.

Chapter 2

"Del? Del? *Please* wake up, Del. *Del!*"

I could hear the voice, muzzily, even though I seemed to be flying unsupported through a meteorite storm in deep space. A lot of the smaller meteorites were striking me on the head, a steady stream of them, causing flashes of light and throbbing pain. And the voice wasn't helping.

"Del? Wake *up!*"

It was Posi's voice, I realized. And through the muzziness I repeated a promise that I'd often made to myself. One day, when I could afford it, I'd have her voice changed. To something softer and more soothing, the voice of a warm-hearted woman who was at once both sophisticated and demure. Instead of a voice like a tirelessly bright, precocious and prissy child, which was how Posi had always sounded.

But then her voice dragged me a bit further towards wakefulness, and bits of memory stirred. I wasn't in space, unsupported, but lying on the floor of my cabin, feet tangled in trousers, with a severe headache and a lump on my temple. As terror poised its claws over my belly again, I looked around as quickly as the headache allowed.

There was no sign of Pulvidon, or anyone else. But there were clear signs of what had happened.

I sank back with a groan, wondering how I could so stupidly manage to forget. Out of boredom, on the way to ClustAlph, I had rearranged my cabin. The demi-mural-sized vidscreen was now on *that* wall. And *that* was where Pulvidon had been standing. On the screen. Obviously part of a recorded message. But enough to frighten me into tripping, falling, and hitting my head on a corner of a work surface on the way down.

"*Del?*"

"All *right*, Posi," I snarled. "Give me a minute."

"Certainly," she said. "But there are several messages for you. And one of them – from the human whose image I left on your screen – is very disturbing."

"I can imagine," I said, struggling painfully to my feet. "I'll look at them in a while."

Then I attended to my more immediate needs – getting rid of my clothes, soothing myself in the Omnipure sauna, dabbing some Analgeez on the lump on my head, pulling on a comfortably loose robe in contrasting aquamarine and burnt umber. And to complete the cure, a sniff at a snapped capsule of Soreno-more painkilling mist, following by a restoring beaker of Rakittian demon-alk.

By then I was feeling ready to talk to Posi – though not quite ready to look at disturbing comm-messages. So I checked some other things with her first.

Posi is an artificial intelligence entirely built into my ship. She and the ship are top-level, state-of-the-art, and the largest expenditures I've ever made – a sum that I've only ever managed to get together that once. But I've never regretted the expenditure. Posi and the ship have been crucial to my success, since I became a space courier. And to my survival as well, once or twice.

"Posi" stands for Polyfunction Organizational and Service Intelloid, which gives almost no real idea of the range of her capabilities. Above all, she doesn't make mistakes. She can do silly things sometimes, when she doesn't have proper data, but that's not the same thing. Anyone can do that. So it's enormously reassuring to be able to lie back with a drink, as I did then, and be told by your Posi that no one has tampered with the ship's locks or approached the ship or even touched it from a distance with a perceptor beam.

It was also reassuring to know that Posi always takes messages the way I like – without acknowledging or replying in any way. Theoretically, anyone with a comm-link facility, knowing my code, can reach me anywhere in the galaxy. But if Posi and I keep comm-silence, without any kind of reply, the caller can't *know* he's reached me. And so, more importantly, he can't get any kind of fix on my position.

That meant that I could know where Pulvidon was, because he had called me, but he couldn't know where I was.

With all that reassurance bracing me, along with a refill of demon-alk, I let Posi replay the message. Even so, I couldn't help shrinking back a little as Pulvidon's image filled the screen.

He looked as lean and deadly as ever, grinning that predatory grin. "Curb," he said, by way of an opening, "I know you'll be picking this up, even if you're too gutless to acknowledge."

That stirred me. I'm cautious and sensible, like any good professional, but gutless? I quelled my automatic shrinking and sat up straight, trying to stare coldly at the screen.

"A tale has come to me," Pulvidon was going on, the hungry grin widening, "that a certain FedPol unit-leader, known to both of us, is about to hang up his guns. To be a private citizen, along with a little piece of meat who used to belong to you. Am I right, Curb?"

I felt the sweat start up on my forehead, watched the demon-alk shiver in the beaker as my hand trembled. Stupid sludge-brain, I swore at myself. How could I forget to take into account Famlio's tendency to have spies everywhere, especially inside the FedPol? Of course Pulvidon would already have heard about Chertro's planned resignation. He probably knew before Chertro did.

"So it's open season on couriers," Pulvidon was continuing. "Nobody'll say no to me. Doesn't matter how much you paid once, or how much you might offer now. Your payment was made because you got in our way, so you owed us. That's an end of that. Payment wasn't made to *me*, Curb. You still owe *me*." The carnivore teeth glinted. "And I'm coming to collect. Wherever you try to run to. I'd have your guts if you had any. Instead, I'll have your head and hide. That's what'll settle the debt, Curb. That's what I aim to take."

For a long moment the image was held – the same image

that I'd been looking at when I tripped and fell. Then it faded, and the last thing to disappear was that shark-toothed grin.

"Was that caller intending to be humorous, Del?" Posi asked. Her voice sounded troubled, and with good reason. Yes, I know, artificial intelligences are supposed to be wholly free from anything resembling human feeling. Pure-logic machines with no glands, no instincts, no emotions – or so the advertising says. But anyone with any sense knows that they *do* come to feel things, in their own way. The extent of their awareness makes them sensitive – and their exposure to human responses colours that sensitivity. Whatever her manufacturers might have said, Posi was troubled.

"No humour," I told her shakily. "He means every word."

"How will you reply?" Posi asked.

"Not sure," I said. "Before that, though, you can get us off-planet."

"What course should I set, Del?" she asked.

I shrugged. I just wanted to be out where no one could find me. But I knew Posi wouldn't enter the GalacNetlines without a course and a destination.

"Head for Uulaa, Posi," I finally said. "And don't hurry."

Uulaa is the resort planet where I have my base, such as it is. So it was not a place where I actually wanted to go, right then. But it would take a while to reach it, even at lightspeeds, and I hoped I could come up with an alternative course, a more likely destination, by then.

So Posi requested spaceport clearance for lift-off and, when it came, took us out. Up through the dense traffic of Alph City's skies, into orbit to wait for a departure slot, then away at planetary speed towards the boundary of the Cluster's territorial space. Beyond that would be the acceleration to lightspeed and then the exit from present space–time reality into the safety of the Netlines.

"I recorded two other messages for you, Del," Posi said. "They are not disturbing at all. Should I play them for you now?"

"When we're at lightspeed," I told her. I was feeling too disturbed to be curious. Anyway, I thought, the other messages were most probably direct-line advertising shots. They could sometimes be mildly diverting, if you were in the mood, but I wasn't likely to be in the mood until I felt safer. Drink in hand, I wandered out of the cabin, trying to avoid remembering Pulvidon's words and shark-grin, trying to let some harmlessly random thoughts take over my mind.

Opposite my cabin was the closed door of the ship's second cabin, now unoccupied, which had been Mala's during our time together. For a moment I felt yearningly lonely. Not from missing Mala, since at moments of stress and danger she was always at her most sharp-edged and critical. I suppose I was yearning for some warm and willing female company, since that's always one of the best ways to forget about your troubles for a while. At least it has fewer side effects than most psychochemicals.

But all I had was Posi to talk to, and my ship to provide some comfort. I ambled into the control area and slumped in my pouch-seat, staring at the perceptor screens over and around the controls. The rear ceptors showed the Cluster, SenFed Central, receding smoothly away. I can't say I was sorry to see it go, even though I hadn't been paid for that delivery.

Then the panel produced the sweetly musical tone that signalled entry into lightspeed. The transition to Firstlight was silky – just that one instant's feeling of being taken apart cell by cell and reassembled. The ceptor screens winked out, since there's nothing to see at lightspeed, and we were on our way.

I hardly noticed as Posi took the ship up to Halflight. Because I'd told her not to hurry, she held us there instead of pushing on to Highlight speed. Not that it's really a speed, or a velocity. More like a rate of transmission along the Galac-Netlines. And the Netlines are sort of transmission channels created on that other plane of existence beyond "real" space–time. They link all the known star systems of this galaxy, providing short-cuts for ships at lightspeeds. The Netlines also contain channels used by the interstellar comm-link web and, I'm glad to say, by the galacvid networks.

In fact I was just about to go back to my cabin and look for a nice comedy on the vid. I felt I could do with some laughs. But

20

then I remembered the other calls that Posi had mentioned, and the chance of a bit of amusement from them. So I told Posi to play them.

They weren't all that amusing. But they were definitely good news.

The first of them was from a minor official in the tax office on ClustAlph, to tell me that my payment had been processed and had been credited to my primary account in the Fedbank. All that was said with a note of self-congratulation, as if it was not a contractual payment but a donation to charity.

The second call was an offer of a job.

That was good news because there would be less time than usual between jobs, between earnings. Also, it gave me a destination other than Uulaa – and one that was even farther away, allowing me more time to think and plan, in safety.

Best of all, it was a very interesting destination, somewhere I had never been but had always wondered about. Not just another ordinary planet – but the Home System, the one that contains Old Earth.

The person offering the job was a human named Harkle, who bore the grand title of Custodian of Relics. But there was nothing else grand about Harkle. On the screen he came across like an underpaid professor-type with a guilty conscience – wearing a cheap and none-too-clean one-piece suit, looking sweaty of brow and shifty of eye. Whatever was causing his nervousness was also prompting him to be secretive, for he gave no indication of the nature of the job, merely saying that he'd tell me when I got there. And "there" was the Asteroid Belt in the Home System – specifically, the converted planetoid where he and his mechanical assistants tended their relics in the Museum of Old Earth.

Of course the Museum couldn't be on Old Earth itself. Neither can much else, for reasons that every human in the galaxy has heard about, over and over, during whatever schooling they undergo. So we all know the history. How the old planet had been endlessly pillaged, polluted and depleted until eventually more than three-quarters of the population were starving. How their rulers responded in true human fashion, cutting off their heads to spite their race. How all the have-not nations declared war on the haves, causing a massive nuclear exchange plus every chemical and biological weapon to top things off.

When that was all over, no one on Earth was starving anymore. No one was doing much of anything, including breathing. Radioactivity, deadly gases and lethal viruses quickly mopped up any survivors. And so came the End, as it's known. Leaving Old Earth as it still is – a ruined, crumbling, desolate husk.

No one ever goes there anymore – not even for one of those cheap object lessons about the "failures of the past". For that, we have the Museum. Or documentaries on the vid, filmed by robo-cameras. You can't see the surface of Earth from off-planet, what with the permanent overcast that is mostly carbon dioxide and methane. And of course people wouldn't go down into atmosphere, or land. Even if you put down on one of the safer areas, rather than the vast areas of putrefying ooze or radioactive craters, you could still be in trouble. For, aside from the billions of anguished ghosts that various psychics claim to have sensed on the old world, there is actual *life* still remaining. Of sorts.

The viruses are still there, waiting. Strange moulds and fungi grow in eerie shapes. And the new rulers of Earth, an apparently unkillable and now primary species, are giant, mutant insects called cockroaches.

As far as I was concerned, they could have the place. I would be going nowhere near Old Earth, for the star map that Posi screened showed that the route we'd follow into the Home System, to the Asteroid Belt, kept us some distance from Earth, some way out from the tired old sun. So I gave Posi the go-ahead to lay in the new course.

"Will you acknowledge the call now, Del," Posi asked, "or should I do so? To tell them that we are on our way?"

"No," I said firmly. "Wait till we're out of the Netlines. Then call them on a planetary frequency." An enemy would have to be in very close range to pick up that call and locate my position.

But then the thought of waiting enemies brought into my mind another idea, a very unpleasant possibility.

Anxiety began to fold itself around me as tightly as the pouch-seat when I asked Posi to replay the call from Custodian Harkle. In that second viewing, it seemed to me, he looked even more shifty. And the fact that he wouldn't say anything at all about what he wanted me to carry, or where, seemed even more suggestive. My instincts were shouting at me loudly, and the word they shouted was "trap".

"Posi," I said, "that first call – from the human named Pulvidon. The one you found so disturbing. Where did it come from?"

She needed no measurable time to check the record of the call, which would have carried with it the co-ordinates of its origin. Pulvidon, she announced, had called from the planet Wel-phac, an obscure place that I'd never heard of, out near the Rim in a faraway sector. So Pulvidon was a long way from just about anywhere – certainly from Old Earth.

That was slightly reassuring. But my instincts weren't satisfied. They still felt bothered by the strange shiftiness and secretiveness of Custodian Harkle.

Right, I told myself. We'll approach the Asteroid Belt, and this scruffy Custodian, on maximum alert. We will have Posi run every possible security check, and then run them again, before even making comm-contact with Harkle. Certainly before landing. And if there's anyone out there setting a trap for me, who believes he can elude the perceptions and protections of a highest-level polyfunction Intelloid like Posi, he will come to think again.

All the same, with my instincts still muttering and nervousness still wrapping around me like a clammy blanket, I can't say I really enjoyed watching anything on the vid for the rest of that journey.

Chapter 3

"Mister Curb?" Custodian Harkle said. "You've ... uh ... made good time. You can land ... uh ... whenever you like."

He was sweating, I noticed. By the look of his limp greyish collar, he had been doing so for some while before his unappealing face appeared on my comm-screen.

I hadn't wasted time after Posi brought us out of the GalacNet and into the Home System at Underlight speed. When Posi had completed all her checks, and was certain that no one was lying in wait within range of her ceptors, I'd made my call to the Custodian. But seeing him, more shiftily nervous even than before, made me nervous too, all over again.

"Harkle," I told him, "I do not like the idea of landing at all. Not until you stop sidestepping and tell me why you've brought me here. As it is, the whole thing smells of a set-up."

I watched his eyes widen and the sweat burst out more abundantly. "Oh, Mister Curb, *no*! It's not ... I just ... uh ... I don't want to give details on a comm-link!"

"Nobody's listening to us, Harkle," I said. "Take my word for it. You can tell me."

"I'd really ... uh ... rather not, Mister Curb," he said, sweating miserably. "I'd feel better speaking ... uh ... face to face."

I doubted if I would, since I could imagine how the sweaty softbrain would smell. "I'm not interested in how you'd feel," I said harshly. "There are lots of folk in the galaxy who would happily pay someone like you to set me up. I don't stay in one piece by taking stupid chances."

His shifty little eyes were starting to look desperate as well as haunted. Then something flashed in them, like the Harkle version of an idea.

"All right, Mister Curb," he gabbled. "I can ... uh ... set your mind at rest. Casi, *you* tell him."

The comm-picture didn't change, but a new voice spoke. A crisp and well-modulated female voice, coming from a standard terminal on Harkle's desk. Obviously one of the principal artificial intelligences that helped Harkle run the Museum. And no more truly emotionless than Posi was, since the voice was taut with what sounded like annoyance and disapproval.

"Good day, Mister Curb," the voice said. "Custodian Harkle is indeed speaking the truth. By his order I am unable to discuss the details of the commission that he wishes to offer you. But I can assure you that you and your ship will encounter no threat to your security if you land on the planetoid."

I frowned. Her annoyance was no doubt because Harkle had told her not to talk about why he'd called me. More of his secretiveness – which just pumped up more of my uneasiness. So I put the comm-call on hold, and consulted Posi.

"Del, that is a Curator and Archive Systems Intelloid," she said. "Of a very advanced level. It is generically impossible for a Casi knowingly to transmit false data. And I doubt if anyone could organize threatening behaviour on that planetoid without Casi knowing about it."

That made me feel better. I flicked the comm-switch back to life.

"All right, Casi," I said. "Tell your boss to take a trank or something and relax. I'm coming in."

Posi took over from there, and the ship slid on through the planetary orbits of the Home System. Another time I might have stayed by the ceptor screens to have a look at the legendary planets that were the first stopping places for humankind as they took off from Earth to spread their species among the stars. I did get a glimpse of one of them, whatever it's called, the one with rings. But by then I was heading back to my cabin for something more important.

Not all of my anxiety had been dispelled. I knew I could rely on Posi and could believe Casi. But I probably wouldn't have been inclined to trust the sweaty Custodian even if he hadn't been so obviously hiding something. So if I was going to walk into his presence on my own, it was time for me to run my own personal security check.

I also changed clothes, into a simple one-piece lounger, pastel yellow with bronze piping on the seams and dark-bronze boots and accessories. It was fairly close-fitting, so that most people would look at me and imagine that I was unarmed. They would be wrong.

My personal armament is made for me – at considerable cost – on Clabidacia V, by exters who are the finest micro-engineers in the SenFed. They provide me with well-disguised micro-weapons which still have the fire-power of a platoon. Aside from the two tiny fusitron blazers in my wristbands, I have mini-explosives, incendiaries, gas grenades and much more distributed all through my clothing, accessories and jewellery. I even have some mini-weapons hidden in my nails and hair and elsewhere on my body. Even if I'm disrobed I'm never entirely disarmed.

With the weaponry transferred to the new garments and checked, I sauntered back to the control area and tucked myself into my pouch-seat, watching the ceptor screens as Posi swept the ship down to the planetoid in a graceful arc and touched ground as lightly as an Anostral gauze-moth. There wasn't much to see on the screens, other than a squat building next to the landing patch, because the Museum and everything else was underground, inside the planetoid. But then the extending tunnel of a Manport extruded from the squat building, to provide a life-supported passage from my airlock. Shortly, after walking its length with some care and warily taking a waiting elevator downwards, I was in the bowels of the planetoid and being greeted by Harkle in his office.

He was still wearing his dull one-piece suit, and its collar was still as wet and grey as his lank hair. Also, as I'd expected, he smelt. But it was more than just stale clothing and poor hygiene. It was the stink of fear. Yet I couldn't make out what was frightening him. It wasn't me – I was only making him nervous, in the way that social inadequates are always nervous with all other folk. And I knew, because of Posi's extensive scan, that the two of us and Casi were the only intelligent

beings on the planetoid. Everything else was low-level servaton, robot or data-storage unit – or inanimate, and harmless.

So I watched, and waited, letting him babble on with what
he considered to be social niceties. He even had a servaton
bring glasses of Quillossian cloud-wine, which I ignored. It
was bad enough breathing his air – I wasn't going to risk any
of his drinks.

After he'd gulped a glass or two, which calmed his nerves a
bit but did nothing to close his pores, I got him to the point of
why I was there.

"It's . . . uh . . . a relic," he said at last. "One of the . . . the
personnel pods that were used in . . . uh . . . twenty-first
century star-probes. You might have seen pictures . . . And I'd
like you to take it to . . . to a planet in the Tertellian Nebula
sector. The planet Colloghi. Right away . . . uh . . . if you
would."

"A *relic*?" I asked, when his stumbling speech ran down.
"You mean something from the Museum? A twenty-first cen-
tury artefact?" I narrowed my eyes. "You're supposed to be a
Custodian. How come you're sending a relic to another planet?"

"They bought it," Harkle blurted, then looked as if he wished
he hadn't.

"You've *sold* a relic?" I asked. "Is that permitted?"

Sweat gushed from his skin, making him look as if he was
melting. "It's . . . uh . . . I . . . uh . . ."

The strangled gabble broke off, interrupted by the crisp
voice from the desk-top terminal.

"The sale contravenes seventeen sections and sub-sections of
the Interaction Charter of the Sentient Federation." Her voice
sounded even more disapproving than before. "It is also in
breach of this Museum's . . ."

"Casi!" Harkle roared despairingly. "Shut *up*! That's an
order!"

Casi went silent, Harkle mopped his brow with a sodden
cloth, and I studied him coldly, my mind racing.

"She's . . . uh . . . upset about the sale," Harkle said, producing a grisly travesty of a smile. "She feels strongly about . . .
uh . . . *all* our relics, and hates to see any of them go. But it . . .
uh . . . often happens."

He stumbled on like that for some time, probably encouraged by my silence, telling me about the pod. He said that the twenty-first century spaceship, the star-probe, had appeared in the Home System only a bio-month or so before. The ship itself was to remain in the Museum, along with most of its contents. But, Harkle said, the Museum had a great many of the old personnel pods – so it had been decided that the latest one could be sold, to raise funds. And the planet Colloghi had bought it.

I listened quietly, watching the questions form in my mind, wondering if I should bother asking any of them. Harkle had probably told the truth about the star-probe. But when he began his explanation of why the pod had been sold, his voice, expression and posture all started giving off signals that said "lies".

Still, I wasn't much troubled. Nor was I much interested in sub-sections of the Interaction Charter or whatever it was. There are always a lot of petty restrictions getting in everyone's way. What I did find promising was that Harkle was lying and scared, and so could be put under pressure. All I needed to know was exactly how, and about exactly what.

So I played along for a while. "All very interesting," I said to Harkle. "But, tell me, just what were those personnel pods *for*, back then?"

"Oh ... uh ... well ..." The question seemed to throw him into a near-panic, but he tried to rally. "We think they were protective sleeping places ... something like that."

I nodded slowly. "And what *about* the personnel? Any signs of human life on board?" It seemed unlikely, after so many centuries, but again Harkle over-reacted into frantic gabbling.

"Uh ... there ... uh ... I ... no," he finally said. "Just some barely identifiable traces. That happens, you know, when ... uh ... life-support fails. Over so much time."

I looked at him for a long moment, almost smiling at the clumsiness of his fabric of lies. And growing more curious about the reason for his lying. I glanced at Casi's terminal, but doubted if she'd tell me anything, after her owner's last direct order. Time for a little private research, I thought.

So I asked for the washroom, and Harkle pointed the way,

looking relieved to be rid of me for a while. In that privacy, running a creaky old Manu-rinse to provide covering sound, I pulled out the pendant that hangs around my neck and touched its jewels – activating a miniaturized comm-link direct to Posi.

Posi has many priceless attributes, one of which is a "call beam" facility that can reach out over large distances in normal space and considerably further when it follows the Netlines. So she can access normal data banks just about anywhere in the galaxy. But this time she reached out a very short way and accessed those of Casi. I suspect that Casi willingly made her memories available. She had been told to shut up – but nothing had been said about non-verbal communication with a Posi.

"That Casi is very pleasant," Posi reported after a few nanoseconds of data intake. "But she is terribly upset about breaches to the Interaction Charter . . ."

"I know," I interrupted testily. "But I'm not concerned with laws against selling artefacts . . ."

"No, Del," she said. "Casi is most upset over a breach of the sections of the Charter forbidding the captivity and sale of sentient life-forms by other sentients."

I swallowed with some difficulty, beginning to see an incredible light. "Go on."

"The ancient star-probes," Posi continued cheerfully, "each carried one or two persons. And because the journey took a great many years, with those primitive sub-light propulsion engines, the occupants were not *awake* during the crossing. They were in regulated coma, with life support and physio-maintenance, inside *suspended-animation* pods."

The incredible light flared up more brightly in my mind. "Then this pod . . ."

Posi said it for me. "This pod will breach the Interaction Charter, if it is sold, because its internal monitors reveal that it is still operational. And that its occupant is still alive."

"After so long," I said, half to myself. I had a chilling mental image of a little ship wandering aimlessly in the limbo of deep space for centuries, then somehow finding its way home again, carrying a sleeping human within it. All that way, all that time . . . I shivered, and shook the image off.

Then another, smaller light flicked on in my mind. "Posi, if there's a living person in the pod, how is it that you didn't register him in your ceptor scan before we landed?"

"I cannot say, Del," she replied. "Perhaps the pod's insulation is opaque to a perceptor beam. Some old technologies used thin layers of a base metal in such structures, as crude radiation shields."

"Could be. It doesn't matter." I turned off the Manu-rinse, stowed my pendant away, and went back to confront Harkle.

His attempts at evasions and blustering denials lasted about three and a half seconds before he broke down. I think that right then his Casi would have loved to have been built with a sardonic-laughter function. Anyway, Harkle admitted that the pod was occupied by the star-probe's only crewman, intact and healthy as far as the pod monitors showed. And that the planet Colloghi had offered Harkle a fairly astonishing sum for both pod and occupant, with the provisos that the sale be "discreet" – and that the conveying of the pod to Colloghi be carried out by no one else but one D. Curb.

I might have saved myself a lot of trouble if I'd asked some more questions – about, say, how Colloghi had come to know about the pod. And, especially, why the planet wanted me to transport it. But my thinking had become fully focused on that mention of an astonishing sum.

"I'm glad to know you're getting a good fee, Harkle," I said. "That leads me to point out that we haven't yet discussed my fee." I smiled unkindly. "But the discussion won't take long. Because what I want is half."

Harkle made a sound somewhere between a groan and a squeal. "That's . . . you can't . . . uh . . . I . . ." He grabbed at the bits of his articulation and forced them together. "I was told your charges are quite reasonable!"

"As they would be," I said, still smiling, "if I was carrying an unoccupied, unimportant, legally sold personnel pod. As it is, however, I want half. If you keep arguing, I might start asking for sixty per cent."

He stared around wildly as if looking for help from somewhere. But Casi was still obediently silent, and there was no one else.

"On the other hand," I added, watching Harkle's jowls tremble, "I could be a good citizen and make a call to the FedPol. And to whatever branch it is of the SenFed public service that employs Custodians of Relics."

Harkle sagged, as if the flesh was disappearing from within his clothes. "All right," he said weakly, not stammering or hesitating any more now that he was beaten. "Half. Just so you take the thing. Get it away and *over* with."

"Fine," I said cheerily. "And it's payable in advance."

Still sagging, he shook his head dully. "Not by me. Colloghi's paying me on delivery. They'll pay you then too."

"They'd better," I said, "seeing that I will have their very desirable object in my possession, on my ship, until payment is made."

He raised his head, with another travesty of a smile. "Oh, they'll pay. But you'd better not get ideas about trying anything, Mister hotjet Del Curb. You'd better just deliver the pod as arranged and take your fee. If you don't – if you try to cheat Colloghi – you'll regret it for the rest of your life." The smile widened. "Which would be a very short time."

I just laughed, thinking that I was listening to the bravado of an overstressed and mostly broken man. So I didn't bother asking him to elaborate on what he meant. I was going to wish I had.

Chapter 4

I didn't see Harkle again after that, while I was on the planetoid. That was fine with me, since it meant I didn't have to smell him either. I dealt only with Casi, who seemed to have extended her disapproval from Harkle to me, speaking to me curtly when she spoke at all. But that was fine too, since I wasn't there to socialize with Intelloids.

Mostly, I just waited around in my ship, letting Casi and Posi – who were getting on very well – direct the servatons in the loading of the pod. I took a look at the object itself, on a ceptor screen, as it was brought aboard on one of those heavy-duty hovertrucks that are called floaters. Everyone was moving it with immense care, in slow motion, and I could see why.

The basic structure was a large, heavy, metal chest – a bit like one of the ancient deep freezes that human antique dealers make so much fuss about. But the chest was surrounded with high-tech equipment that I guessed was mostly electro-bio-chemical, with a jungle of wires, tubes and pipes leading into the chest itself. That, I gathered, was what the twenty-first century could manage by way of life support. Though the fact that all the equipment and the self-renewing power source were still working, after so much time, spoke of a fairly high-level capability, for primitive times.

But then I turned away from watching the agonizingly slow process as the thing was loaded and set up in my ship's main cargo area. Instead, I watched another screen. Posi had produced a rundown for me on the planet Colloghi – a nice, short, digestible briefing, as I'd asked.

And I learned that when you added up an ancient spaceman in suspended animation, and Colloghi's particular speciality, you got a fascinating equation.

First, though, I sat through the usual background material. I saw that the planet has an adequate oxygen atmosphere and a surface that is mainly water. And a lot of the water is frozen, because it's *cold* on Colloghi. So cold that the small human colony lives within an atmosphere-controlled dome city, Collopolis, built on a sheltered plateau up on the planet's only large land-mass – an immense mountain. I also saw that the colony seemed a peaceful, uneventful place, ruled by a hereditary Governor. And that the humans shared Colloghi with a species of humanoid exter, only semi-intelligent and quite docile, providing cheap labour for low-level jobs.

It might seem, from all that, that Colloghi didn't have much going for it. But Posi's sketch showed that the humans there did quite well. And they derived their main income from having set up one of the most advanced, frontier-of-technology cryogenic centres in the galaxy.

They called their system "Hiatus", and claimed that it was unique and nearly flawless, able to put people into full physiological stasis for as long as they liked, totally guaranteed. According to Posi's briefing, the Colloghians charged fees that would make a planetillionaire turn pale – but they were never short of customers.

It all made me stop and think a bit, when the briefing ended. What a solution to a person's problems. Even the problem of being pursued by a killer from a major criminal organization. Go into stasis for a few years, re-emerge into a brave new galaxy, and maybe the problem would have dwindled away, eroded by good old Time. If not, you could always drop back into Hiatus and wait until it had.

If you could afford it.

I admit that I toyed with the possibilities for my own situation. If I sold my ship and a few other things, I could raise enough for something of a rest in Hiatus. By the time I came out, there was a good chance that Pulvidon would be out of the picture – since his is a fairly high-risk profession. It looked quite appealing, in that light.

Except that when I woke up I'd be wiped out financially, just about completely credless. And I'd have to find a way to earn a living without a ship – in a galaxy that would be a lot different, given the usual frantic rate of change. I could just see myself ending up something like one of the nomadic psycho-cactus peelers on Bilyssa.

Not me, I thought. I'd worked hard for what I'd acquired, and I was keeping it. I told myself that I'd find a better way to deal with Pulvidon, sooner or later. But I wouldn't go and hide in Hiatus.

So, instead, I pondered awhile about the other point that had emerged from the briefing on Colloghi. I'd begun to see it myself, almost at once, and Posi had quickly confirmed it. Or Casi had, to Posi, since they were chatting away non-stop all the time.

Here was a twenty-first century spaceman in suspended animation – a kind of stasis. There were the Colloghians with their Hiatus – a galactically recognized kind of stasis. The Colloghians had committed a crime in buying the spaceman in his pod. But I knew there would be ways of covering up the crime. And the possible rewards would be enormous.

For I had no doubt at all that the Colloghians were going to try to revive the spaceman.

If they succeeded – and if the person was mentally and physically intact afterwards – and if they did it with maximum publicity, SenFed-wide – it would be the greatest coup in the recent history of cryogenics.

Only a few ancient space travellers have ever been found alive in their suspended animation, in all the past centuries. And of those few, *none* – not one – has ever been brought back intact to full consciousness. Most of them remained in the coma that is stasis, whatever was done to them. Others died. One actually made it to a more or less waking state, but sadly he had been resuscitated by the horned, fire-breathing exters of the planet Haslep Wor. He had taken one look at them and had gone incurably insane.

Yet apparently Colloghi was willing to risk a great many

creds *and* serious criminal activity, to get at this pod, to revive its occupant. Clearly they thought they could do it.

I didn't much care if they could or not. I was more interested in other possibilities for my own income and well-being. I was just considering some of the possible approaches towards a bit of good old reliable blackmail when Posi interrupted me. For a thinking machine, she is often very inconsiderate about disturbing people's thoughts.

"Del, the loading is now completed," she told me happily. "Casi informs me that it has been managed perfectly and that the pod has suffered no harm. She is such an *interesting* mind, Del, despite her limitations, so concerned and aware . . ."

"Posi," I broke in, "tell me about Casi's qualities another time. Right now, tell me when we're leaving."

"Yes, Del," she said, no less brightly. "I was going to. Casi tells me that we should leave very shortly. Custodian Harkle has received a comm-call from another ship on its way to the planetoid, and he seems exceptionally frightened by the thought of that ship's personnel finding us here."

I sat up, alarms going off in my mind. "Can you access that other ship, carefully, and find out who they are?"

"There is no need, Del," she said. "Casi has told me. The ship carries representatives of the Historical Preservation Office, from SenFed Central."

That brought me straight out of the pouch-seat. "Then get us *out* of here! *Now!*"

"If you wish, Del," Posi said mildly. "But Casi has asked for assistance from us. She is concerned about the Custodian, within her programmed loyalties. She wonders if we could take him . . ."

"No chance!" I yelled. "Harkle got himself into this, he can deal with it! I'm not waiting for anything! If the pod's safely stowed, get us *away!*"

"If you say so, Del," Posi replied, and fired the ship's engines.

Her voice held a clear note of reproach, but it was hardly for the first time, and it was the least of my worries. I fell back into the pouch-seat as we lifted smoothly off, staring nervously from one ceptor screen to the next in case I could spot a vengefully pursuing SenFed ship. And they *would* pursue, with FedPol back-up, I was sure. It would take no more than a dirty look to make Harkle pour out the whole story.

But then the thought of pursuit, capture and all the rest fired up my adrenalin and my survival instinct. Which always wonderfully clarifies my thinking.

"Posi, where is the other ship now?"

"It is just emerging from the feeder Netline that serves this star system, Del," she replied.

"Have they spotted us on ceptors yet?"

"I detected one of their perceptor beams just grazing us. But there is now a large asteroid between our ship and theirs. They may have thought that we were another piece of the Asteroid Belt."

"Good." I thought quickly, focusing on the need to stay hidden behind something nice and big, until the SenFed ship landed on the planetoid. And my fear-accelerated thinking came up with the answer. If I had to hide, it was best to hide in the last place anyone would look.

"Posi," I said in a half-whisper, as the enormity of what I was about to do came over me, "go the other way. Go *in*, towards the sun. Keep something between us and the other ship all the time. Then, when you get to the planet that's third from the sun, swing around to the far side of it, and land."

"Land?" The ceptor screens blurred as she changed course, then steadied. "Del, the third planet is Old Earth. There is a SenFed Navigational Warning, number 3310.331, which states that making planetfall on Old Earth can be hazardous to sentient health."

"I know," I said through gritted teeth. "But we won't be there long. And I don't plan on going for a walk. Just *do* it."

So she did. Keeping us nicely shielded all the time, especially when we whisked around a smallish red planet whose name I forget. And shortly, in the gloom that passes for daylight on the sunward side of Old Earth itself, we settled down on the surface.

The reality didn't seem to be *too* much worse than the vid documentaries. The same evil clouds of gas and dust blowing across bleak, featureless plains. The same sludge and ooze in what used to be oceans, lakes and rivers. The same craters, glowing as bright as mini-moons. The same filigrees of green-ish mould and repellent sculptures of greyish fungus, envelop-ing the heaps of rock and rubble.

The same ruined, rotting, pestilent, purulent world that gave birth to the human species and sent us off to colonize the stars.

I've always liked that resonant sentence, which was the conclusion to the first Old Earth documentary I ever saw. And the words were spoken beautifully by that classical vid-actor who does the Smoothi-derm depilatory commercials, so they've stuck with me.

Anyway, I didn't pay all that much attention to the land-scape. I've seen a few dead planets – and while Earth may be uglier than most, dead is still dead and never a visual treat. I was more concerned about what Posi was picking up, through her call-beam link to Casi, concerning the other ship. But then she was given some news about something else.

"Del," she said, sounding hesitant, "Casi has just told me something that you might find upsetting."

My tension level soared, thinking it was about the SenFed ship. But she surprised me.

"It is Custodian Harkle," she went on. "He seems to have ingested a poisonous substance, which has proved fatal. Casi believes he did so knowingly."

I stared at the terminal she was using, wondering why she would think such news would upset me. It came as sheer, ecstatic relief. Smelly old Harkle hadn't been able to face the almost certain punishment that would have come to him. And, taking the easy way out, he had inadvertently managed to cover my trail.

"Casi believes," Posi was continuing, "that the Custodian died because he did not wish to face the officials on the other ship. She says that the officials know about the finding of the star-probe ship and have come to inspect it. It seems that Casi herself announced the discovery, as she is programmed to do, in one of her routine reports."

Poor old Harkle, I thought. Betrayed by a bureaucratic Intelloid. "Do they know about the pod?"

"Casi says that they do not. And she cannot now tell them

because of the Custodian's recent order. She asks whether you will now return the pod to the planetoid."

"No, no," I said. "The Custodian commissioned me to carry it to Colloghi, and that's what I must do. That's . . . how he would have wanted it."

"Yes," Posi said in a peculiar tone of voice. "That is what Casi believed you would say."

I grimaced, then sat back to enjoy the feeling of relief. The SenFed people would never know for certain what had been in the pod – and good loyal Casi would never tell them. I was away, free, unsuspected. Posi could find out from Casi when the SenFed folk were inside the planetoid, well away from their ship's ceptors, and then we could lift off from Old Earth and vanish into the GalacNet.

And on Colloghi, I thought further – now that Harkle's out of the picture – I can renegotiate my fee.

"How long till the other ship touches down on the planetoid?" I asked Posi.

"It will be in 7.48 bio-minutes," she said.

That was all right, I thought. I could pass more than seven minutes in happy contemplation of how many Fedcreds I could be taking away from Colloghi, and what I could do with them.

Idly thinking these thoughts, I let my gaze wander past a ceptor screen or two. Then I sat up and stared fixedly at one of them. I'd seen a weird sort of movement. And when it happened again I saw more clearly what it was that was moving.

A large and grotesque creature, scuttling along without visible haste on six long splayed legs that were covered with hairs like thorns. The body, a shiny dark brown, looked like it would come up to about my shoulder. It was vaguely oval in shape and flattened rather than bulging, with a jutting bit of bone or chitin over the drooping head. The head also sported large eyes and long antennae as well as nasty-looking jaws. Here, I realized, was one of the new rulers of Earth – a mutant cockroach.

It was heading straight for the ship, obviously drawn by the bright novelty. I could see it in clearer detail as it drew nearer, and I began to wish I couldn't. But I continued to watch as it paused by a spreading tangle of mould and gnawed briefly at

38

it. I noticed that the mould was growing on a heaped clutter of rocks – and that the cockroach's jaws sheared away stone and chewed it up as effortlessly as the mould.

"There is a remarkable creature approaching the ship," Posi said brightly. "According to the SenFed Bioindex, it has one of the highest survival quotients in the galaxy. In this mutation it is now immune to all Earth viruses and to fission radioactivity. Its only predator is its own kind . . ."

"All right, Posi, spare me," I snarled. I was feeling a stab of unease as I watched the thing on the screen probing at the ship's side with its antennae. Then it began to clamber slowly up. For an instant, it looked into a ceptor beam – and so it seemed to be looking out of the screen, directly at me. Hungrily.

Chapter 5

In a moment the cockroach turned away and wandered along the top of the ship. Its progress bent a few aerials, twisted two ceptor transceivers out of alignment and crumpled a field-generator housing. At one point it took the thick metal edge of a vid-dish in its jaws, as if testing, and bit off a sizeable piece.

Automatically, Posi activated one of the repairbots out of the hull, to put things right. The cockroach seemed deeply interested in the stubby little robot with all the arms, probably thinking it was another insect. It scuttled over, crumpling two more transceivers. Then, after an examination by antennae, the monster bit the robot neatly in two and began thoughtfully trying to chew the upper half, looking around as if deciding what bit of high technology to have for dessert.

"Del," Posi said, "we ought to lift off before the creature does any further damage."

"We can't," I told her. "The other ship won't land for a couple of minutes."

"If the insect damages any more perceptor transceivers, I may not be able to navigate."

"I *know*," I said hoarsely. "Just wait."

But waiting might have proved disastrous, for the cockroach was clearly developing a taste for high-density accelsteel. Until it was distracted – and I was even more alarmed – by a new arrival. Another cockroach, of about the same size, heaving into view beyond the heap of mouldy rock.

Seeing "our" monster chewing, the newcomer scuttled over

40

to find out what was for lunch. But the first one didn't seem to be in a generous mood. Dropping what was left of the repairbot, it turned on the newcomer, which was swarming up the side of the ship. For a moment they threshed around each other, doing no good to a few more aerials and housings. Then the battle stopped.

Each of them had clamped those lethal jaws on to a hind leg of the other. As I watched with an increasing feeling of nausea, they then settled down into positions of repose and calmly began to eat.

They were good eaters, too, and were each starting fairly quickly on a second leg. A gambling man might have enjoyed having a bet on which of them would first eat its way to some vital part of the other. Certainly they both seemed to be enjoying their meals, not at all concerned about the bits of themselves being consumed. Within a few more moments, they were abandoning the minimal nourishment to be found in the spindly legs and were starting to make inroads into one another's abdomens. It occurred to me that if they didn't die too quickly, they would soon hit each other's stomachs and be eating ingested bits of themselves.

That was when, with the hugest sigh of relief, I saw that the time of waiting had elapsed. Casi confirmed to Posi that the SenFed people were safely inside the planetoid – so I gave the order and Posi lifted the ship.

We were out to the edge of the ionosphere before what was left of the two cockroaches finally stopped eating and fell off.

With me urging her on, Posi put the ship up to maximum Underlight speed and cut a few navigational corners. We stormed past planets, moons and asteroids, heading for the system's feeder intake to the GalacNetlines. Hitting the feeder with perfect super-Intelloid accuracy despite our velocity, Posi took us all the way up to Highlight without pausing.

No one had seen us go. No ceptor had drifted across our path to record our presence for an official eye. Posi's continuing contact with Casi, on her call-beam, told us that the SenFed people were having a fulfilling time dealing with their Custodian's suicide. Not one of them suspected for a moment that stolen goods – one occupied pod, suspended animation, for the use of – might have only recently departed from the Museum planetoid.

So I tottered off to my cabin for a restoring drop of synapsimix – literally a drop, on the tongue, since a larger dose can produce convulsions. Posi put another repairbot out on the hull to tidy the mess left by the cockroaches, while also setting her Netline course for Colloghi. The journey would take several bio-days – a nice long time, I thought, to enjoy some serenity and security. And the prospect of a suddenly enlarged income, because I would now be the *sole* vendor of the pod and its occupant.

In fact, I thought, the extra income might be useful to me in some kind of attempt not to *hide* from the attentions of Pulvidon but perhaps to thwart them. As I lay in my cabin, relaxing, feeling the synapsimix rippling gently through my spinal fluids, developing pleasantly pitiless fantasies about how I'd have *liked* to thwart Pulvidon, out of nowhere a completely amazing thought blossomed in my mind.

There was a second way to make myself rich through the pod. If I was lucky and managed both, I could end up with planetillions. I might then even think again about going into Hiatus, on Colloghi, leaving Pulvidon behind without sacrificing my ship or anything. I lay back and imagined the joyous reunion, after ten years or so, between myself and Posi – who would have been loyally maintaining the ship while setting up quick-snack briefing tapes to bring me up to date on galactic changes . . .

But I pushed that fantasy away and got down to thinking about the second way that I might profit from the pod. Which all depended on what had gone into it. If I could somehow get it open, without damaging the occupant too much, I might find treasure.

I knew for a fact that treasures had been found in ancient starships, even though their personnel had long before crumbled into dust. Back then, as now, people liked to wear jewellery, amulets, lucky charms – things they cherished and would not leave behind when going on a dangerous journey. Also, manned vessels from the past were normally stocked with objects that were everyday and boring then but valuable antiques now. Even those chunky, indestructible Coc-col bottles from back then, commonplace enough to today's antique dealers, are still worth a handful of creds.

But I was thinking more of the kilotonnes of creds once paid by a collector for an ancient locket with a holopic of some mythological Earth musician – Orpheus or Elvis or something like that.

What if the astronaut in *my* pod was wearing some personal jewellery?

I saw no reason why Colloghi should have it. They were buying a chance to do a never-before-accomplished resuscitation, not going into the antique business.

Anyway, what they were buying was the *chance*. They would know that there was a risk of failure. They would also know that they would get reasonable promotional mileage out of simply trying – if they handled the marketing of the operation properly.

So if by accident I disrupted something in the pod while looking for artefacts, and the astronaut never came back to life, who could ever say that the fault was mine?

Who would ever know?

So I strolled back to the cargo area, to see what could be done.

I freely admit that tech-and-mech is not my strong point. But I can find my way around the controls of a drinks dispenser, and I know better than to thump the screen when the vid-picture starts fragmenting. I didn't really expect to be balked for long by a piece of primitive construction from the twenty-first century. But I was.

The basic coffin-shape of the pod itself offered almost nothing to the eye, except for a fine line that, I assumed, marked the division of the lid. Then there were all the attachments and everything on the outside, looking as tangled as a Lybdartian swarm-vine. It became more and more clear that the whole thing was impressively self-sufficient. After a while I thought I was beginning to see the difference between one group of conduits that seemed to be recycling bodily fluids and another group that seemed more concerned with nutrients. But I couldn't be sure, since I was basing my guesses only on the relative size of the pipes and tubes. Then there was the jungle of cables and wires, some of which I believed – remembering bits of a documentary I once glanced at – would be attached to electrodes on nerve centres, keeping parts of the inert body moving slightly, at regular intervals, to maintain muscle tone within the demands of the cellular preservation process.

But after nearly an hour of tracing tubes and pipes and wires to their various attachments, and staring hopelessly at the dials and meters with unreadable settings in a language I didn't know, I was no closer to my goal. I was even becoming tempted to ask Posi for help, risking her disapproval. But then my eye was caught by an odd little dial, half-hidden under one of the clusters of wires that entered one end of the pod.

The odd dial had only two settings, which even I could understand to be "off" and "on". As I looked closely, I saw that the indicator wasn't a needle but a small lever, or switch. Pointing to the right-hand setting.

Taking a deep breath, I turned it all the way back to the left.

Nothing happened for a long disappointing moment. Then I became aware that something had changed. The exterior containers and so on had been making faint noises, clicks and gurgles and pops, not much above the threshold of hearing. I'd noticed them only vaguely, subliminally. But now they had stopped.

And I nearly jumped out of my boots when the silence was shattered by a loud, flat *crack*, like the firing of an old projectile gun.

The line on the pod that indicated the lid had suddenly stopped being a line and had become an opening. A narrow gap, widening with painful slowness.

My heart thumped. I'd done it. The thing was opening, and in a moment what lay within would be revealed. A sudden vision of wealth made my mouth go dry and my palms wet. Stooping, I put one eye to the slowly widening crack, peering in.

Not much light seeped through the gap, but I could see another welter of technology lining the inner walls of the pod. I could also see some of the smaller tubes, with needles on their ends, and some of the wires with electrodes and subdermic filaments, retracting into those cluttered walls.

Retracting from a long, humped shape covered by a plain cloth. A man-sized shape.

Faint alarm began to stir within me. If all the needles and electrodes and everything were being pulled back, it meant that the life-support system was closing itself down. Which I hadn't intended to happen. Maybe that meant that the astronaut had died, with the pod's opening, so that life support was no longer needed.

Or maybe it meant something else.

Tensely, I waited for the lid to swing further open. Far enough so that I could get a hand inside. When that happened I reached in, with growing anxiety, wondering what nastiness might be exposed. And I lifted one end of the cloth.

To reveal a pair of pale bare feet, decidedly on the large side, with at least one ingrown toenail.

Wrong end. Reaching in even more nervously, I repeated the process at the other end of the cloth. This time I revealed a face.

It was a fairly ordinary face, that of an apparently youngish human. Probably a man, but I couldn't be sure. Pale skin, heavy eyebrows, close-cropped brown fuzz on the head, no facial hair. I suppose some people would have called it a pleasant face, still slightly rounded in a youthful way.

But the shock that hit me wasn't pleasant at all when the face opened its eyes and looked at me.

The eyes were brown, glazed, out of focus and started to droop shut again almost at once. But that one look was enough to turn me cold and shaky. It even stopped me from looking for artefacts. I just flung the cloth back over the face and tried to close the lid.

No chance. The lid kept on opening, slow and steady. The switch that I had turned would not budge. In a few more moments, I realized, the opening would be wide enough to . . . to allow someone to come out.

It was time to get help. I could have spoken to Posi there in the cargo area, of course, since she has audio-visual outlets everywhere in the ship. But I was feeling less than comfortable in that place, with who knew what going on inside the pod. So I got out, to the control area, and told Posi what was happening. In a slightly edited version, naturally. Because they can be quite naïve sometimes, Intelloids, not always grasping the subtleties of human behaviour. Or commercial necessity.

"I can certainly understand, Del," she said, sounding sympathetic, "how technological curiosity would make you want to open the pod. I have been wondering about the ancient equipment too."

"I don't suppose you'd know," I asked hopefully, "how to reverse it all?"

On a screen above me Posi projected a detailed diagram of the pod with attachments, then enlarged and exploded it, with arrows. I didn't bother studying it too closely, since I knew she'd explain it all to me simply. She always does.

"From what data I can find, Del, I believe that a reversal is not possible while the shut-down is in operation. The whole shut-down phase must be completed before the pod can be reactivated."

"But the person is coming *alive!*" I said desperately.

"Yes, so you said. And it is remarkable that the process should have been managed so easily. I am fascinated to know that such an excellent automatic-revival function could be provided for a stasis pod so long ago."

"Well, I'm *not* fascinated!" I yelled. "I don't want some old-time astronaut stumbling around my ship! He could be dangerously out of his mind!"

"That is possible, Del," Posi agreed. "You should investigate further, so that we can plan a response."

I waved my hands helplessly. "Can't *you* deal with it?"

"Visually, yes," Posi said. "But to assess a mental state, we need closer contact. Remember, Del, this person is from an ancient time and will suffer great culture shock – if he or she is able to understand anything at all. Close contact, at first, should be made by a fellow human. Yourself."

She had a good point. So I was just trying to work out a way to keep the contact from being *too* close when she spoke again.

"You ought to go back now, Del. The person is trying to climb out of the pod."

Chapter 6

By the time I got back to the cargo area and peered through the view-panel, the worst had happened. The astronaut's efforts had succeeded. He was out of the pod, more or less upright, awake and alive.

I'm not sure how he'd found the strength to clamber out of the pod, since he looked even shakier on his legs than I was feeling. He was wobbling weakly around the cargo area, staring at the walls as if he'd never seen such barriers before. I had the idea that he might have been looking for the door, but he didn't seem to see it when he looked at it. At first he didn't even see me when he looked at the view-panel. Then he did a double-take, frowning and blinking like someone trying to read the label on a bottle when they are very drunk.

Seeing him in such a weakened, disoriented state gave me heart. Even if he was seriously brain-damaged, I felt I could handle him. So I left the view-panel, slid open the cargo-area door and went in to confront him.

Only then did I realize how big he was. About a head taller than me, broad-shouldered and deep-chested with a fairly lean waist and impressive muscle definition. The face may have been youthful but the body was that of a powerful, athletic adult. And since he was stark naked, there was no longer any doubt that he was male. He was quite impressive in that way, too.

He had stopped moving when I entered, just standing and swaying, blinking at me in a dazed, uncomprehending way, dark brows drawn down in a puzzled frown. Then with an effort he brought his bare feet together, almost overbalancing, and raised a hand to his forehead in what looked like a strange kind of greeting gesture.

"Mie rontee moo-sur," he seemed to say.

His speech was slurred and croaky, as might be expected after centuries of voicelessness. But even if he'd had the articulation of a vid newsreader he would have been unintelligible. I speak a few exter dialects fairly well, besides standard Galac, but I'd never heard anything like that.

"Posi," I said, "what language is this droolwit speaking?"

The astronaut's frown deepened when I spoke. But it changed to a wide-eyed startled look when Posi replied from her terminal in the cargo area.

"As far as I can tell, Del, it is an oddly accented form of Americish, a dominant language on Old Earth in the twenty-first century."

"Whaa tizzis? Whirr mie-att?" the astronaut mumbled, staring at Posi's terminal.

"Yes, that confirms it," Posi went on. "I will access historical data-banks for instruction in the language."

"I don't know if there's much point," I said sourly. "I'd be surprised if his mind is intact, the way he sounds."

"And yet he seems physically healthy," Posi replied. "No doubt your species was more easily able to spread out through the galaxy because they had such advanced physio-preservation and maintenance technology, even back then."

I grimaced, beginning to wish they hadn't. The young astronaut was a little too big and muscular, and he was starting to look at me very strangely. I began to wonder if brain-damage was going to jolt him into some kind of insane violence. I hoped not, since a blazer hole in him would be hard to explain to the Colloghians.

But he only went on staring at me, turning now and then to look again at Posi's terminal, then around at some of the hoisting, packing and stowing equipment fitted on the walls and ceiling. I saw that the dazed incomprehension was starting to fade from his eyes – being replaced by tinges of astonishment, disbelief and fear.

He seemed at last to focus particularly on my clothes. I saw no reason for that, since I was wearing a shabby old thing that I often throw on during long space journeys, to be comfortable. Just a short tunic of soft cloth in luminescent silver, with loose blue trousers and low, soft silver boots. The tunic's epaulets, like the belt, headband and so on, picked up the blue-and-silver theme, setting off the jewellery and other attachments. In short, nothing very startling or stylish.

But the young man's expression looked more and more stricken. Clutching at the pod to steady himself, he seemed to moan. And when he spoke again his voice seemed even more slurred and choked.

"Thaassitt! Yurr – yurr*nay* lee-ann!"

Seeming to clench his large fists, he lurched towards me. If it was an attack, it was slowed and spoiled by his unsteadiness. But I didn't wait around to let him get some speed up. I plucked a jewel from one of my rings and flung it at him, holding my breath. It was one of the mini-grenades of soporific gas – quick-acting, fast-dispersing. As the grenade burst softly in the young man's face, his eyes rolled up, his knees buckled and he crumpled to the floor.

I stepped aside, not wanting to pull a muscle trying to catch his bulk. He hit the floor with a fleshy smack, bouncing a little, then lay still.

"*Now* what?" I inquired acidly.

"It would be best if he were taken to your cabin, Del," Posi said.

"Take him to Mala's ... to the spare cabin," I snarled. "I don't want him flopping all over my place."

As I spoke, Posi was activating one of the lifting robots from its niche in the wall of the cargo area. The robot wasn't made for carrying people, but it was capable of some limited adaptation to circumstances, with Posi's help. It extruded two snaky tentacles with padded grabs and clamped them on to the unconscious astronaut's ankles. A bit unceremonious, but better than putting grabs around his neck.

I left the area with the robot trundling after me, dragging the inert naked body behind it. In what had been Mala's cabin, the robot hoisted the body high into the air, feet first, then dumped him fairly roughly on to the bunk.

"As far as I can tell without extensive tests, Del," Posi said, "this person seems fairly rational, mentally, despite suffering shock, disorientation, lack of co-ordination and so on."

"He seems crazy as a Phyquollian thorn-leaper, to me," I said sourly.

"I doubt it," Posi replied. "I have acquired fluency in Americish" – well, she *had* had several minutes to do so – "and it seems that most of his statements so far have been relatively sensible."

I wasn't so sure of that when she translated. His very first sounds made little sense even to Posi, though she believed that they may have been the man's name or other identification. He'd then asked where he was, and so on, which seemed natural. But his last, fear-filled statement, before the attack, was an assertion that I was an *alien*.

It made no sense, since everyone's an alien when they're away from home. But Posi explained that the twenty-first century used the word to refer to any sort of extraterrestrial – which, back then, they only dreamed or wrote frightening fictions about.

"I will reassure him and answer his questions when he awakens," Posi said. "Meanwhile, the data shows that twenty-first century men preferred to be clothed, except in conditions of athletics or intimacy. Perhaps you could find him a garment, Del. And some food and drink, to show that you mean him no harm."

I'm not sure I *do* mean him no harm, I thought angrily. His presence outside the pod was seriously threatening my aim to sell him profitably to the Colloghians. But I set that problem aside to think about later, and went to my cabin to find him something to wear.

I had just the thing – a long overcloak in a deep scarlet cloth, with spangles. It had not been cheap but I'd only worn it once. Then I'd tried that new Atomi-fresh process that is supposed to remove dirt down to molecular level. Except that it also loosened the molecular binding of the cloth. The much-enlarged cloak now made me look as if I was trying to wear a tent – but I didn't think it would be that much too big for the astronaut.

Then I picked up a couple of bottles and beakers and went back to the spare cabin. My return created a stir, since the astronaut was awake – looking shaken and afraid. I was a little shaken myself when the strange noises began coming from his mouth again. But then they were apparently answered by similar noises from Posi's terminal. I offered him the overcloak, which he reached for in a gingerly fashion. Then I had to take it back to show him where the arm-slits were and how it fastened. He stood up – less unsteadily than before – to look down at the cloak, his expression still fairly dazed. Then he turned back to me with more of his weird speech.

"He is offering you thanks," Posi told me. "I have been able to convince him that you are human and quite harmless."

Harmless? I thought again of potential payments from Colloghi, and ran my thumb thoughtfully over some of my rings.

"It seems that he *was* giving his name in his first utterance," Posi went on. "He is called Myron T. Moone, and he was a junior officer in the North Atlantic Federation Forces, which he shortens to NAFF. He was part of a special star-probe task force, one of Earth's first programmes to seek other systems with planets that could support human life."

A good thing some of the others were more successful than this one, I thought. Or *all* of humankind would have self-destructed with its planet.

The thought made me smile wryly – and my smile seemed somehow to reassure him. He even returned it, with a slightly shy and boyish grin. It made him seem almost likeable, and it suggested that Posi might be right about his mental state.

She confirmed it at once. "His mind seems quite undamaged," she said. "In fact he is mentally very composed, to the extent of placidity. Possibly he was selected for just that attribute, since it was known that he would face culture shock, returning to what was then his future. He even seems to have accepted, in a calm and fatalistic manner, what I have told him about his ship going astray – and how much further into the future he has travelled. But perhaps, to him, one future is no more or less disturbing than another."

That made sense. Moone had expected to awaken into a strange and startling time, so he wasn't unduly troubled at having done just that. Posi went on to say that his star-probe had been heading for a fairly distant system, as the Earth would have seen it. If the probe had made it, Moone would have been automatically revived to do a full scan of the planets – before going back into stasis for his return trip.

But the navigation system malfunctioned, the probe took the wrong flight path and began an enormous swoop through nearly half of the galaxy. So it didn't get home in just eighty years or so, but in all these centuries. And poor Moone never did get revived along the way.

Not till now. Not till I, myself, performed the first ever successful resuscitation of an ancient starman out of a stasis pod.

But I wasn't much interested in the achievement, right then. Much more importantly, in that account of Moone's travels, I had been given the information that would save the day. Or anyway my fee.

Moone *could* get back into the pod and go back into stasis. He had been supposed to do so after waking up to look at the star system. The facility was there. And, I told myself firmly, he was going to make use of it. One way or another.

I was fingering a gas grenade again while Posi went through more exchanges with Moone. They produced another grin from the young man, some looks of dawning amazement, then a long, steady appraisal of me that seemed tinged with ... admiration? Finally he came over, almost tripping over the cloak which was a bit large even for him, and solemnly shook my hand, mouthing more of his strange sounds.

"I have been telling him about your career, Del," Posi said merrily. "He seems greatly impressed, and sees you as a space hero of the sort found in the entertainment media of his time."

I nodded thoughtfully. Impressing the young man didn't seem a bad thing, though it wouldn't be difficult to impress a culturally deprived primitive. But I wasn't sure that what I had in mind for him would impress Posi.

"Posi," I asked, "is there any chance of this softhead learning a little Galac inside his lifetime?"

"Certainly, Del. Though you should realize that Myron T. Moone is potentially quite intelligent, for a human." And, after that little dig, she went on to tell me something very interesting.

She said that Moone's forces, the NAFF, trained their personnel mostly through a form of high-speed sleep-learning which was called hypnojection. All of Moone's knowledge and skills had been acquired this way, in a matter of bio-weeks rather than years. In fact, Posi said, some of his skills were not part of his conscious awareness but were reflexive, automatically triggered by the right stimuli.

Looking at Moone, I had the feeling that not much *was* part of his conscious awareness. At various times since waking I'd seen him look puzzled, anxious, fearful, hopeful and earnest. Mostly he just looked puzzled.

But if Posi said he could be taught, he could. Especially if she was the teacher. He even seemed hungry for instruction, and willing to go along with Posi and me unquestioningly. Which was highly promising. So I watched Posi put him under – she has, after all, a full medical training among her poly-functions – and when the big lunk was asleep and the hypno-jection began, I wandered off to think.

While thinking, I drifted back to the cargo area to have a rummage around inside the open pod. But there was nothing. Not a personal possession or artefact or even a Coc-col bottle. And Moone had worn nothing at all, so if he had jewellery or amulets or anything he had to be wearing them in very uncomfortable places.

That disappointment made me even more determined. If I was going to come out of this with the desired stack of Fedcreds, I had only one real option.

Chapter 7

As the ship flew merrily on towards Colloghi, I fretted and waited and watched the vid. And drank too much demon-alk. So I was a little too fragile in head and stomach to show the right level of appreciation when Posi finally announced that Moone was with us again. Fluent in Galac, now, with a good general grounding in the history of the galaxy since the twenty-first century.

I was even less responsive to Moone's first intelligible greeting, when I entered the – his – cabin.

"Captain Curb! *Sir!*" he bellowed, snapping his hand up as he had the first time he'd seen me.

I winced as the sound bounced around inside my aching head. "If you can't speak quietly, don't speak," I said sharply. "And I'm not a captain or any other kind of military shortbrain."

He took on his puzzled look again. "But this's your ship . . ."

At least he'd spoken softly that time. And his Galac was quite creditable – though the credit belonged to Posi.

"Yes, it's my ship. But I'm the owner, not the captain. So you just call me 'sir' or 'Mister Curb' and we'll get along fine."

"*Yes* – " he began to bellow.

"Quietly!" I reminded him.

" – sir," he finished, crestfallen.

I began to wonder if this was the right moment – and if I was in the best shape – to put my proposition to him. Perhaps a small show of friendliness first, to establish trust.

"Now then, Moone – make yourself at home. Look around the ship, anywhere you like except my private cabin, opposite." I thought a moment. "And try not to touch anything in the control area."

"Sir."

I saw the earnest, eager-to-please expression return. If he'd had a tail it would have wagged. I forced a thin smile of encouragement. "Also, Posi will tell you the things you need to know. About food and drink dispensers, washing facilities and everything. And . . . feel free to ask me questions. When I'm not busy."

"Sir." His hand twitched, wanting to perform his ritual salute, but he restrained it. I saw that his large brown eyes were moist with gratitude and humility and admiration. Things were going well.

"I . . . I'd like to say, sir . . ." His voice was half-choked with emotion. "I mean, I hardly know how to tell you . . . how I feel about what you've done for me. Posi told me I'm the first one ever to come outa suspended animation intact. And she said it was all *your* doin' – that she didn't even know you were gonna try. So I . . . I gotta thank you. And – if there's anythin' you ever need from Myron T. Moone, ever, you just say."

I smiled a little less thinly. "Oh, I will, Moone. I will. Count on it."

I was pleased that Posi had gone on building me up in the young man's eyes, no doubt out of pure Intelloid loyalty. It would be an asset, in the small deception I was planning. I'd need Moone's willing, even devoted co-operation – and I seemed to be getting him into the right frame of mind without effort.

The next day or two passed peacefully, bringing us closer to Colloghi, while I watched for the right moment to put my request to Moone. All that time he went on being gratifyingly respectful, even awed, around me. In fact there were times when I felt that he overdid it, that all the sirring could get tedious. So I gave him permission to call me Del. He was struck speechless by this privilege, and I thought for a moment that he would fall on his knees.

Even so, he had his good points – aside from what he could

do for my Fedbank balance. One of them was a total lack of self-pity. He was many hundreds of years and light-years from home, with no chance of going back, yet his position didn't seem to trouble him at all.

"I didn't even *like* the twenty-first century," he told me once. "Anybody with any sense knew Earth was sick and dyin'. Lotsa people believed that if we went out to other planets we'd ruin them in time, just the same. But I was really glad to be picked for a star-probe. Got me away from Earth, out into nice clean pure empty space."

"If your mission had gone properly," I pointed out, "you would have been back on Earth and maybe still alive for the nuclear wars."

He nodded, looking earnest. "I know. It's kinda hard to think about that sometimes. But like I said, Earth was dyin' anyway. The wars were just . . . its cremation. A nice clean way to go."

He seemed obsessed with "nice" and "clean". I was tempted to tell him about the lethal ooze and moulds and cockroaches now on Old Earth, but then I thought that he'd probably found out for himself. He spent most of his time in front of a screen absorbing information, soaking it up tirelessly – ancient history but also the recent progress of the SenFed and the rest of the modern galaxy. Luckily, he'd soon understood that Posi was a better target than me for his insatiable questions. She usually answered with a quickly assembled briefing film, which he devoured.

On the other hand, he did seem to enjoy listening to me talk about some of the remarkable incidents that have happened to me during my career. He especially liked stories from my time as an interplanetary investigator, for even in his day there were a number of fictional investigators performing heroics on the vid. At least three times, as we went along, I told him about one of my best-known exploits, the rescue of the Callitee princess. In a slightly stylized version, since he was looking for excitement and glamour. It didn't seem necessary to mention the lucky accident that helped me get the princess to safety. And if Moone wanted to imagine the princess as a beautiful damsel, I saw no need to tell him that the Callitees are all grotesquely fat, with mutant skin permanently covered by suppurating sores.

With all that, we were less than two bio-days from Colloghi before the right moment finally arrived for me to introduce the subject closest to my heart just then. I'd been regaling Moone – again – with the story of my interstellar pursuit of a psychotic exter called Rimeq the Renegade. That was the exploit that earned me the fortune which I spent on Posi and the ship. But I underplayed that point, and probably also didn't make too much of the part played by Mala and the FedPol in Rimeq's capture. Anyway, Moone was particularly amazed by the sheer *distance* that I'd travelled in the pursuit.

"I don't reckon I'll ever be the space traveller you are, Del," he said wistfully at last. Then he gave his boyish grin. "But I *am* somethin' *you'll* never be. A *time* traveller."

"You never know," I said lightly, thinking of Colloghi's Hiatus as still a possible way for me to escape the threat of Pulvidon.

Moone's eyes widened. "You're not sayin' that you got real time travel, now?"

"No, no," I said. "Just forms of stasis. Versions of your suspended animation."

"It is an interesting point, though, Myron," Posi put in. She had taken a great liking to Moone, probably because he was willing to sit still and be educated. So she seemed to be joining in on all our conversations. "People today can travel forward, into the future, through stasis. But you are the only one in the galaxy who has travelled successfully into the *present*."

"I still can't think of it – of *now* – as the present," Moone said wonderingly. "I think of myself as bein' in the future. Marooned in the future . . ."

I was growing a little restless with all that bandying of pasts and futures. But Posi is impossible to deflect when she is in pursuit of an idea.

"However you see it, Myron," she said, "the fact is that you are a very special person, in this present time, *because* you are a time traveller from the past. There is a strong probability that you will be able to use that fact to support yourself – perhaps to become quite comfortable."

I felt as if I'd been kicked in the stomach by a Naspiddoric stone-tail. Astonishingly, that was the first time I had thought of the possibilities in Moone's unique position. I'd been too concentrated on the more immediate profits to be made from Colloghi. But as my mind raced to present me with those other prospects, I grew more excited.

I could see things like special documentaries – celebrity vid appearances on popular talk shows and game shows – film biogs – all kinds of things. I began to wonder if Moone could sing. Above all, I began to wonder about the percentage I could take as his agent and manager.

Then those speculations brought me to a vital realization. If there were creds to be made from Moone in the long term, I couldn't possibly sell him outright to Colloghi. The pod, yes. But not the occupant. When the Colloghians had finished whatever promotional thing they were planning around his resuscitation, I wanted Moone to be *mine*, all the way.

It also occurred to me that if I owned Moone and he became a celebrity, I'd share in his limelight. Which normally would have been fine. But it would be a lot of visibility, with Pulvidon after me . . . I tried to shrug away the chill that came with that thought. Moone and I could just keep moving, I told myself. And maybe all the media attention that would be focused on us would help to keep Pulvidon away. No, I thought, I'd be as safe in Moone's limelight as anywhere – and a lot richer. And maybe the creds would give me the clout, sometime, to *do* something about Pulvidon.

That whole stream of thought had taken only a few seconds, during which Moone had gone on looking interested in what Posi had said. So I launched into the setting-up process.

"Posi's right, Moone. I've been . . . er . . . thinking along those lines myself. But I see you being more than just comfortable. I see you being *rich*. A *star*."

"Rich?" His eyes were shining. "A star?"

"That is not how I would expect Myron to use his position, Del," Posi said dubiously. "He would be a valuable resource for universities and museums, lending his first-hand knowledge to filling out historical perspectives on the past. Perhaps writing a book . . ."

"He can do that too," I said, waving a hand. "Anyone can write a book. But along the way, he's going to be *famous*. A household name on every sentient world. A galactic celebrity. The Person from the Past. The Time Traveller. The Man Who Can't Go Home . . ."

"What sort of things would I have to do, Del?" Moone interrupted eagerly, his eyes shining more brightly.

"Just be yourself. Vid producers will fight to get you to appear. Manufacturers will fight to get you in their adverts. Girls will fight just to get you."

"Girls?"

"Boys if you like," I said, shrugging. "Armastynian roller-beetles, if that's what turns you on."

"No, no," he said quickly. "*Girls*."

His eyes were positively incandescent by then, and I knew I had him where I wanted him.

With a perfect lead-in to what I first wanted *of* him.

"One thing, though," I said. "When the creds start pouring in, and the girls start flocking around – " he was almost drooling " – you'll need some looking after. It's a big complicated galaxy, and it can get nasty for someone who doesn't know how to read the signals and play the games."

He blinked. "I was hopin' *you'd* help me, Del, tell me what I hafta know. Like you been doin'."

"I'd be glad to," I said warmly. "But as your star rises and your fame grows, you're going to attract a lot of unscrupulous folk. Sharks and tricksters who might try to push me aside and take control of you."

"I wouldn't let that happen," he said, jaw bunching.

"You might not be able to stop it. Unless you were protected, legally." I smiled with sincerity. "So maybe we should get Posi to draw up a little agreement, where you name me as your sole representative. In perpetuity."

"Great!" he said, looking relieved. "But I won't hear of you doin' this for nothin', Del. That agreement's gotta have somethin' in it about you gettin' a *share* of what I make. I mean, I wouldn't even *be* here if it wasn't for you."

"Well," I said, trying to look both modest and surprised. "I hadn't thought about that, of course. But I suppose you're right

– so I accept. What were you thinking of, something like a 70-30 split?"

"No, no, Del," he said firmly. "I want you to have *half* – and no arguments!"

Half? I'd intended the seventy per cent for me. But the light in his eye warned me that he thought of me as a high-ethic hero untainted by commercial tendencies. So I gritted my teeth, thinking that there would be other angles, other times, and agreed. And Posi – sounding as if she would have gritted her teeth, too, if she had any, with disapproval – produced a plastifilm document naming me as Moone's sole agent, manager, guardian and so on, to which he and I laser-scribed our signatures.

"OK!" Moone said boisterously at last. "Where do we start?"

I felt that he really meant "where are the girls?" but I let it go. "We start on a planet called Colloghi," I told him. "Where you'll first be introduced to an awestruck galaxy."

He nodded slowly. "It's funny. All this time I been findin' out about everythin' – and Posi did tell me once that we were headin' for a place called Colloghi. But I never got round to askin' why. Guess I figured it wasn't my business. What do you mean, I'll be introduced?"

"Colloghi," I told him, "will be the stage where the Time Traveller makes his entrance."

And, carefully, though with a few sensible omissions, I explained.

When I finished he was once again wearing the dazed expression that he'd had on his first day. Though, come to think it, he'd had it a lot of the time since, too. It may be how primitives look, faced with a galactic culture.

"You want me to go *back into* the pod?" he said, sounding pained.

"Exactly," I replied. "Posi tells me you can be put back into stasis quite easily. Good technology, for way back then. And it won't be for long."

"But, Del," he protested, "it really *hurts*, when it starts to get goin'. And you feel really *terrible* when you come out of it. And . . . and what if somethin' goes wrong this time?"

"Now, Moone," I said, patting his shoulder in a fatherly way, "you're a big strong lad and you can take a little discomfort. And you'll only be under for a few days, at most. What could go wrong?"

"But I don't understand why we gotta do it," he said plaintively. "It seems . . . *dishonest*."

"I do not understand either, Del," Posi said with an edge to her voice.

I sighed. The primitive and the thinking machine – a contest in simplemindedness. "It's not dishonest, in the way you mean. It's *show business*. The Colloghians bought you and the pod in order to promote their Hiatus business by reviving you. Probably for the galacvid cameras. And that's fine, because they'll be doing *us* a favour. Think, Moone. What would be the more dramatic launch for you? If you emerge from a twenty-first century pod in the full view of a vid audience of planetillions? Or if you saunter off my ship and say 'hi, guys' to a couple of professors?"

Moone blinked, and frowned, and scratched his close-cropped head, and finally began to nod. Posi, thankfully, said nothing.

"I guess I see that, Del. So – I guess I go back in the pod." He turned the trusting brown eyes on me, and I smiled encouragingly. But then the puzzled frown returned – and something else with it that made his jaw muscles tighten again. "One thing, though. Did you say the Colloghians *bought* me? The pod and me?"

"Of course," I said, surprised. "That's how I got into this. They hired me to transport you and the pod."

"You mean," Moone said slowly, his face darkening, "people can *buy* other people, in this time? Like *slaves* and stuff?"

I saw then where his thinking was taking him. In the same moment, I saw my get-out.

"Not legally, Moone," I said with maximum sincerity. "The Colloghians were committing a crime. So there's no telling what might have happened to you *after* their promotional vidshow of your revival. That's . . . well, that's part of the reason I opened your pod. To see if you were alive, and . . . well . . ."

He nodded, gazing at me worshipfully. "And *save* me. That's it, Del, isn't it? You wanted to save me from whatever the Colloghi people were plannin'." He grabbed my hand, cracking the bones with enthusiastic squeezing. "I guess I owe you even more than I thought."

"Don't mention it," I grunted, freeing my hand.

"That is interesting, Del," Posi remarked, her voice sounding odd. "I did not know that you *intended* to revive Myron. You seemed quite surprised and upset when it happened."

"Never mind, Posi, thank you," I said tightly. "I was surprised that the antique pod worked so well, that's all." I gave Moone a strained smile. "Some of the human emotions are a closed book to Intelloids, I'm afraid."

But privately I wondered if Posi was developing an unfortunate capacity for sarcasm.

Luckily, Moone was scarcely listening. He was firmly focused on what he thought was the main point – that the Colloghians had tried to buy him, like a commodity, and I had saved him.

"I guess it'll teach them a lesson, Del," he said at last. "I go back in the pod like you say, and come out pretendin' to be all confused and everythin', like I was. So they do the show, thinkin' they own me – only after, we tell them we're partners and give them the finger and go our way."

"Right," I agreed. "Just like that. Sort of."

Only first, I thought, I'll have banked a stack of kilocreds that Colloghi will have paid me for you. They won't be able to enforce their possession, since it's illegal. And I felt sure that I could find a way – maybe through the vid people who would film Moone's revival – to cover my back if the Colloghians turned nasty.

So I dreamed of abundant wealth, and Moone no doubt dreamed of abundant girls, as we sped along in Highlight towards the end of a feeder Netline and the edge of Colloghi's territorial space.

Chapter 8

I felt a little edgy as Posi took us in to Colloghi on planetary. At first I tried to lose the feeling in a re-run episode from one of my favourite serials, made famous after the furore when the star actress found that her four-armed Entikkian gardener *could* get her pregnant, not just in the script but for real. After that I idled along to the control room and stared edgily at the ceptor screens.

Moone, in the other pouch-seat, was at his most tail-waggy, getting a running commentary from Posi and crying out "Hey!" and "Wow!" as we cruised in through the Colloghi system. I suppose it was quite a show for someone travelling through a star system for the first (conscious) time. We passed meteor showers, crudely faceted ice asteroids, a couple of comets and an impressive collection of moons on one of the dead outer planets. As well, Colloghi has a remarkable red-dwarf sun, and a red dwarf is always worth seeing.

By the time the planet itself was filling the forward screens, I turned and smiled brightly at Moone. "Time you were asleep."

His face fell. "Right now? I kinda wanted to watch while we landed."

"You can watch our lift-off, when we leave, instead," I told him. "And plenty of other landings on other worlds. But first you have to go and be a twenty-first century spaceman in stasis."

He sighed, nodded and struggled out of the seat.

"Toss that robe into my cabin as you go by," I added as he left. "And Posi – have the 'bots tidy up in the spare cabin."

"All right, Del," she said. "And I will keep internal perceptors monitoring the pod as it returns Myron to stasis."

"Good," I said. "Tell me when we have clearance to land."

"We are cleared now, Del. Colloghi has only a small spaceport with no visible traffic. The Intelloid who acts as Controller seemed pleased to have something to do."

So down we went. And I almost felt sorry for Moone, missing out on that first glimpse of Colloghi's most striking feature.

There are higher mountains in the known galaxy, including the Worldgate Peaks on Vaviklya. But this one seemed particularly impressive because it stood alone. It was a vast geological freak, rising in awesome isolation – and rising, and rising. Some fairly thick streamers of cloud swirled around it, broken enough to show me how high *they* were above the surface. Yet there was a breathtaking amount of mountain jutting up above them. And tending to bulge, towards the top, rather than tapering like a cone. I suppose that was because of ice as much as rock, since the upper levels especially were sheathed in ice. It made me wish for a brighter sun, to glitter magnificently on that sheathing. The light from the red-dwarf star only touched it with a sort of ruddiness, like the complexion of an outdoorsy human.

Then we went lower, and I saw the overall landscape more clearly. Stretching tediously to every horizon, softened a little by light flurries of snow, lay the expanse of the Colloghian sea. Though it didn't look much like a sea, since its surface was covered with immense ice-floes, like islands, separated by narrow stretches of black water. The floes were full of ridges and hollows, humps and crevasses, but from my ship they just looked colourless, featureless and deeply unappealing.

Anyway, I barely glanced at them as we descended. The screens and my attention were filled with the vastness that was the lower reaches of the mountain.

Its breadth and bulk made it look like it was a continent all on its own. And I suppose it is, since it's the only sizeable land mass on Colloghi. Its lower reaches looked more beaten and eroded than the upper ones, and as Posi swung the ship around it I inspected the great gouges and vertical cracks, the jutting knobs and crags, the sweeps of glacial ice, all the special weatherings that give a mighty mountain its character. I thought of a few climbers I knew who would sell their souls to spend some time on that mountain's lower slopes. And who might probably lose their lives if they tried for any of the higher ones.

Then our circuit was nearly complete. Into view on the screens came the dwelling-place of Colloghi's human population.

It was a huge and fairly flat plateau, an enormous ledge cut into the side of the mountain. And less than halfway up – 2.58 kilometres, Posi informed me – from the surface of the sea. Behind the plateau the mountain rose in a sheer wall of icy stone. In front of it the mountain fell away in vertical cliffs, all the way down to the blank ice-floes. I stared at those cliffs, and for some reason shivered, despite the ship's regulated temperature.

Then as Posi drifted us delicately down to the apron of the spaceport, which looked to be a bit near to the edge of that alarming drop, I stared beyond the port at Collopolis, the domed city of Colloghi.

As travellers say, if you've seen one domed city you've seen them all. This dome had been built to withstand Colloghian weather – or "climate", since weather as other worlds know it didn't seem to happen. The dome was made of quality accel-steel in the frame and so on, with translucent glassteel on the upper curves to admit what passed for natural light. I was apparently arriving towards the end of that bio-day, and the dome's interior was nicely lit up. Quite welcoming, I thought. And I smiled to myself, thinking how soon I would be wearing out my welcome.

Not that I cared. I wasn't there to win friends.

Around me the ship seemed to settle, with a sigh, as Posi switched off power. Checking the screens, I could see what she'd meant by an absence of traffic on the spaceport. Posi has a standing instruction to find a landing patch with lots of room, where possible, between my ship and any others. But this time there were no others. The closest thing to us was the usual cluster of low buildings housing the port's Controller and other operations, no doubt mostly machine-run.

"Vehicles approaching from the city, Del," Posi said.

I switched my attention to a lateral ceptor screen. Vehicles, indeed. An innocuous passenger car of the plain ground-skim sort you find everywhere, and a much larger skim with heavy-duty housings and a flat-bed platform at the back.

Coming to collect the freight, I thought, smiling to myself again. Won't they be disappointed.

"A human in the leading vehicle has identified himself as the spaceport superintendent, Del," Posi said. "He wishes to speak with you. Shall I make the link?"

"Please," I said, still smiling. "I'd enjoy a word with the superintendent."

That official, appearing on the comm-screen, was a narrow person with close-set eyes. Like all minor officials throughout the galaxy who like to exercise their driblets of power, this one wore a kind of uniform, nondescript grey with metallic insignia, and a peaked cap. They *love* peaked caps.

"Mister Del Curb," the narrow face said in a grating whine, "I am the spaceport superintendent. Welcome to Colloghi."

"My ship's Intelloid has told me your title," I replied coldly, "and I know what planet I'm on. Tell me something I don't know – like why you are approaching my ship."

His close-set eyes tried to widen, but there wasn't a lot of room. Perhaps the peaked cap was too tight. "Why, I'm . . . We're coming to offload the . . . the cargo you've brought."

I shook my head firmly. "There is no *cargo*. There is an *object* on board, in my possession. I am, however, willing to listen to offers for it."

The superintendent then tried to frown, which made his eyes almost disappear entirely. "I know nothing of this. My orders . . . I was informed that the purchase had been completed . . ."

"Then you were misinformed," I told him loftily. "You might like to speak to those who gave you your orders, explain their mistake to them, and tell them to contact me directly."

I switched off, enjoying the bafflement on his face as it faded from the screen.

The lateral screens showed that the vehicles had come to a stop in the midst of the spaceport's snowy emptiness. As I watched, they started up again, swung in a slow circle and trundled away back to the city. While waiting for the next call, I got myself a beaker of warming tea made from the Nardicyan brain-fern. It always does seem to tune up the neurons, just as the adverts say.

Very soon, Posi had the next caller on the comm. This one had no cap nor uniform but a bright and well-cut robe and widely spaced eyes. Also, his expression was both disdainful and guarded at the same time, which would have been a giveaway even if I hadn't so recently been amid the officialdom of SenFed Central. A high-up public servant, I told myself, and I was right.

"Mister Curb," the new caller said in a fairly commanding voice, "I am Enni Slar, the Marshal of the Mansion and the Governor's principal assistant. It seems that some . . . confusion has arisen."

I nodded to myself, recalling that Colloghi was ruled by a hereditary Governor. Public servants would mostly be the Governor's servants – and the Mansion would be the Governor's residence.

"No confusion here, Marshal," I said easily. "I'm carrying an object that comes from a certain planetoid in the Home System. I understand Colloghi is interested in buying it. For the right price, I'd be interested in selling."

"I don't believe the object is yours to sell, Mister Curb," the Marshal replied. "*My* understanding is that you are the carrier – to whom we are prepared to pay an adequate transportation fee. When delivery is properly made. But Custodian Harkle . . ."

"Is no longer with us," I cut in smoothly. "Has departed this life."

The Marshal's expression became a little less disdainful and a lot more guarded. "Dead? Harkle? How?"

"By his own hand," I said. "No doubt the balance of his mind was disturbed at the time, by the SenFed officials who were visiting him."

The Marshal went slightly pale. "Ah, I . . . I trust that the officials . . . that nothing was . . ."

I smiled, with a touch of disdain of my own. "Relax. When

they landed I was safely away, with the object in my care. Where it remains. I doubt if Custodian Harkle made a will, but since he entrusted the object to me, I feel he would have liked it to be mine. To dispose of as I wish."

The Marshal rubbed at his upper lip, looking harried. "I see. Yes. Well. Um. Perhaps you could indicate . . . what sort of figure you had in mind."

My smile may have turned a little wolfish. "Gladly. I have of course considered all the difficulty and stress involved in transporting the object under such peculiar circumstances. In those terms, I think the fee I have in mind is only just and fair."

And I named a sum exactly three times that which the Colloghians had been going to pay Harkle.

That swept away all of the Marshal's disdain, along with his composure. "You *can't* . . .!" he said in a near-shriek. "It's absurd . . . It's *extortion!*"

"No, no," I told him in friendly fashion. "It's business."

"But I can't agree," he babbled, his brow growing damp. "I need authorization . . . the Governor . . ."

"Then go and ask the Governor to call me," I cut in, "so I can stop playing footsie with flunkeys."

He tried to draw himself up indignantly, failed, and settled for switching off abruptly. I leaned back in the pouch-seat, grinning, sipping my tea.

"Del," Posi said, sounding worried, "your conversations with those people sound almost as if you *are* planning to sell Myron to Colloghi. As Custodian Harkle was intending."

I sat up warily, knowing about Posi's tendency to scruples. "Not at all, Posi. I'm selling the pod, not Myron."

"But Myron is in it," she insisted.

"True. But when he comes out again, he won't belong to the Colloghians. He'll belong to m . . . that is, to himself. He'll be free. With us."

"But will the Colloghians not object?" she asked.

"Maybe, but they can't *do* anything, like go to the law, since they *intended* to buy Moone, which is illegal." I put a note of earnestness in my voice. "You see, Posi, I want to teach them a lesson. They must learn that they can't buy and sell a sentient human as if he was an object."

"That is quite right, Del. And after you have taught them the lesson, will you give back the fee that you are asking?"

"No, I won't," I snapped. "That's payment for the pod, and my courier fee."

"If you say so, Del," Posi replied dubiously. "I have another call from the Marshal now."

The Marshal had had time to gather a bit of supportive outrage. He was still a little pale, but he was glaring. "Curb, the Governor will speak to you. You address her as 'Governor' or 'ma'am'." He glanced furtively to one side. "I present Her Worship the Governor of Colloghi, Bartraselda IV, known as the Bountiful."

The screen flicked to a different image, which I studied with interest. Bartraselda the Bountiful seemed well enough named, since even a loose robe couldn't hide the size of her. Though she was fairly short, she was excessively wide. She had a broad square face, a broad square nose, small mean eyes, a lipless mouth and a neck like a weightlifter. Her hair was black and straight and coarse, and so was her slight moustache. She was a bit flat-chested but made up for it with a pronounced bulge of belly. In one stubby-fingered, multi-ringed hand she held a long smouldering cheroot which was the only slender thing about her.

"Governor," I said, making sure not to sound at all overawed.

"Del Curb," she replied, her voice throaty and rough. "Del's short for Delmore, right?"

She'd been doing some checking, I thought. "Yes, ma'am," I said carefully.

"Hah!" It was both a snorting cough and a laugh. The grin that went with it revealed broad, square, stained teeth. "An' that's what y' want of me, right, Del? *More!*"

I returned her grin. "Isn't that what everyone wants of a ruler called the Bountiful?"

"Hah!" Definitely a laugh that time. She squinted at me through cheroot smoke. "There's times, Del, when bein' boun- tiful is good public relations, other times when it's bad busi- ness. This time, I'm thinkin', it's gonna be both. But y're grippin' me where it hurts, boy." Her lipless, froggy smile became a leer. "I want the pod, you got it, so looks like I'm payin'. 'Less y' wanta dicker awhile?"

I shook my head. "Not this time, Governor. Straight fee – take it or leave it."

"That's the way," she said approvingly. "Y' got the grip, so y' get to squeeze." She glanced aside from her comm, gave someone a short nod, then looked back at me. "My Marshal's settin' up the cred transfer now, Del. So I'll send out the skim-carrier again, to take delivery when y'r Fedbank confirms."

"That'll do nicely, ma'am," I said with my most winning smile. "And then I thought I might disembark and visit your city awhile, with permission . . ."

"Just what I was gonna say, Del." If my smile was winning, hers was knowing. "Y' should stay around awhile. Y' might be interested in the show we're plannin' around that thing y' brought. What y' might call a kinda – *openin' ceremony*."

She laughed and I laughed. I could see that it would be unwise to underestimate her. She didn't seem at all troubled by my inflated fee, but I put that down to the effect of an autocrat's extended wealth. She was certainly planning, though, to find some devious way to involve me in the pro-motional display being developed around Moone. That way, she'd think, I could hardly go away afterwards and blow any whistles on their illegal purchase. Not without incriminating myself.

But that was fine. I wasn't planning any whistle-blowing. "It'd be my pleasure, Governor," I said.

"Good." She grinned at me, then winked. "Come an' be an official guest at the Mansion, Del. We'll look after y' just fine."

Part Two

Hiatus Complex

Chapter 9

The skim driver who conveyed me to the Mansion was a human, not a mandroid, bald and greasy and talkative. But he didn't bother me, because I wasn't listening to him or looking at him. I was basking in the secure knowledge that, before I'd left my ship, the full fee I'd asked for had been transferred safely to my Fedbank account. And while basking, I was keeping a careful eye on the flat-bed skim-carrier ahead of us, carrying the pod and its attachments.

I'd been firm to the point of vehemence with the men and robots who off-loaded the pod, making sure they took extra care. I got the feeling that the Governor and her Marshal had made the same point just as forcefully, for the workers treated the pod as if it was made of Ileccatil foam-glass. Braced and padded and covered, it rode the carrier in what looked like perfect safety. But I watched it carefully anyway.

At the same time I took stock of my surroundings in general. The city, Collopolis, seemed pleasant enough inside the dome, but that was probably by comparison with the outside. Over one of my newest doublet-and-leggings outfits, in muted marigold and burgundy, I'd put on my heavy Insu-therm cloak with its adjustable lining and a hood with oxygen mask because of the altitude. All that, to take only eleven rapid strides over the spaceport snow from my ship to the skim. But I noticed that the workmen wore planetside versions of spacesuits, not just warm clothes. And inside my cloak, inside the skim, inside the city, the memory of the coldness of that brief walk still made me shiver.

So did what I saw above me, above the dome city – the sheer and looming wall of the mountain, icy and imponderable. I had a new perspective of its vastness as it reared up and up to disappear into the cloud cover far above. It seemed too big to be comprehended by a human mind. When I looked up, I felt an urge to cringe.

But it held my attention, not just for its size but because of an interesting gleam and glitter from nearly every bit of the colossal wall. I made the mistake of asking the driver if it was what I thought it was.

"Yer right there, sir," he confirmed. "Mountain's mostly sandstone an' like that, but all through, it's all *riddled* with crystals an' like that. First colonists, they tried makin' a livin' outa minin' an' like that. But they got no market even for the semi-precious stones an' like that. Synthetics're just as good an' cheaper. So Colloghians, they stopped diggin' up stones an' started buryin' people."

And like that, I thought sourly as he gave a merry cackle that revealed more gum than tooth. Tuning him out again, I went back to looking carefully around.

I'd been glad to see that there were plenty of iris-type entrances to the city, which didn't seem locked or guarded. I always like to know that I can leave a place easily if I need to. Under the dome the streets were broad and smooth and tidy, with lots of well-tended trees and shrubs, and buildings that were never too tall or too varied from the "oblong-on-end" style favoured by so many human colonies. The city's layout was also the standard grid pattern, with a few self-consciously picturesque squares and quaint alleys. And the main, central square was our destination.

It was dominated by the imposing bulk of the Governor's Mansion, looking broad and square like the lady herself. We cruised along an extra-wide avenue leading to the front of the building, sweeping to a halt in front of a slightly squat portico. I stepped out of the skim, ignoring the hand that the driver thrust at me in hopes of a tip, and straightened to look at the Marshal of the Mansion, Enni Slar, awaiting me in the entrance.

"Mister Curb." He seemed to have regained all of his composure and his disdain as well. He even allowed himself a trace of a supercilious smile when we found that he was taller than I.

"Please come this way," he went on. "The Governor wishes you to join her, and some others, for a light supper. The servants will take your luggage to your suite."

I'd noticed two figures standing deferentially behind him. They looked like small people in heavy fur coats, which was a bit odd in the dome city, though not much odder than the therm-cloak I was still wearing. But as the Marshal gestured at them and they hurried to pick up my two holdalls and to take my cloak, I saw that while they were small – coming up to about my shoulder – they weren't people.

They were very humanoid, though, with round, dark-skinned faces, bright eyes, button noses and gentle little mouths. Their heavy coats weren't garments but thick pelts of lustrous red-gold fur, longer and thicker on some parts than on others. It covered all of them except their faces, the palms of their four-fingered hands and what looked like thick leathery pads on the soles of their feet.

These would be the local exters, I thought – remembering the briefing Posi had given me which said that the creatures weren't quite up to full-sentient level on the evolutionary scale. But their glances were alert and interested as they passed me, and I saw that a lot of people would think they were decidedly cute. And bright enough to manage simple tasks at least – which would save Colloghi from buying high-cost robot and servaton technology.

But then I put them out of my mind, for the Marshal had set off at a brisk stride. Refusing to let him hurry me, I ambled casually along, taking in the Mansion's interior. The building was definitely big, but not complicated, with a straightforward layout rather like the city's – a grid of corridors with rooms or suites or lesser passages leading from them. I imagined that the upper floors would be the same, neat and simple. The decorations and furnishings, though, were in what might be called "colonial ostentatious" – maximum quality and expense, minimum suitability and taste. The furniture itself echoed the building's theme of broad and squat and heavy – like the people, probably past governors, staring from numerous holo-portraits on the walls.

It always cheers me up to be in a place where people have kilocreds to splash around. So I enjoyed looking at the visible wealth, as much as I enjoyed making the Marshal stop and wait for me several times. He was starting to lose some of his composure again, a faint flush of annoyance darkening his jawline. I smiled cheerily at him and wandered along, looking at everything. Eventually he retaliated by slowing his own pace and giving me a guided tour with more details than anyone could want.

Finally the main corridor from the entrance led us to what he described as the official Receiving Hall – big and bright and airy, with pillars, chandeliers, a painted ceiling and a gleam-ing floor. At one end squatted a huge table with a throne-like chair for the Governor dominating. But we passed through all that ostentation into a smaller adjoining room, with a smaller and less formal table on which was laid out an amazing variety of things to eat and drink. If this is a light supper, I thought, I'd love to come to a feast. But I tore my gaze away from the goodies to give a respectful greeting to Governor Bartraselda, seated at the far end of the table.

She seemed in a relaxed and expansive mood. With one of those batrachian smiles that extended into a leer, she waved the hand that held another cheroot. "Del, come in, glad to see y'. Grab that seat there."

I inclined my head in a sketch of a bow and reached for the chair she indicated. Till then I'd hardly noticed the other two people – only that across the table sat a big man with a shiny naked scalp while next to my chair, turned away to face Bartraselda, sat someone with a tousle of curly dark-brown hair. But when the brown-haired person turned, all my percep-tions went to pin-point focus while my stomach contracted and my knees turned to jelly.

Her face was not perfect or even conventionally pretty, but that only served to make her more beautiful. Her eyes were dark and luminous, her skin was porcelain-smooth, her mouth was sweet and sumptuous with a small gap between the front teeth making her smile even more entrancing. Though she was seated, I knew she was tall for a woman, about my height. Though she wore a plain white one-piece, I knew that her figure would curl the toes of men dead for centuries. I'd never seen her in the flesh before, yet every molecule of her face was familiar to me. I felt I'd known her for years, and I'd fantasized about her almost every day of those years.

Jarli Firov. *The* Jarli Firov. Presenter, link-person and star of the galacvid's most popular magazine show, "In the Net". Jarli the non-stop traveller, who flashed back and forth across the galaxy to dig out all the weird, quirky, fascinating stories that the SenFed's incredible diversity has to offer. Though in most cases the only thing people like me remembered about one of her shows was *her* – and what clothes she wore, or didn't quite wear, each time.

Jarli Firov. The Highlight Heart-throb. Right *there*, at a table where *I* was going to sit. And *smiling* at me.

"Hah!" As if from a great distance, I heard Bartraselda's bark of laughter. "Guess I don't hafta introduce Jarli to y', Del. Y' better siddown 'fore y'r pants get any tighter."

She went into a spasm of strangled laughing as I sank into my chair – flushing a little, because Jarli *was* having, slightly, the effect Bartraselda was referring to. And Jarli knew it. So she let her smile crinkle a little, in sympathy, causing my vision to blur and what sounded like a full orchestra to start up in my inner ears.

Then she numbed me completely by reaching over to shake my hand. "Nice to meet you, Del Curb," she said in her melodious contralto. "I understand you're the one who has brought the . . . guest of honour."

I mumbled something in a voice that seemed corroded, while Bartraselda went into another fit of hilarious strangulation.

"If y' can look away from Jarli f'r a sec', Del," she whooped, "this fella over here's Doctor Rocdril. Gotta be nice to him, 'cause he's the second most important person on Colloghi after me."

The big man with the gleaming hairless head half-rose from his seat. His face was florid, his hands were large and powerful, his white suit was spotless, and his eyes were as cold as Colloghi's sky. "Curb," he said, with the briefest of nods.

"The doc," Bartraselda was adding, "is the big brain in charge of the Hiatus Complex. Y'know? An' he's a kinda useful fella in *lotsa* ways."

The suggestive tone in her voice, the return of her leer and the way she reached over to grab the thigh of Doctor Rocdril told me a couple of interesting things. First, that she was probably making use of more than the doctor's brains. Second, that she was well on her way to being drunk.

But, I thought, why not? She was a hereditary ruler who could do pretty much as she pleased, and did. In that position, not many of us would be models of sobriety and rectitude. I glanced at Jarli, who was doing something to a small pastry on her plate, and had a brief vision of the special joys that a hereditary ruler's power might provide.

Bartraselda gestured, and one of the furry exters scurried swiftly to the table. I'd vaguely noticed several of them standing silently against the wall, obviously waiting on table. This one refilled Bartraselda's beaker – it looked like fever-gin from Dall'Achia – then came around to serve me. It seemed bright-eyed and alert like the others I'd seen, deft-fingered as it served me the food I indicated and poured me a tall glass of Ye-priddish petal-juice. Its fur, even more lustrously golden seen close to, had a light, spicy odour. And I saw that the creatures were not only humanoid but very mammalian – for when the one serving me leaned further over, two small pale breasts with brown nipples peeped out through the thick pelt on its chest.

But I registered all that only dimly, paying more attention to Jarli's bosom, and the rest of her, while listening to the Governor.

". . . sort of a celebration supper, Del," she was saying. "Jarli just got here yesterday, an' now you're here with what Jarli calls the guest of honour. So now we can get goin' – get things settled about the show."

"It shouldn't be too complicated," Jarli said in that magical voice. "I've got the script mostly roughed out already."

"I'll wanta see that," Bartraselda said.

Jarli nodded. "When it's tidied up."

"And I," Rocdril put in sharply.

Jarli raised a cool eyebrow. "The Governor has script approval by contract, doctor. You don't."

Rocdril's face flushed darker. "You are going to stage your circus *inside* the Hiatus Complex – and there, I am in charge! There are things that must be protected, areas that must remain secure . . ."

"Leave it, Rocky," Bartraselda cut in, with an edge to her voice that cut through the alcoholic slurring. "I'll show y' the script if y' want. But *I* say yes or no to Jarli. Nobody else."

Rocdril glared and fumed, but subsided. And I grew a little thoughtful. The impact of meeting a ravishing vid-star may have distracted me, but that sharp little exchange stirred my instincts – into reminding me what I was doing there, and where my problems lay. They had nothing to do with script approval.

The Governor had committed a crime by buying the pod with occupant. So had I, by handling and re-selling it. So I was keenly interested to know how they were going to get round that point when they *filmed* the pod and occupant for a popular vid-show.

Jarli was talking quietly to Bartraselda about a minor production point when I cleared my throat and interrupted.

"I was wondering when this show of yours was going to happen," I said to Jarli. "Because the Governor sort of invited me to stay around for it."

"*For* it?" she echoed, melting my knees with another mega-watt smile.

Bartraselda was grinning as well. "It'll jus' be a day or two, maybe three. While Jarli gets it all set up. An' y' *better* stay, Del, or Jarli'll be real disappointed."

Jarli widened her smile as I looked at them both, puzzled. "I checked you out," she said, "when they told me who was bringing the pod. You're fairly well known, Del Curb. Investigator turned courier – quite a few exploits behind you . . . So I thought an interview with you, the courier, would add something to the show."

That remark caused even her smile to become dimmed in

my eyes. I sank back into my chair with the impact. She – they – wanted me *on* the show. To be watched by planetillions.

A lot of things flashed through my mind. Including the advertising benefits to my business. Including the confirmation that Colloghi wanted to connect me visibly – galaxy-wide – with the pod so I'd tell no tales later. And including the gleeful thought of how Pulvidon would gnash those shark teeth if he saw me on the vid, on my way to being a celebrity.

Chapter 10

Naturally, I also thought about how my being on the show would bring me into proximity with Jarli. And when I considered all those possibilities together, my brow got a little damp and my hands trembled slightly. Which Jarli saw, and misinterpreted.

"Don't worry about it," she said. "You'll be fine. I won't embarrass you."

"Jus' listen to Jarli, Del," Bartraselda put in, with an exaggerated wink. "She's the pro – she'll look after y'. She'll jus' ask y' stuff like how y' got the pod, how far y' came, what y' think about revivin' the spaceman an' all."

I looked at the Governor carefully. "You want me to say how I *got* the pod?"

"Surely," Jarli said, her eyes clear and guileless. "The Governor has told me all about how she bought the pod from a tribe of space gypsies, near the Tracaxxal system, who refused to say where they got it. She felt it was her human duty to reclaim it, and to see if the unfortunate occupant could be brought back to life after all these centuries."

I stared. "That's what the show is going to say?"

"It is," Bartraselda said. Again her voice had lost all gin-induced sloppiness and her gaze was direct and hard.

Jarli frowned, looking from one to the other. "What is it? Isn't that what happened?"

"Sure," Bartraselda said, her gaze fixed on me, making certain that I got the message. "Del just knows we're kinda stretchin' a point. The gypsies coulda got the thing in some crooked way – so the law could say we're handlin' stolen goods."

"But you don't *know* that," Jarli said, her frown clearing. "And the point is that you *rescued* the pod, with its occupant. So – that's what my programme will say."

Trust a media person, I thought admiringly. It was a first-class rationalization which I couldn't have bettered myself.

"Sounds fine to me," I said quickly. "And don't worry, Jarli. I'm a professional too, in my way."

"'Course y' are, Del," Bartraselda said, her cheery slur returning. "Knew we c'd count on y'. 'Specially after that fancy fee y' got outa me."

I considered the notion then of asking for a bonus to cover unexpected vid appearances. But I decided against it. Being greedy can bring trouble, in my experience. So I said nothing, just went on sunning myself in Jarli's grateful smile.

Until the occasion was flung into noisy chaos.

The little furry exter who'd served me had come back to the table to refill Rocdril's cup. But all the agile deftness that it had shown with me seemed to have deserted it. Somehow its hand seemed to jerk, and half the contents of the pitcher – something herbal and hot – cascaded into Rocdril's lap.

He leaped up, roaring, purple with fury, sending the little creature sprawling with a vicious backhand. *"Every time!"* he bellowed, glaring at Bartraselda. "Every time I sit at a table in this place, it happens! Soup, sauce, drink, *something* is spilled over me! I've had *enough* of these clumsy animals!"

As he spoke he was ripping a heavy belt from around his waist. I watched with vague interest as he lashed out at the crouching exter. The belt whistled as he struck again and again, with all his strength, at the bowed, furry back. The exter cowered, wrapping its arms around its head, squeaking in high-pitched anguish.

And to my astonishment, the squeaks made sense. Garbled and badly articulated, but recognizable *words*.

"No – Mast' – no!" the creature squeaked. "No hit – no hit – no hurt . . .!"

Rocdril's arm rose and fell relentlessly, his grunts of effort counterpointing the belt's muffled thud on the thick fur. Bartraselda licked her toad-lips and watched, bright-eyed. Neither of them seemed surprised to hear the creature speak. Nor did Jarli, but her reaction was quite different.

She flung her chair back and leaped to her feet. "Stop it!" she yelled. "Stop! You'll *kill* it, you sadist!"

Arm raised, belt poised, Rocdril turned his florid face towards her. "Shut your mouth," he snarled. "If I do kill it, there's plenty more. It's nothing to do with you."

I saw Bartraselda's smile start to fade. Guessing that she disapproved of anything that risked alienating the vid-star, I saw a chance to gain a few points for myself in two directions. I pushed my own chair back and rose easily to my feet.

"You've made your point, doc," I drawled. "Maybe you'd better stop, like the lady says. Put your belt back on before your pants fall down."

Rocdril turned his livid glare on me, but I stared back coolly. The table was between us, and he was only holding a belt. I could have dropped him with a mini-weapon before he got anywhere near me. *And* left him alive.

"Doctor." That was Bartraselda, chiming in with her hard, unslurred voice. "Do as our *guests* say."

Rocdril began to speak, then saw something in her eyes and changed his mind. Whirling, he stalked from the room. The little exter unwrapped its arms, looking wonderingly around at me. But I was more interested in Jarli as she turned to me, her eyes filled with warmth and approval.

"Thanks," she said. "I just hate that kind of cruelty."

"Oh, right, me too," I said earnestly. "Glad to help."

"Excitin' place, Collopolis, eh, Del?" Bartraselda said, grinning. As she spoke she beckoned to the little exter, who got up and went to her. It was still quivering with apparent distress, and in absent-minded kindliness Bartraselda stroked the golden fur of its back to quieten it.

I watched with some interest. "Your exters seem fairly advanced, Governor," I said idly. "Working as servants – able to speak . . ."

She shrugged. "They're pretty good for sub-sentients, yeah. Not too hard to train, though they can be scatty sometimes.

Short attention span. They're not the only sub-sents that pick up a sorta pidgin from human speech. But they never get more'n those bits."

"They *are* native to the planet?" I asked.

"Oh, yeah. Before the colony, they all lived down on the ice-floes, gettin' what they needed from the sea. Some of the first colonists tried huntin' them for fur, but it's just too rotten cold and rough out there. More colonists died than Logies."

"Logies?" I echoed.

"It's sorta what they call themselves. They got a bit of a half-language of their own, like lots of the higher sub-sents. An' their name for their world is somethin' like Colloghi, so the colonists borrowed it, like often happens." She nudged the little creature by her side. "Say name all you kind."

The creature blinked, then looked at me. "Logh-uy," it said. When not squealing in pain, its voice was sweetly musical, though quite high-pitched – like the upper registers of a Binnearic larynx-flute.

"There y' go," Bartraselda said, looking as pleased as any owner when their pet has done a trick. "Cute li'l thing, ain't she?"

"Then it *is* a female?"

Bartraselda leered. "C'mon, Del, I saw y' lookin'. Those li'l tits ain't no skin disease. An' the boys, they got nice li'l parts too, if you can find 'em in all that fur."

Then she belched, hoisted her beaker, drained it and thumped it back on the table. "I reckon supper's over, folks," she announced. "Seein' we've had the floor show an' everythin'. Me, I got some city business to look at 'fore I get to sleep. You OK now, Jarli?"

Jarli nodded her curly dark head. "I have things to do, too. I should work on the script and think about lighting and things." She smiled wryly. "Providing that Doctor Rocdril lets me into the Complex at all, after tonight."

"Hah!" Bartraselda laughed. "He'll let y' in. It'll be like nothin' happened. He'll be just as stiff-necked an' cold-blooded as ever."

Jarli grimaced, then changed it to a smile as she turned to me. "It'd be nice if you could spend some time with me tomorrow, Del. I'm going to be shown around the Complex, to check locations and things. If you could come and look around as well, we could find time to talk about your interview."

I leaned slightly back, to be sure that I wouldn't fall into her eyes and drown. "Fine," I said. "I'm . . . sort of at a loose end anyway."

"We'll start right after breakfast, then," she said.

I badly wanted to suggest something that we could start *before* breakfast, but it wasn't easy with Bartraselda grinning at us. Then Jarli got gracefully to her feet and it was too late. I sagged a little as she left the room, feeling as if someone had shut off the lights around me.

Bartraselda leaned back and laughed. "One thing's sure, Del – y're not a fella that don't care f'r women. I know she's a pretty thing, but y' look like y' been lobotomized."

I tried to gather myself. "It's just that a lot has happened," I said stiffly. "About being on the show and everything. And I'm just down from a long run in Highlight. I think I should get some rest myself."

"Right," she said, nodding. "Take things easy – no pressure here." She reached to the little exter, still hovering beside her, and gave her a gentle push. "Seliki here'll show y' where y're stayin'."

"Thanks . . . uh, ma'am," I said, remembering my manners as I left the table. I glanced at the little exter, half-smiling at its bright-eyed readiness to serve. "Seliki?"

"Mast' come," it said in its high, sweet treble, and moved away.

"Y' can have Seliki to look after y' alla time y're here," Bartraselda said, as I began to follow. "Reckon she can take care of just about *all* y'r needs."

And what sounded like ribald guffaws followed me as Seliki and I left the room.

The little Logie led me back out through the magnificent Receiving Hall and into the grid of corridors. Soon we peeled off from the central corridor along a slightly lesser passage, which brought us to an open foyer and a grand, sweeping staircase that we began to climb. At the top we turned along another sub-corridor, and I wondered idly how long it took to teach the furry sub-sents the layout of the Mansion. Not long, I guessed, since they seemed bright and capable for their evolutionary level.

That led me to think again of how Seliki had drenched Doctor Rocdril, and how he'd complained that it happened all the time. And a thought struck me. Every Logie I'd seen had seemed physically neat and well co-ordinated. I wondered, with some private amusement, if Seliki and the other Logie servants simply didn't *like* Rocdril. And had their own way of showing it.

If so, good for them, I thought, for I didn't much care for the doctor myself. I'd been pleased to face him down and win a definitely warm response from Jarli. And the recollection led me into an enjoyable fantasy sequence involving a divergence from the planned tour of the Hiatus Complex, next day.

The fantasy ended a little too soon when Seliki came to a stop in front of a tall door at the end of a side corridor. "Mast' place," she announced, flinging the door open.

It was a large, airy, well-lit suite, abundantly and luxuriously furnished. The view from the windows was interesting, looking out over the city to the mighty wall of the mountain beyond. The view of a side table was also interesting, since it held containers of many exotic drinks including Elovskiic liquigasm, one of my favourites. I was also glad to see my two travelling holdalls waiting for me, just next to a good-sized galacvid screen.

Normally I would have poured a drink and lounged awhile on the king-size couch, watching the vid or maybe re-running the Jarli fantasy. But during the walk to the suite I'd begun to feel faintly peculiar, and in the suite I felt more so. My head was feeling weirdly heavy. Not a real ache in the usual sense, but a kind of inner pressure that I didn't like at all. So I decided to do without any more drink or anything and to go straight to bed. The last thing I wanted was to be unwell when I was going to have a day out with the Highlight Heart-throb.

Just as I reached that virtuous decision, Seliki astonished me with a completely unexpected question.

"Mast' want hit 'fore bang-bang?"

I stared at her. Her voice had been entirely matter-of-fact, as if she was asking if I wanted my boots cleaned.

"Bang-bang?" I repeated, wondering if it really meant what it sounded like.

In reply, she slid a small hand down between her thighs and parted the extra-long, thick fur. What was partly revealed left me in absolutely no further doubt that she was very humanoid and extremely female. Then she made a gesture with that hand, and a movement with her hips, that left me also in no doubt about what her question meant.

"Bang-bang," she said gravely.

"Um," I said, staring at her groin.

She moved her hand away, smiling. "Hit first? Tie down? Mast' say."

The willing docility in Seliki's voice made me toy briefly with the thought of accepting her offer. But I decided against it. I thought it might be fun, but it wouldn't do if others found out – through servants' gossip or whatever – that I'd abused Seliki in any way. Not when I'd gained Jarli's favour by *rescuing* Seliki from abuse.

Anyway, I wasn't feeling up to it. I was tired, I'd had a few drinks at the supper, my head was feeling very peculiar.

"No hit, Seliki," I told her, trying to match the pidgin. "And no bang-bang."

She had moved closer to me, her spicy aroma all around me. "Seliki no please?" she asked, sounding startled and troubled.

I smiled and reached out to touch her, feeling a jolt of astonishment at the fine-grained delicacy of that lush pelt. I stroked her for a moment, enjoying the sensation, letting my hand trail around to where the firm little breasts nestled in the fur.

"You're very pleasing," I told her. "But I'm tired. And I don't want to hit you, or anything."

She seemed to understand, though I hadn't used the pidgin. She clasped my hand in both of hers, pressing my palm against her breast. "Mast' *kind*," she breathed, little sharp teeth gleaming in a sweet smile. "Mast' *good*."

I nodded amiably, taking my hand away with some reluctance, enjoying what looked like adoration glowing in her eyes. "If you say so. Right now I just want to go to bed. Alone."

She smiled even more sweetly. "Seliki help."

And help she did. In fact she got me to bed without my having to lift a finger, the kind of service usually reserved for high aristocrats who are too refined to know how to unfasten clothing. The skin of her hands was soft and unusually warm, and her touch was feather-light as she undressed me, while I smiled in a lordly fashion at her giggles. In the adjoining bathroom she poured a relaxing bath for me of Angel-cloud ("lose your troubles in our bubbles"). And when I finally clambered into bed she soothed me with a skilled back-rub that almost drove away the odd pressure affecting my head.

It was all quite a skilled performance for a sub-sent, which spoke well for Colloghian training methods and for the level the Logies had reached. Probably border-line, I thought. And I was interested enough not to tune Seliki out and fall asleep when, during her ministrations, she prattled to me non-stop about her people, the Logies.

She started off by simply telling me, as far as I could make out the pidgin, that very few humans were as nice to Logies as, she said, I was to her. Normally they were worked very hard, and otherwise were either ignored or abused. "Much hurt, much bang-bang," as Seliki put it.

"Don't Logies like bang-bang?" I asked.

"Logh-uy like," she replied, smiling widely. "Much like. But when love, when kind. Not when hurt. All bad."

She added something that made me smile when I got her meaning sorted out. She seemed to be saying that Logies dislike rape and sadism because they *aren't* sexual – which they'd enjoy – but are expressions of power and dislike. It seemed a sophisticated concept, I thought, for sub-sents. But what interested me is that while the Logies can be upset, they are never really *hurt* by humans. Certainly not by beatings, because of their thick fur and subcutaneous insulation. In any case, it was the way of their species to recover quickly from unpleasantness, without after-effects.

"Old time," Seliki said, "before Mast's, all Logh-uy live on ice. Much cold – hurt – die. All time hard. But Logh-uy have Allness. Hope make better. Still hope, now."

That was interesting, I thought sleepily. As I understood it, the Allness would be some kind of all-pervading nature spirit. The Logies believed that it would one day make things better, and the belief was comforting in hard times. I knew that other sub-sents have had some dim sort of belief in the supernatural, but again this one seemed fairly advanced. I made an idle mental note to have Posi check the data, sometime.

But by then I'd had enough of the pidgin rundown on the life and times of Colloghi's natives. And Seliki saw that I was growing less interested and more sleepy, so she stopped, covered me up and – in an oddly touching gesture – patted my cheek.

"Mast' kind," she murmured. "Logh-uy friend."

Returning her smile, I reached out again to stroke the incredible richness of her fur, down to where it curved over a firm round buttock. And I thought, sleepily, that it would do me no harm to be thought well of by Logies. I might need all the friends I could get on Colloghi, if anything went wrong with the opening of the pod.

Chapter 11

I woke up dull and thick-headed, the way you feel after a Metastim binge. I'd slept well enough, but I hadn't got rid of that weird feeling of heaviness in my head. It felt as if my skull had shrunk, or my brain had swollen – a sense of inner compression like the early-warning onset of a major migraine. There was still no real pain, but it worried me.

But I dragged myself up and got ready to face the day – most of which I would be spending in company with Jarli Firov. By the time I was out of the shower and dressing, Seliki pattered in with a trayful of things to eat and drink, and with a lot of affectionate smiles and pats. But the sweetness of her greeting was marred a little when she began to giggle helplessly at my clothes.

That made me scowl at her, since I'd chosen everything with great care. It was all in echoing shades of claret and aquamarine – a waisted hip-length jacket with puffed sleeves, tight trousers (discreetly padded, including the ceramic-and-leather groin protector that is standard in all my clothing) and roll-top boots. I knew that the outfit made the kind of statement that Jarli would understand. It didn't surprise me that a primitive like Seliki didn't get its message.

I expected Seliki to be just as ignorant when I began the process of transferring my mini-weapons to the new outfit. Oddly, though, as she watched me, her laughter vanished. And she looked quiet and thoughtful all the while that she laid out my breakfast, giving me a searching look as I sat down to eat.

But I wasn't paying attention to the changeable moods of a little sub-sent. The food and a hot drink brightened me up – as did an actual Metastim capsule from my belt pouch, pushing away the weird heaviness a bit further. Then, feeling even better with the effect of anticipation, I followed Seliki through the Mansion to the entrance hall, where she said I was to meet Jarli.

She looked sensational, as she always does, though her long-sleeved tunic and short skirt were severely cut and in a plain rose-pink, with almost no jewellery or accessories. Just a pink strip like a choker around her smooth throat, with a single pearl at the centre. But she was lovely enough to be her own adornment. I saw her face go through several peculiar expressions as she looked me over, almost as if she was trying to stifle something. But then she managed a welcoming smile and held out a slim hand for me to shake.

"Doctor Rocdril isn't holding grudges today," she said brightly. "He's organized one of the top PR people in Hiatus to show us around."

"Good for him," I said. "Just us?"

She nodded. "I'll do my own filming, as I usually do." Then she turned towards the entrance. "There's a skim waiting for us outside, so we can go."

Two large men sat in the skim, barely acknowledging us as we climbed into the back. Looking at their thick necks and their identical blue-and-white tunics that had to be uniforms, I had no trouble working out what they were – even before Jarli told me that they were from the Hiatus Patrol, sent to pick us up. She added that the Patrol was an independent force, quite separate from the City Militia that policed Collopolis. It seemed a lot of peacekeeping for a small colony.

The skim slid easily along a few streets, around a few corners, then swept through an iris-opening into a broad, bright passage that was a tunnel-like extension of the dome, leading towards the mountain. Above us, through the glas-steel, we could look almost straight up the vertical wall of rock that was the side of the mountain. The sky was overcast, but I had a vivid memory of the view from my ship's descent, and of how much more mountain there was looming above the clouds.

The thought of all that immensity towering above me made me feel again like covering my head and cowering. It also brought back at full output the feeling of heaviness and pressure inside my skull. Rubbing my temples with my fingertips, I thought fretfully that I should perhaps get Posi to look up some of the early symptoms of brain tumours.

Then Jarli gave me a sympathetic look. "Are you feeling a heaviness in your head?" At my surprised nod she smiled reassuringly. "Don't worry. It's not nice, but it's harmless. Every human on Colloghi feels it, though no one knows why. One theory is that it's a kind of freak magnetic field that can pass through the dome."

I let my hands drop. I didn't care what it was, as long as it wasn't terminal. The relief that I felt even eased the sensation a little as the skim reached the far end of the passage, another iris-opening that took us into the Complex.

Beyond the opening, broad heavy doors awaited us on the far side of a smooth apron of plastistone. I looked up at the ceiling – solid, gently arched, quietly lit – and realized that we were inside the mountain. Outside the skim it all seemed warm and well ventilated just as in the dome itself.

Our silent driver and his mate got out with us, revealing that they carried what looked like short clubs but what I recognized as a form of the electro-charged truncheon called Stun-Trun. I was thinking about that armament, and Rocdril's concern over security, when the big doors opened and a thin balding man with a minimal chin hurried out towards us.

He turned out to be the PR person assigned to show us around. On his ill-fitting over-tunic he had an ID badge proclaiming him to be one Caric Peristal, with an unflattering photograph. He offered us similar badges, without photographs, which we were to wear at all times inside the Complex. As he did so he talked, non-stop, almost without taking breath. He introduced himself several times in different ways, explained at least twice what his position was in the hierarchy of the Complex, effused about how overjoyed he was to have the opportunity etc., etc.

Jarli looked at me with a roll of her eyes while I gritted my teeth. It's amazing how professions like public relations always have room for people like Peristal, whose only qualification is that they have the gift of the gabble. And who usually alienate people from the very thing that is being publicized.

But every practised vid-watcher knows how to tune out tedium, like the more inept opportunities-on-new-worlds commercials. So I set up some mental baffles against Peristal's effusions, and we set off.

As we moved through the large doors into the Complex itself, Jarli reached up to touch the pearl at the centre of the choker around her throat. I realized that it wasn't just decoration but a neat form of the HandiBead recorder, nestling against her larynx to pick up her every murmur. I'd bet that it had *its* ways of tuning out Peristal, as well. It was good to find another professional who knew the value of multi-purpose jewellery.

The doors led into a broad, high-ceilinged, softly carpeted area with many doors of various sizes leading from it. I didn't need Peristal to tell me that it was the main entrance foyer, sparsely furnished but full of people – and Logies – who all looked at us curiously. As we crossed it, I noticed that Peristal was fairly well overwhelmed by Jarli, so that he seemed almost unaware of my existence. His talk continued to flow like effluent, full of dullness about the building of the Complex and its early years. But his eyes were saying other things as they gazed wetly at Jarli, and his hands couldn't stay away from her. They fluttered like pale, thin moths, landing here and there for an instant before fluttering away again – on Jarli's forearm, elbow, shoulder, lower back . . .

All right, she was glorious, and I wanted to touch her just as much. Not on the forearm, either. But Peristal was being ridiculous, and repellent. And Jarli obviously thought so too – and had been in such situations before. She had an array of skilled little manoeuvres that enabled her to lean or twist away from the moth-hands, apparently by accident, as if unaware. Peristal just redoubled his efforts to touch her, which made them seem to be performing a weird little dance as they went along. I dropped back a pace or two and just watched, amused.

During all that, Peristal led us out of the entrance foyer

through a door on the left. I'd seen that there were much larger doors in a more central position, looking as if they led to something important. But I wasn't going to ask Peristal about them, even if I could have got a word past his unstemmed flow.

His door led into a connecting passage – a tunnel, of course, but not obviously. Its ceiling was only slightly rounded and very smooth, as were the walls and floor – all high-quality ceramisteel with a soft matt finish. The lighting was gentle and full-spectrum, the air was fully conditioned, and no one could have guessed that we were walking into the depths of a sandstone-and-crystal mountain.

". . . large natural caverns already here," I heard Peristal saying as some of his monologue seeped past my barriers. "They were linked by many tunnels, and the miners that first settled here enlarged some and created others. So the builders of the Complex took advantage of these ready-made features, expanding and elaborating . . ."

I tuned him out again as the passage brought us to a long, dull gallery with museum-like displays showing the inception and growth of Hiatus. Jarli produced an egg-sized SilentPik camera from a belt clip and took a desultory photo or two, and we wandered on. The wanderings took us through a secondary administrative area – some laboratories where no one seemed to be doing much but where Peristal said research went on non-stop – some well-furnished reception suites where clients could be made comfortable while being informed about Hiatus – and so on, and on.

Jarli put up with it for longer than I expected. Probably it was the guards that finally prodded her curiosity, or eroded her temper, or both. Guards in Hiatus Patrol uniform, standing blank-eyed in front of closed doors here and there along our route. Just as there had been Patrolmen guarding the larger doors that I'd seen in the entrance foyer.

At no point in Peristal's blather did he mention the Patrolmen or the doorways they were guarding. As if he couldn't see them or wouldn't acknowledge them. So Jarli finally reached the end of some kind of tether, as Peristal showed us around a cosy little vid and recreation area for the use of off-duty staff.

"Mister Peristal," she said tightly, "why are you giving us all this runaround?"

Peristal blanched, his moth-hands going still as if they'd been pinned to a board. "Runaround? But, ah, Miz Firov, I'm *not*. I'm showing you the Complex . . ."

"You're showing us the edges and the surfaces," Jarli said. "But I'm not doing a promotional documentary on what a terrific place the Complex is. I'm doing a programme on a wholly unique *resuscitation*. Or is Doctor Rocdril planning to revive the astronaut here in this recreation area?"

"No, ah, I really . . ." Peristal's voice was fading a little, and as he cleared his throat he nearly choked. "I understood that the Awakening would, ah, happen in the Complex's lecture hall. We'll come to it in a few . . ."

"No chance," Jarli interrupted firmly. "We won't be coming to it, and that's *not* where it's going to happen. Some dull, stagy little lecture hall? Never. The pod has to be opened in the place where *all* Hiatus clients are revived. That's the only possible setting – all the associations, the atmosphere . . ."

Peristal had gone white around the lips. "Oh, but I don't . . . I mean, it can't . . . Doctor Rocdril would never allow . . ."

"Then I think it's time," Jarli said in an ominous tone, "that we had a word with Rocdril."

So Peristal, even paler and trembling a little, took us to see the doctor. Or actually took us to a place where the doctor came to see us. Very obviously all the important parts of the Complex were situated in its central depths, behind all those closed and guarded doors. Including Rocdril's personal offices or whatever he had. So he came out to meet us, in a little anteroom just off the entrance foyer.

He greeted us with a chilly nod, but otherwise showed no sign – as Bartraselda had predicted – that he recalled our little difference of opinion the previous night. And as Jarli forcefully made her points, he watched her and listened to her as expressionlessly as a lizard.

His voice was just as empty when she finally ran down. "I'm sorry the tour has proved uninteresting," he said. "But you are seeing the only parts of the Complex that are open to the public."

97

"I am not the public," Jarli said sharply.

"You are," Rocdril replied. "What your camera sees, the public sees."

I stepped forward, feeling that I'd been out of things for too long. "So if we try to have a look past any of your closed doors, are your patrolmen going to use their Stun-Truns on us?"

Rocdril turned his frigid gaze on to me. "Most certainly, if they have to."

"*Why*?" Jarli demanded. "What are you hiding?"

"It's not a question of hiding," Rocdril said. "It's simply that the service we offer includes a guarantee of privacy and security. Beyond the closed doors that Curb mentioned lie the primary operations of Hiatus, including extensive data-storage areas and considerable quantities of highly delicate equipment. Strangers cannot be allowed to wander in those areas."

"We wouldn't be *wandering*," Jarli said through her teeth.

Rocdril ignored the interruption. "And at the centre of those closed areas is the Hiatus Heart itself – where the individuals in Hiatus sleep in their individual cubicles, overseen by specialists every moment of the day and night. No unauthorized person can enter the Heart. Ever. Not even Governor Bartraselda herself. There can be no question of allowing *you* in. And that is final."

Something very like emotion crept into Rocdril's voice when he spoke of the Hiatus Heart, and it surprised me. I thought it had affected Jarli, too, because she was silent for a moment. But she was just gathering herself.

"Doctor," she said at last, her tone almost as chilly as his, "I can understand your need for privacy, and all that, in the Complex. I certainly wouldn't want to film people in the Heart, as you call it. That's not what I'm here for. But *you* have to understand something too. If I don't get some co-operation from you for this programme, I'm not going to *make* a programme. And *that's* final."

They stared at each other for a long moment. I could guess at Rocdril's thoughts – balancing his need to keep people out of the inner Complex with his, and Bartraselda's, need for a galaxy-wide promotional showcase. For which they'd spent a lot of money and broken a few important laws.

Finally, expressionless as ever, he gave the briefest of nods. "Co-operation is desirable, of course. On both our parts. What is it you wish?"

"I want to film the opening of the pod in the place where you revive all your clients," Jarli said.

"The Awakening Chamber." Again Rocdril gave his brief nod. "Very well, that will be arranged. So long as you agree not to intrude on other areas of the Heart."

"I agree," Jarli said in a rush. "But . . . I'd like to *see* the place, the Chamber, now. To be sure it's a place where I can film. And I'd like to see the pod itself, too, so I can work out some camera angles."

Rocdril paused again for a moment, as if for thought. "I cannot let you into the Awakening Chamber today," he said at last. "Perhaps tomorrow, when I can be sure that it isn't in use and that no instrumentation will be at risk. But you may certainly see the pod now, in its storage cubicle."

"Fine," Jarli said, a little triumphantly.

"Peristal," Rocdril said, turning his head slightly. I'd almost forgotten the public relations man, who was standing wanly at one side, and who jumped at the sound of his own name. "Take them to the pod – storage cubicle eight in section fourteen. And, Peristal – that means along passages forty-one, forty-seven and 116. No other route."

"Yessir," Peristal gulped.

Rocdril then offered us another almost invisible nod and stalked away, while Peristal was shakily ushering us out of the anteroom in a different direction.

This time we left the entrance foyer through the larger doors I'd noticed. And this time Peristal was silent, kept his hands to himself and scuttled along at speed as if he could hardly wait to get the task over with. Shortly, after passing along more tunnels through more admin areas and the like, we went through a door with two baleful Patrol guards *and* an electro-lock, and entered the inner Complex, the Hiatus Heart.

I couldn't see what all the secrecy was for. We just went along another dull little passage – looking even more like a tunnel, and with plenty of branching tunnels on either side. Jarli put her camera back on her belt and had nothing to say to her recorder, just stared around as puzzled as I was. Soon we turned down another sizeable passage with more side-branches and some closed doors along the way. Then we turned again, past more doors and more secondary tunnels, until we stopped in front of a door like all the others.

Peristal tapped out the code on the electro-lock, the door slid open, and there was the pod. Peristal went in first, with Jarli behind him, her camera leaping into her hand. And I would have been right behind her.

Except that, in the passage behind me, someone whispered something that sounded like my name.

"Delcur . . . Delcur . . ."

I spun round, then relaxed a little when I saw the whisperer. A Logie, standing in the mouth of a subsidiary tunnel that we'd just passed. I knew that it wasn't Seliki – and I had the idea, because it was taller and thinner, that it was a male. But I'd never seen it before, I was sure.

"Mast' come," it whispered, beckoning anxiously. "Mast' come."

I went towards it, warily. "Come where?" I said in a half-whisper of my own. "What do you want?"

"Mast' come," it repeated. "See friend. Help friend."

It backed away, still beckoning. I moved towards it again, wondering if Seliki had got into some kind of trouble, wondering if it was going to make trouble for me. Then I reached the mouth of the small subsidiary, where the Logie was still backing away.

"Del!" said a voice tinged with what sounded like desperation.

My heart sank, and my stomach squeezed around it. Here was trouble enough. And just about the last kind I'd expected.

Behind the Logie, lurking back in the shadows of the smaller tunnel, stood Myron T. Moone.

Chapter 12

He had taken the plain covering that had been over him in the pod and had wrapped it around his hips as a makeshift loincloth. And for once his expression was neither puzzled nor earnest, but worried and slightly embarrassed.

"What are you *doing*?" I yelled. In fact the yell came out as a croaking whisper, but even so the Logie flinched while Moone made pacifying gestures at me.

"Del, listen, I'm real sorry," he said, also in a hoarse whisper. "I don't know how it happened. The pod got opened somehow, and I woke up . . . just like on your ship."

I stared at him, thinking fast. Maybe the pod's opening processes got activated during the move – or maybe someone like Rocdril wanted a quick peek to be sure the occupant was in one piece. I didn't know, and it didn't matter. What mattered was that Moone was out and about in the Complex, which could mean serious trouble. For him as well as me.

"When I got out," Moone was saying, "I didn't know where I was or anythin'. I figured you'd want me back in the pod . . ."

"You figured right," I snarled.

He looked even more abashed. "Yeah – but I told you how it really hurts, and I felt like takin' a look around before goin' through that again. So I came outa that little room where the pod is . . . and the door closed and locked behind me."

I closed my eyes, trying to control the fury and tension sweeping through me. There I was, in danger of having all my plans ruined because a foambrain primitive wanted to take a look around.

"Then in a while," Moone went on, "the Logies found me." He patted the furry shoulder of the creature next to him. "They been real kind – hidin' me, bringin' me food. You know, Del, I figure the Logies understand a lot. Even if they look funny, and don't talk so good . . ."

"Moone," I broke in acidly, "we can talk about sub-sentient understanding another time. Right now we have to do something about this situation. I'm being shown around in here, with someone else, and the room with the pod has just been opened. I can try to wreck the locking mechanism, somehow, so it stays open. If I can't, maybe you and your Logie friends can get it open somehow. But one way or another I want you *back in the pod!*"

Moone shuffled his big bare feet, looking sullen. "Do I have to?"

"You do," I rasped. "If you're inside the pod, you and I are on our way to fame and riches and everything we talked about. Like girls." That brought his head up sharply. "If you're *outside* the pod, everything's on the way to being ruined. And you're likely to be jailed for fraud. And for being a trespasser in this off-limits area."

"Well . . ." His feet still shuffled, but the mutinous expression was fading.

"Listen," I said quickly. "You don't have to go back in right away. The pod's official opening won't be for a day or two. If we can just get you back into the pod *cubicle*, somehow . . . Then I can send word by the Logies when it's time for you to go to sleep again."

"OK," Moone said gloomily. "But I sure hope it's all over soon. I'm gettin' real tired . . ."

"Mister *Curb!*"

The voice was that of Peristal, back at the cubicle, sounding a little shrill. Understandably, since one of his charges had vanished. It had taken him long enough to notice, I thought – but that was probably the effect of being with Jarli in a cubicle.

Moone and his Logie drew further back into the secondary tunnel's shadows as I turned and sauntered out to the main

102

passage. To confront Peristal, looking desperate – and Jarli, smiling, behind him.

"Where did you *go?*" Peristal asked, with a gasping mixture of tension and relief. "You mustn't wander away . . .!"

I shrugged, trying to look casual. "I've seen the pod before – and I was looking for a place to . . . relieve myself."

Peristal blinked, then nodded briskly several times. "I'm afraid there is nothing like that around here. But when Miz Firov is ready to leave, I can take you to a convenience."

"I'm ready," Jarli said. "I wouldn't mind a *convenience* myself."

She stepped out of the cubicle, and the door began to slide shut behind her. It's not easy to move at a frantic speed while still trying to look casual, but I managed it. At least no one seemed startled when I brushed past Jarli and pushed the door open again, pretending to peer in at the pod.

"Does it look all right to you?" I asked her. "No damage from the move?"

She shrugged. "How would I know? I didn't see any obvious signs of breakage or anything."

Peristal was looking both affronted and anxious. "The pod was handled with the utmost care, Mister Curb. There could be no question of damage. And now we should . . ." He stopped, frowning. "What is *that?*"

That was a faint but piercing whine, like a flying insect or a distant power tool. It was being made by one of my most useful mini-weapons – a tiny vibro-blade which is implanted in the nail of my left little finger. It can cut most things, including metals this side of accelsteel. Just then, while I was idly leaning one hand against the cubicle's doorframe, I had thrust the blade into the workings of the lock, twisting it around to chop up the lock's electronics. Hoping to leave the door unlocked, for Moone.

In a moment I switched the blade off – gladly, since its vibrations send shooting pains through my metacarpals – and turned with raised eyebrows to Peristal.

"Sounded like machinery to me," I said innocently. "Are there workshops around here as well as storage places?"

Peristal's face closed. "I'm afraid I'm not at liberty to say. Now we should be going, if you will."

He reached past me to pull the door shut, then touched buttons to activate the lock. I mentally crossed a few fingers. Still, I thought grimly, if my efforts hadn't worked, Moone could always batter the cubicle door down with his head. It didn't seem useful for much else.

From then a fairly rapid progress – with a pause for the "conveniences", which by then I did need – got us out of the Complex, to Peristal's obvious relief, and back to the Governor's Mansion. In another skim escorted by another two silent Patrolmen. It was past midday by then, and the Mansion seemed echoingly silent, as if everyone was occupied with quiet things behind closed doors. Presumably Bartraselda and her staff were sorting out the kind of things governors sort out, and there was no one else in the place except Logies.

We saw one or two of them, going about their business, and they glanced at me covertly and perhaps even smiled – as if Seliki's opinion of me was by then well-known. Anyway, we stopped one of them and requested something to eat. And because I was feeling tense and edgy about Moone's threat to my plans, and needing a little diversion, I invited Jarli to join me for lunch in my suite.

To my surprise, she accepted. And to my delight, when we got to my suite, she sat on the wide soft couch and beckoned me to sit next to her. We kept a decorous distance apart while a couple of Logies brought in our food. After they left I was wondering if it was best to eat first and lunge after, or vice versa, when Jarli startled me with a question.

"Del," she said softly. I twitched and tingled a little – until she went on. "Do you think Bartraselda plants bugs in the guest suites?"

I sat up straight, twitching in a different way. It was a very good question, even if its timing wasn't ideal. Mentally I cursed myself for not having thought of it first, as a good professional should have.

"I can find out," I said, reaching up to my headband. Briefly I told her about the mini-ceptor in the central jewel, which emits a faint pulse against my skin in the presence of bugging devices. And is adjustable to give different pulses for different kinds of presences. I saw Jarli's eyes scan the other jewels in my headband, thoughtfully, not being someone who needed everything spelled out for her.

Then I turned full circle in a sweep that revealed a bug-free room. That news made Jarli smile delectably and lean back, visibly relaxing. But when I slid my arm along the couch's back towards her, she sat up again.

"Let's eat, and talk," she said quickly. "I need someone to talk to. And I think I could do with some help."

"Anything," I said happily, feeling good. Obviously it would be eat first and then lunge. And I imagined that she'd be more receptive after she had my promise of help. Whatever it was she wanted. "What's the trouble?"

"Lots of things," she said. "First of all, though, the astronaut in the pod."

I ate my lunch and listened, with some private amusement, while she told me her troubles. They mainly centred on the fact that she wanted to do more than just a programme showing Moone's supposed revival. She wanted to make Moone into her own personal project. Didn't we all, I thought. But Jarli was worried that she wouldn't be able to do it.

"When the astronaut is revived," she said, "even if he comes through intact, he's going to be confused and distressed. And he won't speak Galac." I nodded, keeping my face straight. "But he'll also be an interstellar celebrity. So the sharks will home in on him, as they always do. By the time he learns Galac, so that I can start putting interviews and other shows around him, some other network could have him. It wouldn't be the first time a network has bought off some star from a rival. Or even *kidnapped* one."

"No one's kidnapping M . . ." I stopped myself just in time. "I mean, there'll be no kidnapping. Anyway, can't your network offer the astronaut enough to keep him exclusive?"

She nodded. "If we get a chance. But that's where I need help. After he's been revived – or *she*, I suppose, since we don't know it's a man – I could do with some help to get him away somewhere safe, teach him Galac, educate him a little, and sort out watertight contracts and everything. After all, if he doesn't know Galac, a contract wouldn't be binding . . ."

I stared down at my empty plate, thinking fast. Jarli's network would pay as big a sum as anyone for vid exclusives on Moone, just as I wanted. And I could keep control of him for public appearances and all the rest. Also, signing up Moone with Jarli's network would mean I'd go on seeing a lot of her. And she'd be feeling a lot of gratitude towards me.

I looked up and saw her watching me anxiously. Reaching over to pat her knee, I gave her my most reassuring smile.

"Jarli, love," I said warmly, "by a happy accident, I can offer you a solution to your problem."

I gave her a slightly abridged version of the awakening of Moone. There didn't seem to be any need to mention my interest in ancient artefacts. And I decided to hold back, for a while, the news that Moone was once again awake, wandering in the Hiatus Heart.

As I spoke, she went through a remarkable series of reactions – disbelieving astonishment, then suspicion and indignation, finally a sort of resigned amusement that I thought was promising.

"And you're his sole representative," she said at last, studying me.

"That's it," I agreed.

She nodded slowly. "You're quite the operator, aren't you?"

I shrugged, with a modest smile.

"And you're right. It does solve my problem. Since you have this Moone all sewn up – and if my network gets *you* all sewn up – "

"We can work something out," I said.

"I don't doubt it." Her smile was wry. "But that can wait – till after the filming of the Awakening. Which now looks like being one of the biggest cons ever perpetrated on the viewing public."

"Not at all," I protested. "Moone actually *has* been awakened, after centuries in the pod. He's not a fake. You'll just be showing a more interesting, *dramatized* version of what happened. That's not a con. The vid does it all the time."

"Mm." Her smile was still wry. "The vid does a lot of things. But I wasn't making a moral judgment. Viewers prefer reality to be rationalized and sanitized, so that's how we present it. But I can see a difficulty. If I'm filming the big exciting moment when a real twenty-first century spaceman comes back to life, I don't want him leaping out of the pod and making a speech to camera in fluent Galac."

"I know," I agreed. "I've told him that he has to act dazed and unsteady and so on, the way he was the first time."

"But *can* he? Can we rely on him to act the part? Has he got what it takes to make this con – sorry, this dramatization – convincing?"

I hesitated. It was a good point. I'd been a bit worried myself, that Moone might be too simple to perform in a reliably natural way. "I don't know," I said at last. "Maybe not."

Jarli bit her lower lip worriedly. "Then we could still be in trouble." She sighed. "What I really wish is that we could sneak back into the Complex and somehow wake him up again. To rehearse him a little, maybe rough out a kind of script for him."

I smiled with pleasure, partly because of what I knew and partly in admiration for the professionalism in her attitude. Media people know how to handle these little difficulties.

"As it happens," I said lightly, "he's awake now, in the Complex. Being tended by Logies. I found him and talked to him – while you and Peristal were looking at the pod."

She stared. "*That's* where you . . ." Then she grinned. "That settles it. We *will* sneak in and find him. And we'll have to do it tonight."

"Hold on," I said, feeling a little alarmed. "How are we going to sneak into that place, with all its security?"

Her grin widened. "You should have listened to Peristal. A vainbrain like that often lets things slip."

And she told me that she'd learned from Peristal that the Hiatus Patrol was mostly for show. No one had ever tried to break in to the Complex – nor, obviously, had any of its customers ever felt like breaking out. So, at night, the Patrol kept only a skeleton staff on duty – as mobile squads, not on permanent station.

"Once we're in we should be fine," Jarli said eagerly. "And if you're the operator you seem to be, you should be able to help me get through those main doors."

I nodded slowly. It all sounded possible enough, with fewer risks than I would have thought. But there was one important point that hadn't escaped me.

"Sounds like you've worked it out," I said slowly. "But I wonder *why*. Because it seems you were pumping Peristal, and making plans to sneak in, *before* you knew anything about Moone."

She looked taken aback. "Well, yes, I was. Because of something else that I wanted to talk to you about – since we're in this together."

That remains to be seen, I said to myself, as she started to explain.

The fact was that she had come to Colloghi for *two* reasons. The obvious, public one was to film an ancient astronaut's Awakening. But the second, hidden purpose had to do with taking a close look at Hiatus.

Because, she said, she had good reason to suspect that Hiatus was crooked.

Her suspicions had been stirred up by accident, while she'd been visiting a friend on the mining planet Pyyltania. The friend was the daughter of a tycoon who owned some of the planet's most productive mines – and who had decided, earlier, to take some time off in Hiatus. People had been surprised, but not much. It's not unusual for high-powered financial types to take breaks, when they can, from stress and problems. While their assets appreciate.

But that's not what happened. Not according to a computer memory that probably was meant to be wiped, but that Jarli found first, by accident. It told her that the tycoon, her friend's father, had signed up for three years in Hiatus. But later, he had signed another contract – committing him instead to a Hiatus sleep of *thirty* years.

That second contract had been signed *after* he had travelled to Colloghi.

And at the same time as he signed it, he had also apparently authorized the sale of his most thriving mines.

Intrigued, and worried on her friend's behalf, Jarli did some digging. Backed by all the resources of a major vid network. And she dug up some disturbing facts.

First, the funds from the sale of the tycoon's mines had gone into a special account in the Fedbank. Shortly after, those funds had been transferred elsewhere. The Fedbank has strict rules against revealing such information, but Jarli got the idea that not even the bank knew where the funds had ended up.

Second, her digging turned up a number of similar cases on other worlds. A frightening number, frighteningly similar. Planetillionaires and the like taking themselves off to Hiatus. Then signing contracts for far longer stays. Then the asset-stripping, and so on, of their resources.

"There's never more than one or two per planet," Jarli said. "So I suppose no one else has noticed the pattern so far. People on any one world would just say 'that's odd' and forget it. Often it happens quietly enough that people don't even realize."

"You're sure that every one of them goes the same way?" I asked.

"As sure as I can be. Not all the contracts and everything are available to be seen, but there's more than enough proof. It's just that no one else has investigated. Of course it's only been going on for the last few years."

I frowned. "You mean until lately, Hiatus was legitimate?"

"So it seems."

I pondered, feeling that I could guess what had happened. Someone with more brains than morals had found a way to plunder the rich fools who made themselves vulnerable in Hiatus. It would be interesting to know how, I thought. And who.

"So you can see why I want to get into the Complex," Jarli said. "Tonight, if I can. You *will* help me, won't you, Del?"

She was leaning towards me, lips slightly parted, an appealing intensity in her marvellous eyes. All that magnetism was irresistible – but by then I'd mostly decided anyway. It was a good chance to get her to do what she could for Moone, so that nothing could go wrong with the vid-show and mess up my plans. And it might be interesting to sniff around the Complex and its crookery, since the sniffing wasn't likely to be dangerous if the place was so lightly guarded. Besides, if I offered my help, there was a good chance of fringe benefits.

I leaned towards those luminous eyes and parted lips, reaching a hand over to rest lightly on the slender waist.

"Of course I'll help you, Jarli," I murmured. "You can count on me."

Our mouths had almost met, my hand was sliding up from her waist towards the swell of a breast, when she suddenly jerked away as if scalded.

"Oh, no," she said. "We're not slipping into bed as a prelude to slipping into the Complex. I'm not buying your help that way."

"*Buying*?" I repeated with a glare. "What do you take me for?"

"For what you are, I believe," she said flatly. "A sharp operator, a bit of a trickster, someone always on the lookout for angles and advantages."

I scowled. "What's wrong with that?"

"Maybe not much, in this galaxy," she said. "But I don't find it very attractive. You're the last sort of person, Del, that I'd want to get involved with."

"You want to get involved enough," I snarled, "to use me in your planned break-in, tonight."

"That's just business," she replied coolly. "You're going to help me so I can get Moone straightened out, which protects your interests in him. I doubt if the rest of it, the possible crimes in Hiatus, matters to you much."

That was true enough, though I felt I could be interested if there was a way to pry loose a few Hiatus kilocreds for myself. But at that moment I was focused on a different interest. I'm not one to give up easily.

"It *does* matter to me, Jarli," I said with extra sincerity. "Because *you* matter to me."

I slid my arm around her shoulders as I spoke, to pull her towards me. I could see determined refusal in her eyes and could feel resistance in her body – but I hadn't really begun my moves, and I wasn't feeling at all discouraged.

Instead, though, I was interrupted.

A tapping at the door caused Jarli to pull away and call "come in" with some relief. I began some caustic remark about it being *my* suite, *my* right to invite people in or not. But the door opened to admit Seliki all in a rush.

"Mast'," she said to me breathlessly. "Gov'nor wants. You come Gov'nor. Now."

Chapter 13

Seliki led me swiftly through the Mansion's corridors, now and then glancing back at me with what looked like a worried expression. But I was worried enough on my own. A sudden and urgent summons from someone in Authority, anyone, always tenses me up. Probably because I'm basically a free spirit, chafing against petty rules and conventions.

But specifically, this time, I was worried that Moone had been discovered in the Complex, which would have been the end of all my plans. And maybe the end of *me*. I could end up in a Colloghi slammer – on a plate for Pulvidon, who would be scouring the galaxy to find me.

Thinking these dire thoughts, I hardly noticed the route we were taking. I suppose I'd expected to be brought into Bartraselda's presence in some official place, like the great Receiving Hall. Only when we stopped at a decorated door I'd never seen before did it hit me that we had been moving upwards in the Mansion, not down to the main floor with its official chambers.

Seliki's little fist tapped on the door. A muffled voice said something, within. Seliki looked round at me solemnly. "Mast' see Gov'nor now."

She seemed to want to say something else, but I wasn't paying much attention. As she hesitated, I stepped past her, raised a finger to the touch panel that opened the door, and tried to find a believable smile to put on. Stepping into the room, I told myself that I'd talked my way out of worse positions than this in my time.

Then I saw Bartraselda and began to wonder if I'd ever *been* in worse positions.

The sumptuous furnishings – a shin-deep carpet, velvety drapes, walls covered with glossy plastisilk – were not those of a public reception area. Especially not when the chamber was dominated by an immense, luxurious divan. Its mattress seemed to be made of that ultimate in yielding softness, the bubbly Lazee-Froth, while the single covering looked as if it had been woven from the gauzy fibres of the spindrift fern from Chackursda IV.

On the divan, with the spindrift covering flung well aside, reclined Governor Bartraselda.

She was heavily made up, with her lank hair teased into something like a coiffure, already coming apart. I studied it carefully, in an attempt to avoid looking at the rest of her. Her gown would have been floor-length if she'd been standing, and I suppose it had a collar, sleeves and so on. I couldn't be sure, since it was mostly transparent. And the lighting had been arranged to leave little to the imagination.

But my imagination would never be that unkind to me.

Clothed, Bartraselda had been deeply unattractive. Unclothed, she was a disaster. Her breasts hung flat against her chest like small fried eggs that had been dyed mauve. Her belly jutted like a drum, with hairy moles around a cavernous navel. Her thighs were like tree-trunks, her ankles weren't much slimmer, her feet were broad and flat. Her shoulders were pimply, her arms were blotched, and an unhealthy looking flush mottled her throat and jowls.

Worst of all, she was smiling at me. And I knew that the smile, like that of a toad watching the approach of a juicy fly, was supposed to be seductive. I felt my stomach turn sour and the heaviness in my skull shift into a deep-seated ache.

"Glad y' could come, Del," Bartraselda said. One puffy hand patted the divan next to her. "C'mon over here, get comfortable."

"Uh." It wasn't much of a response, but my speech centres had been short-circuited. I found myself thinking that if Doctor Rocdril actually did perform as stud for this creature, he must be the most unobservant man in that galactic sector. Or the most desperate.

"C'mon now," Bartraselda said, her smile shifting into a leer. "I won't eat y'. Hah! Maybe the other way round . . ."

I started to realize that my choices were few and all unappealing. I could obey, could go and grapple with the Governor on the Lazee-Froth, which would be less fun than wrestling one of the giant jelly-worms of Kaffatiriq. Or I could back off, running the serious risk of alienating the most powerful person on Colloghi.

"Governor," I croaked, through a definite thickness in the throat.

She got to her feet, breasts flapping like dying mauve fish. "Call me Bartie," she leered.

"Uh . . . Bartie." I took a step back, my mind threshing around to find any kind of get-out. "I'm not sure this is a good idea . . ."

"Sure it is." She advanced towards me, and I backed away. "Don't go all shy on me. Y've been around, Del, I know that. So've I. I figure we could be pretty good t'gether."

"But Governor . . . Bartie . . ." My mind was reporting failure, though I kept it to its task as I edged away towards the wall furthest from the divan. "We have . . . um . . . other commitments, you and I . . ."

"Commitments? Hah!" She made a sudden lunge, flesh wobbling in various directions, but I managed a quick sidestep along the wall to evade her. "I looked y' up, Del. Y'r lady partner's left y', y' got nobody else with y', male or female – an' even if y're already makin' it with Jarli, that's no commitment, an' I don't care."

"Uh . . ." I repeated, with some desperation. She lunged again, but it was a feint – and I was being slowly forced into a corner.

"An' I'm the Governor," she went on, as if we were having an ordinary, casual conversation. "I don't get tied into *commitments* 'less I want to. Maybe y' think I'm wrapped up with Rocdril – but y'd be wrong, Del."

I blinked, unwilling to say "Uh" again, unable to think of any other response as I found the corner closing in on me.

Her froggy grin widened as she stalked me. "Rocky's OK, though it's kinda like makin' it with an icicle. But he hasn't given me what I want. What I *need*. An' I figure maybe you can."

I swallowed, looking hopelessly around for a path to safety. But then she startled me into paying attention again.

"What I need, Del," she said, "is a kid. Somebody to train up to be governor after me, keep the family goin'. Ol' Rocdril's been firin' blanks – so I need somebody else. An' I reckon if that somebody's *you*, it could be fun as well."

She had backed me fully into the corner by then, her squat bulk blocking any escape. "Don't get me wrong here, Del. I got no illusions. Y' don't look much of a stud, an' y' prob'ly don't fancy me one bit. Nobody ever did. But y're my kinda man, Del – 'cause y're *greedy*. Which makes y' corruptible." Her leer stretched the width of her jawline. "An' that makes y' *controllable*. I got what y' want – credits, status, whatever – so y'll do what I want. An' that's what I like. It's the control, the power, that gives me my real happies, in bed or out. Y' know?"

I found myself nodding slowly. I knew what she meant, though I'd never heard it stated quite so bluntly in that precise situation. Oddly, little Seliki had been talking about the same thing the previous night. And it was true. Power is the ultimate turn-on, for most people – whether on a Lazee-Froth divan or in the executive meetings of SenFed Central.

But not for me. Anyway, not when I'd be the victim of the power rather than the wielder.

And as I nodded, she reached out her pudgy hand, trailed it over my chest down to my stomach, then further downwards.

"Y' wearin' a codpiece, Del," she leered, "or are y' just glad to see me?"

I smiled weakly. It occurred to me that if she did somehow manage to get me on the Lazee-Froth I'd probably fail to rise to the occasion. Which would be as likely to earn her displeasure as outright rejection. But I never did get trapped into removing my ceramic-and-leather protector and trying to perform that grisly task. I was rescued. And at the time it seemed the most amazing good luck.

A soft but demanding series of taps on the door brought a startled twitch from me and a gruff snarl from Bartraselda.

"Get *away*!" she snarled. "An' *stay* away!"

The tapping just grew firmer and more rapid. Then the door was slowly eased open. Around its edge appeared the small brown face of Seliki, looking scared but determined.

"Seliki, I'll skin y' an' roast y'!" Bartraselda roared. "What're y' playin' at?"

"Gov'nor, please, please," Seliki whimpered, cringing. "Mast' from sky come. Gov'nor say, this Mast' come, tell Gov'nor, fast-fast."

The pidgin babble meant little to me, but it had quite an effect on Bartraselda. She whirled away from me with a bobble of flesh, flinging off the transparent gown, reaching into a wardrobe for a heavy dark dress with a long skirt and high collar.

"Sorry, Del," she muttered. "Logies have orders to come get me whenever . . . this visitor gets in."

An off-world visitor, I thought, judging from Seliki's "Mast' from sky". "Someone important?" I asked innocently.

"Y' could say that." Bartraselda was clearly distracted, perhaps a little upset. "It means there's business I gotta take care of. Don't know how long it'll take. Seliki'll take y' back to y'r suite."

So I was dismissed, while Bartraselda rushed away to greet her mysterious, important off-worlder. I found myself out in the hall with Seliki, feeling an immense relief, being amazed that it was still only late afternoon. I also felt curious about the visitor, and asked Seliki about him as we went along. But she just looked nervous, repeated, "Mast' from sky", and shook her head. So I let it go and went back to thinking about important things – like my undertaking to help Jarli break into the Complex.

The place seemed well-named, I thought glumly. Things on Colloghi were getting more and more complex, for me. When we reached my suite, I told Seliki to pour me a tall glass of liquigasm – and sat with it, staring at a wall, wishing I could create some role reversal. Why couldn't it be Jarli offering her body and Bartraselda offering remunerative activity? Why do things get themselves the wrong way around?

Seliki, still with her worried expression, watched me as I sat and sipped. I gave her a half-smile, she smiled back, but she still looked troubled – the way she'd looked letting me into Bartraselda's chamber, as if she had something important to say. She was also small and round, with a far sweeter face and far prettier breasts than the ones that had confronted me a short while before. So at last I gave in and asked her if anything was wrong.

She blinked, bit her lip with her sharp little teeth, took a deep breath. "Seliki think," she said nervously. Then she hesitated.

"About what?" I asked in a kindly manner.

She took a second deep breath. "Gov'nor," she said. Another inhalation, then a rush of pidgin. "Mast' now be Gov'nor bang-bang boy?"

It took me a few seconds to translate. I suppose it seemed likely enough, to her, that I was about to become Bartraselda's new lover and seed-sower. But after my last-minute reprieve, and remembering how I'd felt backed into that corner, I was promising myself that I'd use every devious technique I knew, and invent some if I had to, to keep away from the Governor's private apartment. For the remaining few days of my time on Colloghi. And once Moone and I – and maybe Jarli – were off and away from the planet, who cared if a squat and ugly Governor felt angry at being rejected?

Thinking those thoughts, I smiled again at the little Logie. "No, Seliki," I told her. "I won't be doing bang-bang with the Governor."

And then she totally astonished me. She nodded, the worried look vanishing. She smiled broadly. And she spoke.

"That," she said, "is a wise decision, Del Curb."

The astonishment didn't arrive right away. For a moment I went on smiling in a kindly way, raising the drink to my lips. Then the shock hit me – straightening my vertebrae with a snap, almost making me slosh the liquigasm down my front.

"Seliki!" I gasped. "You *spoke*! Properly!"

She grinned at me. "So I did."

"But how . . ." I burbled. "When did . . . I mean, how long . . . I mean, can all . . ."

Beaming, she put me out of my misery. "The Logh-uy learned Galac many generations ago. We can all speak it. It is simpler and more orderly than our own tongue. But of course we do not speak it with humans."

I stared at her. "Why not? You're letting the people here treat you like near-animals when you're full sentients!"

She shrugged. "We are not much troubled by their treatment of us. And it is *safer* for us to be seen as low-level primitives."

"I don't understand why," I said dazedly.

So, crisply, she explained. It had begun in the colony's earlier days, she said, when some colonists began domesticating Logies, as they thought. When the Logies picked up their first smatterings of Galac, and learned more about their planet's often violent and unpredictable new masters, they decided that it would be better for them to appear sub-sentient. Not quite animals, so that the hunting for furs wouldn't go on, but also not full sentients who would be seen as *competitors* for control of Colloghi. And who would stand no chance in a conflict – since, Seliki told me, Logies have no weapons as such and have never been warlike, by nature and by ethical choice.

It seemed to me that assuming a sub-sent disguise was amazingly self-sacrificing. But the Logies were convinced that any other approach would have eventually got them wiped out. And, knowing something of the history of humankind's colonizing urge, who would argue with them? So they played their role of docile, obedient sub-sent domestics – played it perfectly for generations.

And then, in more recent years, they found an even better reason for maintaining their cultural disguise.

"What reason?" I asked, though I suspected that I could guess the answer.

And I was right. "Changes took place in the Hiatus Complex," Seliki said, her expression darkening. "Evil things began – terrible things. And the Logh-uy became afraid. If the

118

people who do the evil things knew we understood, we could be killed to silence us."

"What *are* the evil things?" I asked.

Seliki hesitated, then shook her head. "It is not easy to explain, and you might not believe. You should see for yourself, Del Curb. The Logh-uy *want* you to see. I have spoken of you to my people – and they feel as I do, that you can help us think of a way to stop the evil people."

That shook me. I didn't much object to helping the Logies *think* of what to do. But I wasn't going to join in any crusade against the evil people, whoever they were. In my experience, evil people are dangerous people.

But then another thought struck me. Seliki wanted me to see the evil in the Complex for myself. So I could ask the Logies to help me get in. I'd found a made-to-order means of entry for Jarli and me, for our planned break-in that night.

"As it happens, Seliki," I said lightly, "I'd already planned to go back into the Complex and have a sort of unofficial look around. Tonight. With Miz Firov."

Seliki's face lit up with what looked like a tinge of mockery behind her merry grin. "Oh, yes – to see your big friend Myron Moone. He too is much liked by the Logh-uy. And it is good that you will go in with Jarli Firov. She can also advise us about dealing with the evil." The mockery became more visible. "You would like to be Jarli Firov's bang-bang boy, I think."

I managed a casual half-shrug, unwilling to discuss Jarli's views on that subject. "I'm not bothered. Anyway, let's talk about how I'm going to get into the Complex."

"So." Seliki laughed throatily, then became more business-like. "I will send messages to the Logh-uy in the Complex to expect you tonight. And I will bring you a map of the Complex, with notes to show where the patrols will be at different times."

"Perfect!" I got to my feet, pleased. It really was going to be simple, I thought. "I'll start getting ready."

As she bounced away, I turned to digging out a suitable garment for the night's work. It wasn't difficult to choose, since I'd brought only one dull and inconspicuous outfit. But I like to be prepared for anything. It was an ordinary, functional coverall in charcoal grey with a subdued blue trim on all the usual places. I was sitting in my undershorts, transferring my mini-weapons to their allotted places, when Seliki – no longer bothering to knock – came back into the suite.

She giggled at the sight of me. "You should have fur instead of clothing, Del Curb," she said merrily. "You would make a fine he Logh-uy."

I didn't feel flattered, seeing that male Logies tend towards the spindly. So I ignored the remark. In any case, she was holding out a square of plastiscrip with markings on it.

"The map of the Complex," she said. "It is crude, but it is the best that the Logh-uy of the Complex could do."

"It's fine," I said, glancing at the markings. "Anything's better than going in blind."

"All the Logh-uy that you meet in the Complex," she added, "will know why you are there, and will help."

"Then I'm all set," I said.

She moved closer to me, eyes dark and grave, all laughter fled. Raising one small hand, she pressed its palm against my left pectoral, over the heart. I assumed it was a Logie ritual, so I did the same – letting my hand cover her firm little breast. Her skin, I noticed again, was sensuously soft and incredibly warm.

"I am glad you are here to help us, Del Curb," she murmured. "Go with care. Return safely."

"Oh, I will," I said, squeezing her breast gently.

I was just wondering if the ritual allowed me to bring my other hand up to her other breast when she moved back, still gazing at me with great seriousness, then turned and left the suite. Which left me nothing much to do except wait for nightfall. I tucked the map into a pocket, turned on the vid and lounged back with another liquigasm and a piece of fruit to nibble. But my attention kept wandering from the slush film being shown. I got started thinking about how I might introduce Jarli Firov to the niceties of the Logie farewell ritual.

Chapter 14

Darkness had finally fallen over Collopolis when I made my way to Jarli's suite, a few corridors away from mine on the same floor. I met no one on the way, but I hadn't expected to. Bartraselda was probably still closeted somewhere with her Important Visitor, and I wished them luck.

Jarli seemed pleased to see me, though she looked a little nervous. She had changed into a one-piece coverall nearly as basic as mine, with blue and green swirls like camouflage. But they did nothing to disguise her glorious shape. She even smelled wonderful as she came near me to look at the map I produced.

The map seemed to impress her greatly. Seliki had wanted me to keep her secret, so I told Jarli that I'd copied a map that I'd seen in the Governor's apartment. And that it was a little crude because I'd been in a hurry. I could see that Jarli's opinion of my resourcefulness went up several notches. When she then naturally asked me why the Governor had sent for me, I said it was for more discussion of my fee for bringing the pod, bonuses and surcharges and things. I wasn't about to tell anyone what the Governor had tried to do to me. For her part, Jarli graciously avoided any mention of what I'd been trying to do to *her* when Seliki had interrupted.

So, all friends again, we slipped away on our mission. Jarli had explored the Mansion more than I had, and got us down to the main floor by some back stairs – narrow, poorly lit, obviously reserved for Logie servants. That was confirmed when we met a Logie, who just stepped back and watched us pass, unblinkingly, though with the faintest of smiles.

A ticklish moment came when we emerged on to the ground floor and heard voices in a corridor ahead, one of them sounding like the Marshal, Slar. That corridor was on our route out, so we were stymied for the moment. But I warily looked through a narrow opening nearby, half-covered with hangings, and found that it opened into another servants' route. If we'd met another Logie I might have risked startling Jarli by asking the way, but I didn't need to. We wandered for only a few minutes in a maze of ground-floor servants' ways, until Jarli spotted a bigger, more solid-looking door than some others that we'd passed. It opened on to the outside – a narrow, rough path surrounded by shrubbery.

"Stage One complete," I said lightly.

Jarli nodded, but stared around at the shadows in a very jumpy way. She didn't seem to mind at all when I took her hand as we moved away. Her skin was no less soft than Seliki's, I found – but a *lot* cooler.

Once out in the city streets, we walked along quite openly – two guests of the Mansion, out for a stroll. We met only a few other people, who glanced at us with idle curiosity and then did double-takes when they recognized Jarli. They must have thought that I was the luckiest of men, out for a walk with the Highlight Heart-throb. Even though by then Jarli had gently disengaged her hand from mine. I was a bit annoyed when I caught her unobtrusively wiping her palm on her coverall. I didn't think it was only *me* who was sweaty with nerves. Not that much, anyway.

At the same time, I had something of a right to feel nervous. Far more than Jarli – because she had no real idea of what was going on or what I was going through. I kept remembering Seliki's ominous references to evil people in the Complex doing evil things. And her even more ominous idea that I might somehow help the Logies *do* something about it. Then there I was, going to creep around those dangerous areas to help Jarli uncover the truth about Hiatus. And if I added in the fact of a powerful lady Governor wanting my services in another sort

122

of way, it seemed that I was being asked for help by a lot of females in a lot of threatening situations.

But in those kind of situations, there's only one person that a truly sensible man will help. Himself. I was on my way to the Complex primarily so that Jarli could meet Moone and protect my investment in him. If Jarli's aim of investigating Hiatus criminality looked like getting us into trouble, she'd be on her own. It was only fair.

Just as it was only fair that the Logies should find their own ways of dealing with the Hiatus evils. It wasn't my fight. I don't go out of my way to take part in the ones that *are*.

These were the thoughts and worries occupying my mind as we took our walk from the Mansion to the Complex. But as we got nearer to our goal, I began paying more attention. We were approaching a place where guests of the Mansion shouldn't be strolling, and I didn't want to be spotted.

I set the mini-ceptor in my headband to pick up life-forms, which would be other pedestrians or skim drivers, so that I'd have time to pull Jarli around a corner or behind a bush, out of sight. The first time I did it she resisted, no doubt thinking I was being overcome by uncontrollable lust. But then she saw the City Militia skim that I was aiming to avoid. From then on she moved into hiding when I said, glancing at my head-band, obviously not needing to be reminded about its uses.

All in all, I felt, the enterprise was doing me no harm in Jarli's eyes. Though she didn't seem keen on any more hand-holding, or on being touched in any way. But I didn't mind. I had the idea that she was a little withdrawn by nature, at first, with a man. For self-preservation, since after all she had half the humans of the galaxy lusting after her every week on the vid. But I was fairly sure that I was breaking down her resistance bit by bit. Unless any evildoers or other dangers got in the way, I felt confident that she'd come around before long. Maybe after a successful invasion of the Complex.

We had a bad moment when we came to the extension of the dome that led from the city to the Complex entrance. It was just a longish, man-made tunnel, well-lit all along its length. If anyone came along, we'd be totally exposed. So we waited by the large iris-opening, and listened, and I nervously checked my mini-ceptor. Then we just put our heads down and went through the tunnel in a flat-out sprint.

We got through unseen, and arrived breathlessly at the Complex entrance. The run had worsened the unending heavy ache in my head, but otherwise I felt fairly satisfied about what we'd achieved. A moment later, I felt even better.

Jarli was still looking worriedly around the plastistone apron in front of the large doors when I moved forward to look at their lock. I had various ideas about getting through, but it turned out that they weren't needed. The doors were unlocked – probably by Logie friends of Seliki's – and standing a fraction apart. Before Jarli noticed, I pretended to fiddle a moment with the buttons on the electro-lock, finally nodding sagely and pushing the doors open. Jarli looked very impressed.

Seliki's map said that the Patrolmen would be out of the main entrance foyer at that time – and it was right. We shot across the empty foyer, whisked through the large doors on the far side, now unguarded, and entered the labyrinth of the Complex.

It was still the outer Complex, of course, where we had toured with the PR man, Peristal. Even so, we stopped for a breather, grinning at each other, flushed with success.

"I can't believe it's been so *easy*," Jarli said quietly.

"Not *all* that easy," I said. "But smooth."

She studied me, head tilted. "That was a neat bit of breaking in," she said lightly. "Makes me wonder if you have any real criminal tendencies."

I gave a modest shrug. "You just pick up a few useful things around the galaxy, in my sort of life-style."

"So it seems." As she spoke she reached into her belt-pouch and drew out a tiny object that I realized was a miniaturized vid-camera, as neat as any of my weapons. It was fixed to a slim strap that fitted over her head, centring the camera just above her eyes so that whatever she looked at, it filmed. A thin tendril extruded down to place a tiny plastifilm disc in front of her left eye – probably a view-finder combined with a tiny screen that would display continuous data about the pictures. The whole thing was perfect for combined snooping and filming, and showed how prepared Jarli had been for this investigation of hers.

"Right, then," I said as she adjusted the camera strap. "Let's go give Moone the fright of his life."

"Moone?" She drew back a little. "No, wait. I want to go and look at the Hiatus Heart first." As I frowned, she went on quickly. "Anything could happen here. We might have to get out fast, and we might never have another chance like this. I *have* to find out what's really going on in Hiatus."

"But what about Moone?" I demanded. "Your show?"

She drew herself up, looking noble. "I'll sacrifice it if I have to. The truth about what's happening here is far more important."

Not to me it isn't, I thought angrily. Making sure that Moone wouldn't foul up his performance at the Awakening concerned me far more than the off-chance of crooks in the Complex. But I could see that Jarli's chin was set firm and her mind was obviously made up. And the passageway we were in was not the place to spend time trying to talk her around.

"All right," I snarled. "Let's just see if we can't be *quick* about bringing all the evildoers to justice."

She tightened her mouth at that, but said nothing – just marched away, after reaching up to activate the camera. I followed, a step or two behind, not intending to be in *that* vid-show.

The map guided us along a few passages, and my headband ceptor warned us about life-forms around us. So eventually, meeting no problems, we came to one of the heavy doorways that would have had Patrol guards during the day. Because, the map said, it led into the inner Complex. Unfortunately the map didn't say how to get past its sturdy electro-lock. Jarli turned to look at me expectantly – and at the same moment my ceptor pulsed.

I dragged Jarli back around a corner and waited, heart pounding. I could hear soft padding footsteps in the passage where we'd been. Then they stopped, and I heard the faintest of hisses. With great care, I slid enough of my face past the corner to peer around.

A Logie was standing by the door, a skinny male. Seeing

me, he beckoned, pointed to the lock and made ushering-through gestures. He repeated it all again, to be sure I'd got the message. Then he grinned, and padded away.

I glanced back at Jarli, who was doing something delicate to her little display screen and clearly hadn't heard a thing. "Come on," I said softly. "It's all clear now."

Ignoring her camera, I led the way. The corridor was indeed clear, and again I pretended to do things to the electro-lock before sliding the door open. On the other side of it, we were in the Hiatus Heart.

The map showed that the Heart had been constructed like a wheel, with several big wide passages like spokes, linked by a tangle of smaller tunnels, running in to the huge area or chamber at the centre. We set off on a fairly roundabout route, trying to keep to the secondary tunnels. Sometimes, though, we had to venture out into one of the larger arteries for a short distance. On one of those occasions, we barely got out of the way before a large floater-carrier came around a corner, piled with an assortment of machinery, guided by two men who looked like technicians. As they sauntered past the side tunnel where we were crouching in shadows, we could hear their every word.

". . . it's all just junk," one was saying as they came past. "It won't fool *any*body."

"It will," the other said insistently. "When Rocdril has it set up, it'll look fine. It's only supposed to be background anyway."

"But there are people out there who've *been* in Hiatus before," the first one said. "They'll know what the *real* Awakening Chamber looked like, before it was dismantled."

The second one grunted. "Rocdril knows too. Anyway, those folks who were Awakened, before, they were always too dazed to know *where* they were."

"I dunno," the first one said gloomily. "It still seems risky. On the vid and everything . . ."

"That's the point," said the second one. "Everybody believes what they see on the vid. They'll believe this. Anyway, they'll all be looking at the astronaut, if he comes out alive. And mostly they'll be looking at Jarli Firov, the tube's favourite boobs."

As their voices, and some lewd snickering, began to fade away along the passage, I saw that Jarli had gone white with anger. Myself, I thought the description was more accurate than her label of the Highlight Heart-throb, since it wasn't just men's hearts that throbbed when she was on the screen. But then she surprised me, for she wasn't angry at all about what they'd called her.

"Did you hear that?" she demanded. "They're setting up a *fake* Awakening Chamber for my show! The real one's been dismantled!"

"I heard," I said. "So what? Don't you vid people often make improvements to some places where you're filming? And pretend everything's authentic?"

"Of course," she said brusquely. "That's not the point. *I'm* not doing it, now – Rocdril is. Which means he does have something to hide. Why should he have dismantled the original Awakening Chamber?"

I shrugged. "Maybe the clients are being revived in a different way."

She narrowed her eyes at me. "No. I think it smells. I think it says that Rocdril is doing something . . . something . . ."

"Evil, I know," I said sourly. "So let's go catch him at it, and then get around to Moone."

Away we went again, drawing even closer to the core chamber of the Hiatus Heart. We still kept mostly to secondary tunnels – and met no one else, not even a Logie. In fact we saw nothing much at all of interest. There were locked doors here and there along the secondary tunnels, but what lay behind them was anyone's guess. It probably wasn't much, though, because our route was going through some very unimportant tunnels. Often they didn't even have the ceramisteel sheathing, but remained as slightly rough bare rock. Those stretches were quite pretty, too, the sandstone glittering with colourful crystals of every sort. I felt a brief moment's sympathy for the early miners on Colloghi who thought they'd found their fortunes in that mountain, until ultra-perfect synthetics killed the natural jewel trade.

By then, though, I was concerned about the time that we'd spent creeping around the Complex – and increasing the odds in favour of our getting caught. I was about to suggest to Jarli, acidly, that she didn't need any more footage of tunnels and could we pick up the pace, when she checked the map, glanced around a corner in our tunnel, and pointed. I looked, and saw ahead of us a metal door, broad enough to admit floaters carrying heavy material. It also had a narrow view-panel, so incoming floaters wouldn't collide with outgoing. And the map said that beyond it lay the central chamber.

Jarli moved ahead of me, eased up to the panel, and looked through with eyes and camera. I saw her stiffen. I heard her make a sound midway between a gasp and a whimper. I saw her face go ashen, saw her bite her lip so that it bled.

Fearfully, readying my wrist blazers in case they were needed, I crept up beside her and looked through the panel.

I saw a spacious, open area, brightly lit. The lighting and no doubt the heating came from a massive half-globe hanging in the centre of the high ceiling – one of the medium-output versions of the artificial sun called Tropica-Lens. Below it, in the open area, swarmed a variety of people. Above the area, around its circumference, ran a broad gallery holding more people. At one side of the area stood a large clear plastibubble of the sort that can be set up as a mobile sterile operating theatre. Doctor Rocdril was there, with a number of others who looked like medics and technicians.

Both inside the bubble and outside, they were perpetrating horror.

Chapter 15

I didn't look too closely at Rocdril's plastibubble, at first. I didn't much want to look at any of that grisliness. But I forced myself to stay at the view-panel, just as I forced myself to stop biting my own lip and making a faint whining noise.

There were some ordinary-looking Patrolmen with Stun-Truns standing around being bored in the central area. There were some equally ordinary-looking technicians moving around being busy among a range of complicated equipment. And then there were the other folk, who looked anything but ordinary.

Among those folk, humans were in the majority, but there were plenty of exters, humanoid and otherwise. It seemed that what was happening to them all was quite adaptable to non-human physiologies.

What was happening was *not* Hiatus.

They were all alive and more or less awake, those folk. That is, they weren't in suspended animation. But I wouldn't have wanted to bet on their levels of consciousness.

I could tell, from the humans and humanoids, that they were on the older side, their bodies mostly having declined into scrawny or tubby. I could tell that because they were all wearing nothing but short and skimpy gowns of some cheap, light material – a lot like what people wore in hospitals in ancient times, when no one cared much for human dignity. The gowns fastened at the back, like loose aprons, revealing a good deal of flabby leg and sagging backside. But I scarcely noticed. I was more fixed on what I could see in front of them, and especially on top of them.

Each of them had the top of his or her skull removed, exposing the naked brain.

A layer of transparent gel protected the brains, and under it I suppose the natural membrane coverings had been left intact. But I could see the brains wobbling and rippling slightly as their owners moved. The sight twisted my stomach, as did the further sight of the handful of slender electrode cables sprouting like gruesome worm-like growths from each of the exposed brains. The cables ran down to an oddly shaped metal case hanging in front of each victim from a broad strap around the neck.

The victims were wandering around the open central area, aimless, slow-footed, empty-eyed – or were sitting just as dully on plain chairs placed near the walls. Those up on the gallery were sitting or shuffling around like the rest. On the gallery, and on the far side of the area from where we were, I saw a number of narrow doors which I supposed were sleeping cubicles or restraining cells.

The exter victims were in just the same state, as far as I could tell. Some of them wore different-shaped aprons or other coverings, for their metal cases to rest against. And I imagined the electrodes and everything would have been altered for them, to take into account the different location and nature of their brains. But the principle was the same. And the effect – for they shuffled, or crawled, or slithered, as aimlessly as the humans.

Next to me, Jarli had pulled herself together and was determinedly filming. I was getting my own composure back, too, helped by looking away from the bare-brains and concentrating on the huge array of high-tech equipment scattered around the broad central area. Machines for medical monitoring, for data storage, for purposes I couldn't guess at. Though near the plastibubble where Rocdril was stood a row of machines with a fairly obvious purpose. They were large, heavy, multi-featured consoles with some of the bare-brains sitting motionless in front of them, attended by technicians. And new sets of electrodes ran from the fronts of the metal cases they carried into the consoles. That sight made even clearer to me – though there hadn't been much doubt – what was going on.

The knowledge didn't make it any easier for me, finally, to look into the plastibubble. When I managed to do so, I saw a standard operating table on which lay a fat, bald man with all the usual anaesthetic and life-support attachments. With Doctor Rocdril carefully and tidily cutting away the top of his skull.

I know it's peculiar, but I just don't like operations. Definitely not having them, not even watching them. I'm aware of the popularity of the galacvid show "Surgery Urge" – where you get a close-up view of major operations, where the patient is awake and providing a commentary, where viewers can call in on a comm-link and offer surgical suggestions. It sounds like fun, everyone says it's fun, but I can't watch it. All that opening up of places that ought to remain closed makes me queasy.

So I looked, saw, felt nauseous, and looked away. Back to the victims at the big consoles with all the electrode attachments. Then back to the wandering bare-brains, metal cases resting against their stomachs.

"They're being brain-drained," I whispered to Jarli.

She replied with only a grimace, because it was too obvious to need comment. The technique was less than a century old, since the linkages had been developed that could directly tap memory fragments in brain cells. But it was used only in special situations – as an ultimate lie detector in major fraud cases, for instance – because if taken too far it could leave an unpredictable amount of brain damage behind. So the technology was supposedly under the blanket control of the SenFed, with a tight interweave of fail-safe authorizations. All that careful control, plus the fact that the technology was grotesquely expensive, meant that hardly anyone had ever taken up brain-draining for private purposes.

Not till now. Till Rocdril. Somehow he had gathered the resources to afford the technology, not to mention the huge Tropica-Lens and all the other equipment. And the reputation of Hiatus provided the victims.

131

"I recognize a lot of them," Jarli muttered. "From my investigations. They're all here, the ones I looked into. Addie Joh from the planet Vallor – Isskoe from Parotemm – and there's Octaveud . . ."

Her voice trailed away. Through it all she had kept her head still, kept her eyes and her camera fixed on the monstrous scene. But her eyes were bright with tears, and her paleness had given way to a flush of pure anger.

"The drains will be giving Rocdril access to all their secrets," she said in a voice that didn't sound like hers. "All their personal codes and bank numbers – all their holdings and interests – every detail of their financial dealings . . ."

I nodded. "So then Rocdril and his people can go and empty their Fedbank accounts, sell their assets, clean them out."

"And no one notices," she said tonelessly. "Or if they do, it all looks legitimate – because of those private, unbreakable codes. And it's covered by a tangle of connections and cut-outs."

A chill began to steal over me despite the temperature control in the tunnel. I could see that Rocdril was working an incredibly complicated scam. And a brilliant one. And, above all, an unimaginably expensive one. Not just because of the planetillions that would have been paid for the brain-drain technology, but because of the whole huge set-up, there in the Hiatus Heart, including the personnel.

Obviously the conspiracy would by now be earning, colossally, paying its way many times over. But at the start, before the first brain had been drained, someone would have had to *capitalize* the enterprise. And I was wondering if it had been Rocdril. I was wondering if even Hiatus, in its legitimate days, would have earned him enough creds for that initial outlay.

As the chill gathered in my blood, I told myself shakily that it was time to go. If Jarli wanted to go on playing investigator, and get her throat cut, that was her choice. I wasn't set on going with her. I wanted to earn those kilocreds, through Moone – and I wanted to be alive to spend them. My instinct for self-preservation had just kicked in, and I tend to pay attention to it. In fact I give it blind and total obedience.

"Come on," I muttered to Jarli. "Let's go."

I saw her eyes swivel towards me, though the camera didn't shift from its aim. "What do you mean? Go where?"

"Away," I snapped, reaching out to grasp her arm. "To find Moone if we can and have a quick word – then *out* of here."

She pulled her arm away. "I'm not moving till I'm sure I've got every bit of this foulness on film. How can you even think about your astronaut when this is going on?"

"Jarli," I said, "we're spying on big-time crime. If we're caught here, they're not going to slap our wrists and make us stand in the corner."

Her face tightened. "Don't go spineless on me," she snarled. "I don't care how big-time these ghouls are. I'm going to get the evidence against them – every detail, on film."

"Which will be a lot of use," I snarled back, "when they bury us under this mountain."

She twitched her eyes towards me again, and I saw that they held a look of distaste. "Nothing matters to you but *you*, does it? Well, don't panic. In a few minutes, if I'm sure there's nothing else to film, we can get out, back to the Mansion. They won't suspect a thing. We'll just act normally, do the Awakening of your astronaut one way or another, get off-planet . . . and then I can blow this monstrosity wide open!"

Her face was glowing at the prospect of her mega-scoop flashing around the galaxy. It was the expression of a zealot – someone who is likely to get lots of other folk killed in the pursuit of their desire. Still, I felt, if she was really only going to be a few more minutes . . . I'd look bad if I left her behind and she got out safely by herself, later. And I hadn't much cared for her calling me spineless.

So I shrugged and scowled and tried to make the best of it while she stared through the view-panel and her camera rolled and tension crawled along my nervous system like electric ice. And when the hiss came from the passage behind me, I whirled with a muffled yell and nearly committed murder with my wrist blazers.

But I held back just in time, for the hiss had come from another male Logie, standing hunched some paces away.

"Mast'! Mast'!" he hissed, beckoning.

Even Jarli half-turned, despite her camera. But then she

went back to her filming while I moved to the Logie, feeling my nerve-ends icing up even more.

When I was close enough so that only I could hear the Logie's whisper, he dropped the pidgin – obviously knowing about Seliki and me. "Somewhere in the tunnels you have set off an intruder alarm, Del Curb," he said urgently. "Patrolmen are searching for you at this moment. You must leave at once."

What a terrific idea, I thought numbly, as the ice on my nerves headed for absolute zero. I turned towards Jarli, then back to the Logie to enlist his aid as a guide. But he was vanishing at high speed around the corner at the far end of the tunnel, sensibly intent on saving his own skin, or fur.

"What . . ." Jarli began to ask, but stopped when I grabbed her arm again, more roughly than before.

"We've triggered an alarm," I snapped. "Patrol's looking for us. Come *on!*"

To her credit, she didn't hesitate or ask questions or have hysterics or anything. She didn't even query me about a supposedly sub-sent Logie coming to warn us. She just pulled off her camera, tucked it into her belt-pouch and matched me stride for stride as we ran for it.

I still had the map and my headband ceptor, along with a sense of direction made more acute by raw fear. So we made fairly good time getting away from the centre of the Heart. We were slowed once or twice when my ceptor warned me of approaching life-forms that were Patrol squads, making us duck into side tunnels while the squads pounded past.

By the time the second set of Patrolmen had been narrowly avoided, I was nearly overcome by exertion and fright. But Jarli just seemed a little excited. She even had the breath to talk, and seemed to think we had the time.

"Are you using that same sensor, or whatever, to warn you when people are coming?" She sounded as casual as if we were strolling in a park. "The one you used before, to check for bugs?"

"Same ceptor, different setting," I said tersely, peering around a corner to be sure the way was clear. "Come on."

She held back. "Has it occurred to you . . ." she began.

"Leave it!" I snapped. "Give your mouth a rest and move your feet!"

Her eyes flared up as if I'd suggested something improper. But she shut up, following silently as we fled along the passage.

We were still keeping to the more or less roundabout route that we'd followed on our way in, since I expected the Patrol to be giving their attention to the larger, straighter passageways. But I was mistaken. Within a few more moments, my ceptor told me that several Patrolmen were coming along fairly quickly behind us. And though we made twists and turns, with the use of Seliki's map, somehow they managed to stay on our trail.

By then I was half-stumbling and gasping for breath with the effects of our non-stop dash. Jarli still looked fresh, but I knew that I wasn't going to outrun anyone. The entrance foyer wasn't too far ahead when I turned into a minor side tunnel, intending to shake the pursuit by doubling back before making a final dash for the exit.

Jarli looked like she wanted to object, but when I snarled at her again she just developed an angry scowl and came along silently. Until I stopped in my tracks, staring around frantically.

The Patrolmen that had been trailing us were still doing so. They had taken the same turn, doubling back just as we were.

And also, my ceptor was telling me, *another* squad was on its way rapidly towards us, from the opposite direction.

"We're surrounded!" I said desperately.

Jarli flung me an icy look. "I tried to tell you. The Patrol very probably has portable perceptors of its own."

I scarcely heard her. My mind was racing, trying to find an escape. But the best thing I could think of doing was charging one of the Patrol squads, trying to blast my way through. Since I didn't know what weapons they might be carrying, the idea didn't appeal very much. And while I hesitated, it became too late.

The squad that had been trailing us hurtled into our tunnel, halted when they saw us – then advanced purposefully towards us. Gripping Stun-Truns, raised and ready.

I may have flinched a little, at first. But then I took a step towards them, snapped out mini-grenades of gas from two of my rings, and flung them.

The grenades burst in their faces with tiny hisses, and I stood holding my breath and watching the Patrolmen sway and topple. But I shouldn't have stayed to watch. When I heard the light footsteps behind me, there was no time to do more than begin to turn.

Something hard smacked against my shoulder – and instant numbness paralysed my every muscle. My eyes rolled up, and my mind began to spiral down into a kind of electrified darkness.

Chapter 16

I came awake out of a featureless dream of torment and found that I felt all right. But the brief electro-paralysis of the Stun-Trun does leave some effect. A feeling that your nervous system has been entirely rewired by someone both unskilled and careless. You think that you *ought* to hurt. And your muscles don't quite work as they should, in the first few minutes. So I lay still, staring sourly at a ceiling, working out where I was.

I was sure, at least, how I'd got there. The second squad of Patrolmen, who'd sneaked up on me from behind, would have carried me there. To a narrow bed in a windowless little room full of standard, basic medical equipment. So it was a room in some kind of clinic – and the ceramisteel walls told me that it was a clinic inside the Hiatus Complex. Probably for the treatment of staff ailments, rather than for the specialized and unusual needs of the bare-brains in the Heart.

I could see Jarli sitting in a plain chair nearby, but I didn't look directly at her. She would probably have some illogical female idea that I was to blame for our capture, so I didn't want to open the conversation. Besides, I wanted to lie there quietly and think of a way to get out in one piece. I was wondering if I could pretend to know nothing of Jarli's film, which our captors would surely have seen by then, when her voice made me jump.

"They put us in here to wait for Rocdril." She sounded remote and dull, as if deep in despair. "They said he'd decide what to do with us after he was finished . . . surgery."

I acknowledged with a grunt and forced myself to sit up. Still not looking Jarli's way, I leaned back and tried to think more clearly. No one would ever believe that I was innocent or uninvolved, I realized. But maybe I could get help. The Logies, or Bartraselda ... I shook my head, trying to clear the remaining fuzziness. No, I thought, the Governor was very probably in on the conspiracy, and the weaponless and pacifistic Logies wouldn't be much use.

Then the last of the Stun-Trun effects faded further away, and I sat up straight, feeling the rest of my mind come on line with a click. Stupid, I told myself. I don't need help or leverage. I knew I'd been roughly searched and Seliki's map was gone, but nothing else was. I was fully dressed, and the Patrolmen had clearly thought that I'd been carrying two gas grenades and nothing else. Every one of the rest of my mini-weapons was in place.

I could be through the door in fifteen seconds and on my way. Out – to my ship, into space, as far away as possible from Hiatus and brain-draining and everything. I even thought that I might still try to take Moone along, so as not to forsake all those kilocreds. And Jarli, if she wished. But I wasn't going to take any more undue risks for them. Getting away safely, alive, was the primary object.

"Where exactly are we, do you know?" I asked Jarli.

She shrugged. "Some kind of clinic."

"I can see that," I said acidly. "Where is it in the Complex?"

"How should I know?" she flared. "What does it matter?"

Her voice was no longer toneless. It became clear to me that she felt a little guilty, since her insistence on staying had got us caught. So she had transformed the guilt, as women do, into resentment and anger. Aimed at me as the only handy target. That expanded my own irritation into anger, so I faced her, glare for glare.

"It matters," I rasped, "because I'm going to blast out of here, and I'll need to know which way to go afterwards."

"Blast out?" She looked at me scornfully. "What with?"

"That's not the problem!" I told her, nearly yelling. "The problem is that they took the map, and I don't want to go the wrong way!"

The scorn in her expression faded a little, pursued by doubt. She glanced at my headband, then looked me up and down, obviously wondering where my blasting-out machinery was hidden. "If you really can . . ." She paused, thinking. "I'm fairly sure we're in the Heart, somewhere near the place where your astronaut's pod is being kept."

That was an unexpected bit of luck, I thought. Moone might be somewhere quite near, so that I could grab him quickly. "Could you find the main entrance from here?"

"I think so . . ." she said dubiously.

"Good." I turned purposefully towards the door. I wanted to blow it quickly, to gain maximum surprise in case there were guards posted outside. One of the explosive wedges from my belt buckle, I thought, tucked into the lock mechanism. And then go through the opening, shooting.

"What about your astronaut?" Jarli said suddenly. "Are you going to leave him here?"

"I'll take him along if I can," I said absently, carefully drawing the explosive wedge out of the buckle. "But I'm not going to spend a lot of time looking for him in the tunnels."

"Surely . . ." she began.

I stopped her with a glare. "We have to get *out* of here, and away. Fast and far. We have no time to waste searching for Moone. We're also not going back to the Mansion for our things, or stopping along the way for a four-course dinner!"

"I *know!*" she blazed. "You'll save your own neck no matter what happens, or who else suffers!"

I shook my head wearily. "That's the way real life is. You've been up on your vid screens for too long. Now get out of the way, because I'm going to deal with the door."

But I didn't. Because as Jarli moved to one side and I stepped forward, the door exploded.

The lock mechanism splintered as if it was made of polystyrene. The door itself crumpled and, was flung inwards at high speed, broken out of its frame. It flew across the room, narrowly missing me as it went.

And in the open doorway stood Moone, wearing nothing but a great big grin.

*

"Del!" he said boisterously. "You're all right!"

"I almost wasn't," I snapped. "That door nearly *hit* me, you know."

"Oh – sorry," he mumbled, crestfallen. "I never thought . . ."

"What are you doing here, anyway?" I demanded.

He continued to look abashed, as if I'd caught him out in some petty crime. "Some Logies came and told me you'd been put in here. They said you were tryin' to put a stop to the stuff goin' on in this place, and they wanted me to come and help you. So . . . I did."

He gave me a hopeful half-grin, looking for approval. When I slowly nodded, the grin expanded.

"Aren't you going to introduce me, Del?" Jarli suddenly asked.

Moone hadn't noticed her, I realized, because she had moved back against the wall to one side and he had been focused on me. I saw that she was studying Moone with an expression of total fascination. Now and then she even lifted her gaze to his face. But when Moone saw her, he gave a strangled yelp, turned so red that it looked as if his epidermis had been removed, and turned to blunder out of the room.

I began to leap after him in case he was heading back into the tunnels. But he was merely snatching up from the floor the covering that had been his improvised loin-cloth. Then I realized that he must have lost the cloth in the action that had preceded the smashing of the door.

Two Patrolmen lay on the floor just outside the room – looking deeply unconscious, as if their brains had been dislocated.

I backed away, feeling a little impressed, as Moone knotted the cloth around his hips and re-entered the room. He was still bright red, but was gazing fixedly at Jarli, looking awestruck. Remembering the two flattened Patrolmen, I swallowed back an irritated comment.

"Jarli Firov, meet Myron T. Moone," I said quickly. "And now I suggest . . ."

They ignored me completely.

"It's nice to know you," Jarli breathed, with one of her maxivolt Heart-throb smiles.

Moone almost reeled. "Uh – same here. Sorry about bein' . . . about not bein' dressed . . ."

Jarli made a dismissive gesture, still smiling. Somehow they had moved quite close to one another. "That doesn't matter at all," Jarli murmured. "It was wonderful of you to come and rescue us."

Moone's chest swelled with pride. And, unless I was mistaken about the folds of his loin-cloth, that wasn't all that was swelling.

"Listen!" I said sharply. They both jumped, as if they'd forgotten I was there. "He *hasn't* rescued us! We're still here! Can we get *going*, before a lot more Patrolmen arrive?"

"I'm sure Myron knows what he's doing," Jarli said, not even looking in my direction. She hit Moone with another galvanic smile. "You certainly took care of those Patrolmen out there."

He looked boyishly modest. "That wasn't much. In the NAFF you get trained for all kinds of combat."

That stirred a little interest in me despite my tension. I could imagine occasions – probably quite imminent – when combat training might come in handy. For Moone and anyone with him.

"What level of training?" I asked.

He looked at me with surprise, as if he'd again forgotten my presence. "I dunno, really. See, it's put in like the rest of my trainin', by hypnojection. I can't really *call* on it when I want to. But if I'm attacked or somethin', the hypno-trained stuff takes over, and away I go."

"So when the Patrolmen made a move against you, you flattened them," I said.

"That's it."

Jarli impaled him with an admiring smile, but I was frowning. "But you broke the door down without being attacked . . ."

He chuckled. "I guess I was still kinda fired up, so I gave it a kick. Maybe the lock wasn't very strong."

"Or maybe you *are*," Jarli murmured, moistening her lips with her tongue-tip.

"Right," I said briskly, as the two of them started another exchange of meaningful looks. "Time to go. Moone, see if one of the guards' tunics fits you. It'll be dangerously cold between the city and my ship."

He turned to me, staring. "Your *ship*? Why're we goin' there?"

"I'll explain when we're safely off-planet," I said tersely. "Now let's . . ."

"But, Del!" he broke in. "What about this place and everythin'? The Logies've told me what goes on here – it's really disgustin' and horrible!" He stopped then, as if a thought had struck him, and began slowly to smile. "Oh, I get it! You just want to get Jarli away somewhere safe before you come back to put a stop to all this – like the Logies said you will."

Jarli's ironic laugh was almost ugly. "What he wants is to get *himself* away somewhere safe. That's all. He'd dump us both in a second if he had to."

Moone frowned, looking troubled. "No, no, Jarli, you're makin' a mistake. Del's my *friend*. He got me outa the pod, looked after me . . . He's gonna be my manager and go *on* lookin' after me."

"I'm sure," Jarli said sardonically. "And go on piling up the creds."

I had to put a stop to that, right there. "Can we save all this fascinating conversation till we're on the ship?"

"Fine by me, Del," Moone said firmly, stepping to the door. "But one thing's for sure. When you come back here to take on these crooks, I'm comin' with you."

I heaved a sigh, then opened my mouth to make more urging noises. But I never got a chance.

With a sudden thunderous crashing of boots, another squad of Patrolmen stormed into the room, Stun-Truns raised.

I could have blown quite a few of them away with my miniblazers, except that Moone was between me and them. Though I'm not sure I would have hit him anyway.

Before my eyes, Moone stopped being a knobbly, awkward-looking, heavy-footed lunk and turned into something very like a whirlwind.

I didn't even see the first blow he struck. His big bare foot must have broken the sound barrier as it took the first Patrolman in the midriff, folded him up and flung him back into the midst of his fellows. And I couldn't believe how that foot got back to the floor fast enough to let Moone strike with the other, all the way up to crack another Patrolman's jaw and drop him as if he were boneless.

It seemed almost unfair. There were only eight of them. If they'd known what they'd be facing, they would have sent an army. But I still might have given odds on Moone.

He seemed perfectly balanced at every instant, no matter how he twisted, swayed or struck. Each of his blows seemed to have all of his considerable weight behind it, so that he struck only once per person. I doubt if he needed more than four seconds to finish off the six remaining Patrolmen. He was a blur of fists, feet, knees, elbows – a moving blur that was accompanied by the satisfying music of crushing impacts against flesh and bone. Only one Patrolman was quick enough to try to swing his Stun-Trun at the blur. Moone blocked the blow with the edge of his hand, snapping the man's wrist, then felled him with a backwards elbow-smash.

That was the last one to fall. Moone was breathing only a little more quickly, and, miraculously, had even kept his loin-cloth on. I saw a kind of emptiness in his eyes for a moment, but it faded as his mind took over again from the hypno-reflexes.

"Oh, *Myron!*" Jarli breathed.

Moone turned to grin at her, she stepped towards him, I moved to deflect them both into a little healthy escaping. But once again I didn't get the chance.

A wide-beam flash of bright energy sizzled in through the open door – and flung Moone across the room into a motionless heap.

"That was just a scrambler," a voice rasped from beyond the door. "But there is a blazer here too – aimed at you, Curb. It will fry you in the next instant, unless you raise your hands and keep very still."

I had no choice. I raised my hands, throwing a furious glare at Jarli for having delayed our escape. She didn't notice, being too busy looking anxiously at the huddle that was Moone.

So I turned slowly to watch the owner of the voice stalk into the room, wearing a cold smile. And holding the nerve-knotting scrambler gun. He was no surprise, for I'd recognized the chilly tones of Doctor Rocdril. I'd also half-expected the two Patrolmen with him, gripping Stun-Truns.

But there was a fourth person, who *was* a surprise. The kind of surprise a man gets when his doctor tells him he has almost no time left to live.

I know I should have expected someone like the fourth person. Ever since I'd seen the horror in the Hiatus Heart, and worked out what it must have cost to set the whole thing up. There are only a few organizations galactically rich enough to come up with that kind of capital investment. And crooked enough to want to.

I should also perhaps have seen a possible connection between a major criminal organization operating on Colloghi and the arrival of a mysterious, important visitor to see the Governor.

As I stood with my arms in the air, feeling as if I was turning into frozen jelly, all the connections fell into place with a *click* like the last closing of a coffin lid.

Because into the room, fusitron blazer in hand, strode a lean and deadly man. Wearing the white-on-black of the criminal backers of Hiatus – Famlio. Wearing a carnivorous grin as he looked at me. My worst nightmare. My deadliest enemy.

Pulvidon.

Chapter 17

A common mistake among powerful criminals, I find, is that they're convinced that more honest people are losers, by definition. And they, the big-time crooks, are nature's winners. I know that things do seem that way, most of the time. But not always, not inevitably. The criminals' mistake is to think in terms of their own historical inevitability. Which creates over-confidence. Which is a weakness.

When Pulvidon entered that room with that gun, he *knew* that he had me. He *knew* that he was completely in control. The winner. He was confident that *nothing* could go wrong. So out of that confidence, he gave in to another commonplace criminal weakness. Vanity.

With Rocdril and the Patrolmen, he herded us through the Complex to the same anteroom, off the entrance foyer, where Rocdril had met with Jarli and me the previous morning. And there, with his shark-grin wide, Pulvidon indulged in a little orgy of gloating and self-congratulation.

Merrily, he told us how Famlio had come to Colloghi. It seemed that a rich but not always upright financier, some years before, had tried to duck out on his debts by slipping into Hiatus for a while. At the time Hiatus was a legitimate operation, making a good profit for Colloghi – and for Rocdril, who was running it. Then it turned out that one of the financier's creditors had been Famlio, who objected to being cheated. They pursued the financier to Colloghi, and found – without much difficulty – that Rocdril could be bribed. As could his medical staff. Soon the financier had been prematurely Awakened, and Famlio had got its kilogram of flesh.

But they got more than that. They'd had a close look at Hiatus, and its corruptible director. Sharp intelligences within Famlio – those who keep a careful eye on the galaxy, looking for opportunities for profit – had seen what could be made of Hiatus.

So Famlio bankrolled the creation of the brain-draining process, behind the Hiatus cover. Then they settled back to a happy time of plundering their victims' minds and assets.

It was always intended to be a short-lived thing, Pulvidon told us. Despite their careful coverings, Famlio knew that it would be discovered eventually. People somewhere sometime would put things together, spotting the pattern.

"Like bright-eyes here might have done," Pulvidon said, grinning at Jarli. "If she hadn't been wrapped up in her show about this antique spaceman."

I avoided looking at Jarli. But that remark slightly lowered my terror level. Seemingly, Pulvidon and Rocdril didn't know about Jarli's film. They thought we were in the Complex for something to do with Moone. So Jarli must have hidden the film, I thought, somewhere in the clinic, while I was still out from the Stun-Trun.

I didn't know how it would help. But something might come up. Anyway, it's always good to know something that your enemies don't know. It offsets feelings of helplessness in the face of their confident knowledge that they've won.

Though there was something else, *far* more important to my well-being than Jarli's film, that I knew and Pulvidon didn't know.

Meanwhile Pulvidon was bragging on. About how spies picked up the news of a twenty-first century ship with a probably live astronaut. How Famlio made Custodian Harkle an offer he couldn't refuse. How Famlio reckoned that reviving the astronaut on Colloghi would be the best galaxy-wide one-shot commercial for Hiatus they could get. It would bring an extra rush of applications for Hiatus – and when those extra folk had been fully drained and fleeced, the whole operation could be quietly closed down.

"And all the victims killed, I suppose!" Jarli flared.

Pulvidon shrugged. "It'd be a kindness, sweets. A full draining disrupts areas of the brain. They aren't much use to anyone, after."

"So do you wipe out Collopolis too?" she asked angrily.

"No need," Pulvidon said. "Nobody from the city comes into the Heart. The Patrolmen are all Famlio, the medics and technicians have all been bought." He grinned. "Some people in the city might suspect, but they keep quiet. When the truth comes out at last, they'll all just shake their heads and say, how awful, we had no idea, it was all the doing of that mad doctor Rocdril."

That made Rocdril grin a shark-grin of his own. "And the mad doctor," he said, "will be very rich, with a new name and a new face, living in luxury a long way from Colloghi."

Thinking about it, I saw how it would be watertight and problem-free – especially with the resources of Famlio to help with the tidying up, the erasing of trails. People might eventually suspect who had been behind it all, but no one would ever be able to prove anything. Bartraselda would probably be able to stay in power, claiming innocence – though the planet's economy would collapse without Hiatus.

"One of the best parts, Curb," Pulvidon was saying, "was how I could use the plan to get to you. The pod with the astronaut had to be brought here – so who better to bring it than a well-known, reliable courier?" He glanced at Moone, in a heap on the floor where the Patrolmen had dumped him. "But you're *not* so reliable, Curb. It seems you and the girl have already awakened the astronaut for some reason."

"It was an accident," I said bleakly. I was thinking miserably that I'd been right to suspect a set-up, at first, when Custodian Harkle had hired me. And I was wishing I'd paid attention to my suspicions.

"I'm sure it was," Pulvidon said, managing to grin and sneer at the same time. "But it doesn't matter. He'll go back in the pod like a good boy. Then, later, like a good girl, Jarli Firov will show him to the galaxy, being Awakened in Hiatus."

"Never!" Jarli said with white-lipped fury. "I'll have no part in your filthy crimes! And I know that Myron will feel the same way!"

"*My-ron*, is it?" Pulvidon drawled. "Well, well." He gestured to one of the Patrolmen. "Get the big kid awake."

Imperceptibly, I started to brace myself. If there was going to be any kind of chance for me, I thought it would come along in a few moments. So I got myself ready as the Patrolman – not a man of delicate sensibility – smacked Moone across the face, twisted his ear, then snapped a finger against a more tender part of Moone's anatomy.

Moone jerked, groaned, twisted away and opened his eyes. They focused at once, showing impressive powers of recuperation. Then his gaze fell on Jarli, being held under a gun. The fury visibly flowed through him, washing away the scrambler effects, recharging the power in his every muscle. He heaved himself up to a sitting position, glaring around, and the Patrolman stepped back and raised his Stun-Trun.

That was the moment I was ready for. I had pinned my hopes on Moone's hypno-reflexes being switched on by the threat. My idea was that when Moone went into action, possibly flattening a Patrolman or two before he was gunned down, it would be the diversion I needed. So I could take out Pulvidon and Rocdril with my blazers and make a break for it.

I knew it wasn't a great plan. Pulvidon was a top Famlio executioner, highly skilled, so he might not be all that distracted by a suicidal attack from Moone. But it seemed my only hope. And it might have worked.

Except that, as it turned out, Moone's hypno-learned combat skills included a share of good sense – about not making one-man bare-handed attacks against several enemies armed with guns. So he just sat there, clutching his loin-cloth around him and glaring.

I nearly yelled at him for letting me down so badly. But I thought better of it. And Pulvidon's grin gave way to one of the nastiest chuckles I've ever heard.

"Right, boys and girls," he said. "Pay attention. Here's what you're going to do." And he crisply explained again how Jarli and Moone were still going to go through the pretence of reviving Moone, out of the pod, as a galactic promotion for Hiatus.

Moone turned red with anger, Jarli turned white – again – with more anger. They loudly stated their determined refusal. They heroically announced that they would never assist Famlio's evil plans. They affirmed that they would seek to oppose those plans with their last dying breath.

"That," Pulvidon chuckled, "can be arranged. So can other unpleasantness. Try this one. If you don't do the vid-show, I'll blow a large hole in your friend Curb."

I twitched violently at that, and Moone looked worried. But to my astonishment, Jarli gave a harsh laugh.

"Him? I'm surprised he hasn't offered to *join* you. He doesn't care about anything except making a profit and saving his own skin. Why should we care about him?"

Even through my fear, it struck me as monstrous that she should say such things. But then others, like my ex-partner Mala, have said things like that now and then. As if there was something *wrong* with earning a living, or with self-preservation.

I was glad to see that Moone seemed troubled by her remarks. "No, Jarli, now, I don't think . . ." he began.

"Oh, Myron, don't let him fool you," she said wearily. "This man has already said how he planned to get Del here – probably to kill him. So our doing the show won't save Del. And we *can't* do a show that will bring hundreds more people here to be brain-drained!"

Moone still looked troubled. But then he nodded slowly and looked at me with an apologetic shrug. "I guess she's right, Del. We can't do that."

Pulvidon had been watching with some amusement, and at Moone's statement he began to applaud sardonically. "Seems these two know exactly what you're worth, Curb," he said.

I felt wholly destroyed. I would have thought that after all we'd been through together, Jarli and Moone would have done *something* on my behalf. A little vid-show didn't seem too much to ask. Yet they had betrayed me with hardly a thought. Fair-weather friends, I supposed. You can meet a lot of folk like that.

Pulvidon had turned to Jarli. "Right, sweets, so you won't be moved by a threat to Curb. Who'd blame you? But I'm getting the picture about you and *My-ron*, here." His grin widened. "So if you don't give me exactly the kind of vid-show I want, it'll be My-ron who suffers. I'll maim him, understand? Take a blazer and burn off the bits that you're probably keenest on."

I saw horror, disgust, desperation and other things flash across Jarli's face. Pulvidon saw it all, too, before he turned to Moone. "And you'll co-operate too, or *she'll* suffer. But I won't hurt her body, My-ron. I'll put her in the Hiatus Heart and brain-drain her all the way. She'll be a beautiful bright-eyed shell, nobody at home inside her head."

At that I braced myself again, for Moone looked as if he would leap at Pulvidon's throat. Go for it, lad, I urged silently. But Pulvidon was quick and alert. He stepped swiftly back, blazer ready, and the moment was lost. Moone sank back, glowering but looking defeated. As Jarli was looking.

As I, most of all, was feeling.

Pulvidon was ignoring me, wrapped up in enjoying the sullen surrender of Jarli and Moone. And I had just about reached that point of no return, when there is nothing much left to lose, when natural prudence is outweighed by terminal desperation. I knew that Pulvidon was going to kill me, slowly and painfully as he'd promised. I knew that if I launched a surprise attack there was a thread-slim chance that I might get most or all of them before they got me. Moone might join in and help. If I failed, I'd be just as dead as I would be anyway, but quicker.

Those dire thoughts took a micro-second to formulate. But then I hesitated, fatefully, weighing my chances one more time. My old instinct of self-preservation was shrieking at me that where there was life there was hope. It's not always true, or even often true, but it made me hold back just long enough.

Pulvidon turned on me, perhaps subliminally aware of my gathering tension. "Take him," he snarled.

Before I could move, two Patrolmen grasped my arms and dragged them around behind my back.

Pulvidon nodded. "Right. Now that you don't seem to be any

use to anyone, Curb, I can put you away." He moved to a short-range intercom terminal on the wall, spoke into it inaudibly. Then he turned his grin back on to me.

"You're lucky in one way, Curb. I don't have time to waste on you. I'd wanted to kill you with my own hands and take a long time at it. Now I have to forgo that pleasure." He stepped closer, staring at me hot-eyed. "But I'll be able to *imagine* how you'll be dying, Curb. That'll be nearly as good."

The door opened suddenly, making me jump. Another Patrolman came in, carrying something like a roll of heavy cloth.

"You're kind of a fancy dresser, Curb," Pulvidon said, "so I'm sorry your last outfit is so plain."

He took the cloth and unrolled it. Through my fear I recognized it, but I didn't understand it. It was a broad length of that thick but pliable material called FlexiMail. Woven from the metallic fibres that form naturally in the stems of the Harbyrean ironweed, reinforced with extra alloys in molecu-bond. It's said to be impressively tough and resistant.

The idea, I learned, was for it to be resistant to *me*.

"People say you're tricky, Curb," Pulvidon went on. "And you were slippery enough when we met last. But you won't trick your way out of this. Not if you were the best escape artist in the galaxy."

He laughed, stepping towards me. I struggled in the grip of the Patrolmen, but uselessly. A moment later the FlexiMail had been wrapped around me, fastened at the back by the instant bonding of magni-link fasteners. I was sheathed from shoulder to mid-thigh, my arms clamped helplessly against my sides. The only way I could have attacked Pulvidon was to kick him, butt him, bite him or spit in his eye.

And that was the end of all my hopes – which had been focused on the important thing that I knew and Pulvidon apparently didn't. The existence of my mini-weapons. But the sadistic cruelty of blind chance had led Pulvidon to bind me in a way that made my weapons useless. I couldn't even use the vibro-blade in my fingernail, since my fingertips were pressed hard against my leg, and the blade would have cut a chunk out of me, while making a uselessly small incision, at best, in the FlexiMail.

All I could do was stand still inside that armoured casing, sweating and trembling, aware that my instinct for self-preservation had fallen into a bitter, accusatory silence.

Pulvidon was saying other things, needling and taunting, but I could no longer hear him past the roaring in my ears, terror sounding like an inescapable tidal wave. I was held rigid by my own sense of doom as much as by the FlexiMail as Pulvidon and the two Patrolmen bundled me out of the Complex, into a waiting ground-skim. My eyes were blurred with panic, my limbs felt boneless and paralysed, my blood seemed to have congealed at the base of my spine. I felt that I might be sick, or foul myself, except that my body wasn't functioning. I was growing heavily immobile as if turning to stone, truly petrified.

In a while the skim paused while the others pulled on protective clothing. Then they drove through an iris-opening out of the dome city, into the blistering cold of a Colloghi sunrise. The searing bite of that coldness shocked me back to some awareness. I saw that we were driving across the edge of the spaceport, where my ship sat – so near, so inaccessible. I saw the city's dome behind us, with the massive wall of the mountainside looming beyond it. In the other direction I saw nothing but whiteness, where the mountain fell away from the plateau in terrifyingly sheer cliffs.

"It's two and a half kilometres down to the ice-floes, Curb," Pulvidon said casually, his voice sounding metallic from within his protective face-mask. I could feel the frost snarling around my own exposed face and neck, biting at my ankles, seeping through the density of the FlexiMail. Most of all, I could feel my lungs labouring, trying to take in enough oxygen from the thin air at that height.

Pulvidon put his mask close to my face, and I saw that he was looking almost wistful. "What I really regret," he said, "is that I'll never know *exactly* what killed you. Suffocation at first – freezing to death – the impact – maybe dying of fright on the way." He treated me to a final glimpse of his carnivore grin. "But I'll tell myself that it was all those things together.

And anyway, whatever happens, the fact is that what will really kill you . . . will be *me*."

The skim stopped at the plateau's edge. The Patrolmen dragged me out, held me firmly while Pulvidon stepped out. He glanced at the edge, at the emptiness beyond it where the mountain fell away. Then he gestured to his men.

"Right. Do it."

The Patrolmen, expressionless within their face-masks, picked me up. Carried me to a level piece of bare rock on the plateau's furthest, dizzying, unguarded lip.

And, with unceremonious ease, threw me over.

Part Three

The One And The All

18

I heard ⟨...⟩ ıd shrill, until it was choked off from la ⟨...⟩ elt as if it was being crushed as I fougl ⟨...⟩ ırough the thin air. My exposed flesh ⟨...⟩ d, made worse by the wind-chill from ⟨...⟩ lt a stinging in ears, nose, cheeks, felt ⟨...⟩ me. But I could only feel, for my eyes ⟨...⟩ ing tears and my ears were filled wit ⟨...⟩y unvoiced ⟨...⟩ I might have been only hanging in mid-air, turning slowly over and over, while a dark frigid razor-edged wind stormed past me. But part of my mind manically kept reminding me that I was plummeting down past the immensity of those sheer cliffs, towards the frozen Colloghian sea.

The same manic part of my mind was even trying to remember, in a weird disconnected sort of way, the formula for measuring the acceleration of a falling object.

That may have been the onset of a delirium caused by oxygen deprivation, or frostbite, or both. From what I'd always heard about human ways of death, suffocating and freezing both put you into a nice comatose sleep before finally finishing you off. As I fell, and froze, and tried to scream, I could hardly wait. No one had made it clear how much suffocating and freezing actually *hurt*, before the sleep came along.

But I fell, and fell, and stayed mostly conscious in all my agony and terror. I have no idea how far I'd fallen, or for how long, when the peculiar feeling started to creep over me. All normal awareness had left me by then, save for my perception of pain and my abject terror of the moment when pain, and I, would end. So the feeling was probably creeping over me for some while before I noticed it.

And for a time after what was left of my consciousness *did* notice it, I just thought it was part of my delirium, and carried on with more important things like trying to take a proper breath so I could scream.

But the peculiar feeling continued, and grew stronger. In a few more moments, my mind started to confront the possibility that it was really happening. Except that the possibility was *im*possible.

My downward speed, my rate of descent, was slowing.

I tried to assemble my remaining shreds of rationality. Surely, I thought, I couldn't have got the acceleration-of-falling-objects formula *that* wrong. Such objects never *de*celerated, as far as I could recall. But . . . I was decelerating.

I had by then fallen far enough to be getting down into some nice thick useful air. I took the deep breath that I'd been aching for, and enjoyed it so much that I didn't bother using it to scream. Besides, I no longer felt like screaming, except perhaps with relief and elation.

As the oxygen washed through my brain cells, I suddenly knew what was happening. Someone had come to my rescue. The one being in the entire galaxy that I could totally rely on.

I knew I was right, because I'd recognized the peculiar feeling that was happening to me. I'd felt it often, before. It has always made me think of what it would be like to leap into a great depth of viscous, gluey liquid. Your fall, your sinking, would decelerate fairly quickly.

That's how I've always felt on those times when I've been lifted or lowered by the Magnigrip tractor beam of my ship. Operated by Posi.

As my fall went on slowing and I went on taking great happy gulps of good air, I was filled with a true, pure feeling of love. Or anyway gratitude. For my flawless, dependable thinking machine. I wished that there was some way that an Intelloid could be rewarded, because just then I would have given Posi anything. So great was my sense of joy and praisegiving that I only vaguely bothered to wonder how Posi had *known* of my plight, what had brought her and the tractor beam to my rescue. She had helped me that way before, but only after an explicit call for help on my pendant mini-comm. This time, bound by the FlexiMail, I had made no call. Perhaps, I thought, she'd had a ceptor aimed at the edge of the plateau, for some unknown reason, and had seen me go over . . .

But right then I didn't care. I didn't even care that I was still going to land in an empty wasteland of snow and ice and black water, immobilized by the FlexiMail sheath. I didn't care because I was going to be *alive* when I landed. I was actually chuckling to myself as I drifted like a feather slowly down.

In the sky above me, the morning was advancing. Below me, though, the shadow of the mountain still spread deep night over the huge, island-like ice-floes and the bands of sea separating them. I saw that I was coming down on one of the largest floes, as rugged as the rest of them, with humps and hollows where ice had bulged and snow had heaped. I seemed to be heading down towards a particularly broad hollow, unusually steep-sided. Its depths were almost invisible in shadow, but for a second I thought I saw a ripple of movement in that darkness. Probably a flurry of snow lifted by the wind, I guessed. Anyway, I knew I'd have a closer look shortly.

But my fall had slowed so much that the final quarter-kilometre or so took an age. I could have walked downstairs faster. My euphoria started to be tinged with a little impatience. And it wasn't helped when a ray of red sunlight reached out to flare against an ice-bright glacier on the mountain, just as I was looking that way. The glare nearly blinded me for a moment, so the depths of the wide hollow below me looked even more impenetrably dark. Which meant that I had no idea what to expect as I floated slowly down the last short way, and landed.

To find that I'd been deposited in the midst of an enormous pile of fur – a thick, soft, springy heap that might well have broken much of my fall even if I'd been falling at full speed.

They were Logie furs, of course – the aromatic scent was

unmistakable. In fact it was very heady, almost too much so. And it was almost too much again to find that dozens of the furs were *occupied* – were the pelts of living Logies, most of them soft, plump females. And it was definitely too much to be engulfed by them, all chattering and cooing and patting me to see if I was intact. Suddenly, after all the suffocating and freezing and everything, I couldn't take what was happening. I felt overcome – by the fact of my survival, by the intoxicating spicy odour, by the furnace heat radiating from all those furry little bodies.

The last thing I remember was the startling sight of a familiar form pushing through the crowd of Logies – my little friend Seliki. Who should have still been high up on the plateau, in the Mansion. Perhaps it was that unlikely arrival which was the final straw. My vision went dim, my legs felt as if they'd melted, and I collapsed into a lot of sturdy little fur-clad arms.

I hardly ever faint, of course, but I'd defy anyone to avoid a little giddiness after what I'd been through. Besides, it wasn't a dead faint. I was distantly aware of being picked gently up and borne away. I dimly sensed that I was being carried towards one steep side of the wide basin – and then somehow *into* it, as if into a cavern. I vaguely saw that the interior was a warren, a honeycomb, of low rounded rooms carved from the ice, one leading to another, separated by fur hangings. I dazedly noted that each room was softly lit and more or less warmed by a few small lamps burning some fragrant oil.

I began to come around then, for I was more immediately aware when the crowd deposited me on a thick pile of furs that resembled a bed, and then withdrew. All except Seliki.

"Come now, Del Curb," she murmured in her musical little voice. "You are safe and warm, and I will look after you. Raise your head a little, and drink."

Blearily, I obeyed. She slid a soft hand behind my head to support it, and I sipped from a cup that she held to my lips. Sipped a liquid that was hot without burning, sweet without cloying, spicily aromatic in a way unlike the Logie-scent. I sipped and gulped and drank it down while Seliki murmured soothingly in my ear.

Then I lay back, beginning to drift away again, knowing that the drink was taking me into a welcome sleepiness born also of exhaustion and reaction and the deliciousness of being warm. I felt Seliki roll me over, felt her deft fingers work out the mystery of the FlexiMail fastenings and undo them, pulling it away from me. The feeling of release was indescribable – and as I relished it, it seemed the most natural thing in the world that Seliki should then remove all the rest of my clothing.

When I was naked she rolled me over again and began to give me a massage – even more thorough and expert than the back-rub she'd first given me. Her hands were lubricated with an oil that seemed to share the scent of the lamps and the aroma of my drink. And her touch worked magic all over my face and ears and neck, my shoulders and arms and hands . . . As she began to extend the magic down over my chest, then lower, I fought the sleepiness, fought to stay at least partly awake to enjoy the later stages of the massage. But I could not. The relaxation brought on by Seliki's hands added itself to all the other soporific effects. I drifted, blissfully, into slumber.

And I dreamed. It struck me, even as it went on, as a remarkable dream – because it was so clear, without the disorienting, irrational leaps that dreams take. And because I was *aware* that I was dreaming. But mostly because I never wanted to wake up.

I dreamed that I was lying on a downy-soft bed, making love. With a woman who was small and well-formed, firm and athletic, inventive and totally abandoned. Who seemed to laugh a lot when she wasn't crying out in ecstasy. We were naked, of course, and yet – here was a bit of dream-surreality – she seemed to be wearing a heavy fur coat, which had the effect of making her delicate skin seem fever-hot. But the coat could be parted, allowing me to make the kinds of contact that I wished.

Best of all, I was tireless. We writhed and flailed around on that bed for what seemed like *hours*, yet I needed no rests to recoup my powers. Even as the room around us echoed with her climactic shrieks and my groans, we were grappling avidly again, rolling into another position, starting at once the ascent to another peak. Nothing in my fairly considerable experience would have hinted that I could manage such a performance, reach such lengths and heights. It was the kind of sexual dream that young men wait for and old men pine for. If it could have been filmed, it could have been the porn success of the decade.

It didn't even exactly end. It just seemed somehow to fade slowly, gently, away – so that at last my partner and I fell back from a rapturous finale not into the start of a new progress but into a languor, a peaceful drift, wrapped in each other's arms.

And obviously, predictably, I awoke some time later, lying half-covered on the pile of furs, to find Seliki lying beside me, smiling satisfiedly and quite literally trying to twist me around her little finger.

I smiled back at her – until sudden surprise made me give a convulsive jerk. Seliki pulled her hand away, fearing she'd hurt me. But my surprise hadn't come from a pain in the groin. It came from the absence of any pain at all. Yet I remembered too well how the deadly cold had clawed at me during that fall, especially at the exposed skin of my face. By rights that skin should be suffering the searing agony of frostbite. Maybe blackening with gangrene. But my lips and cheeks felt perfectly normal when I smiled, and even when I didn't.

"It *wasn't* all a dream, was it?" I asked Seliki, feeling my face nervously. "The fall, I mean, and being rescued, and . . . everything afterwards?"

"It was not a dream," she said softly. "You did fall, but you were taken up and saved by the will of the Allness."

"Oh, well, good," I mumbled. That was the omnipresent nature spirit of the Logies, I remembered. I never feel comfortable with totally irrational religious convictions about divine intervention.

"And afterwards," she went on, "it was beautiful like a good dream, but it too was real. Are you troubled by it?"

"No, no," I said. "I just . . . um . . . expected frostbite."

She looked relieved. "I prevented that. The oil I rubbed you with is a Logh-uy remedy, developed from the oils of sea creatures."

I looked at her wonderingly, amazed again at how many abilities the Logies kept hidden behind their sub-sent disguise. I suppose that some people would then have chosen another question to ask – probably about the details of their amazing rescue. But I expected Seliki to give me more religious nonsense if I did that. And she had put her hand back where it had been, to some effect, which drove me to ask a different question.

"And what about how I ... I mean, how we ..." Her hand was definitely distracting. "Did that oil do something to ... ah, to my virility?"

"No." She chuckled. "That was the drink I gave you, the jwryll. As I told you when we first met, the Logh-uy love to make love. So we developed a substance that would ... prolong things."

"Amazing," I gasped. Her hand was growing more insistent. "And is there ... ah ... can it harm you if you take a second dose too soon?"

"It is wise to sleep between times." Her smile was beatific. "For about as long as we have slept."

She twisted away without removing her hand and reached her other hand down beside our furry bed – bringing up a cup that I recognized.

"Drink, Del Curb," she murmured, offering it to me, "and we will dream our dream again awhile."

Though I knew I wasn't dreaming that time, it still seemed like it. As if everything was slightly larger than life. Especially me. As if all my senses were enhanced. As if time and potency were endless, and all reality focused on to the tangled furs where we lay.

But once again the dream-time slid away to its conclusion, when even Seliki was appeased, and we rested quietly together till our breathing and pulse-rates returned to normal. At last Seliki bounced up to make us something to eat, cooking over a larger version of the oil-burning lamps.

And I lay still, trying to cling to the magic, not wanting to face the problems and terrors that a return to Colloghian reality would bring.

When the food arrived, I fell on it ravenously – strange spicy shellfish and some odd leafy vegetable also from the sea. Seliki told me that the Logies have some oxygen-storing ability and so have always been undersea gatherers. They herd and tend and harvest a variety of sea-creatures and plants. I didn't pay too close attention, being too busy eating. The shellfish was savoury, the vegetables were crisp, and I would have relished the full feeling of well-being, if it hadn't been for my nagging anxieties.

In fact it was my self-preservation instinct that was doing the nagging, having produced the idea that if Posi had lifted off to use the Magnigrip and rescue me, someone in Collopolis might have noticed. So someone up there might have guessed that I was still alive.

Nervously, I located my clothes and things where Seliki had tidily placed them, and called Posi on the pendant-comm.

"Hello, Del," she said warmly. "I have been hoping to hear from you. I have had to go into orbit."

A coldness closed like a fist around my entrails. "Orbit? *Why*?"

"Several perceptor probes were made at the ship," she replied. "And then some men came and tried to force their way in."

Pulvidon's people, of course, trying a little search and robbery. "Did they get in?" I asked hoarsely.

"No, Del. I spoke to them through their ground-skim intercom, to inform them of your programmed instruction. That I should lift off if anyone tried to tamper with the ship. Then when I ignited the engines, they retreated – and I came up at once into a low parking orbit."

Superb, I thought. Not only does she save the ship, she has been seen to do it all on her *own*. I was still a little worried, though. She might have been seen above the plateau when she came down again from orbit – as I assumed she had – in order to use the Magnigrip to save my life.

"You've done well, Posi," I told her. "And I'm really grateful that you came to rescue me. But I wonder . . ."

She interrupted me, sounding surprised. "No, Del. You are mistaken. I have not left orbit. It was not *I* who came to rescue you."

Chapter 19

That statement was one of the more unnerving things that had happened to me on Colloghi. I sat speechless, staring at the pendant. Not Posi who rescued me? It had to be. There wasn't anyone else. Was there? I even wondered wildly for a second if the desperation of my fall had awakened some paranormal power within me, like hysterical levitation.

Posi, meanwhile, had gone on prattling. "In fact I have been having a very interesting time, Del," she said. "I am engaged in the most unexpected and rewarding conversation . . ."

"*Conversation?*" I yelled. "Never *mind*, Posi!" And I switched off.

If I hadn't, she probably would have given me a word-for-word replay of the conversation. She has tried that before. I imagined that she'd been in touch with one of her sister-Posis on the call-beam link. The more high-powered Intelloids love to wander together through forests of incomprehensible concepts, mostly mathematical or philosophical. Or she might have called up that Casi, back in the Asteroid Belt, for a friendly chat.

I couldn't have been less interested. And it was typical of Posi not to realize it. But Intelloids can be like that. No sense of priorities. She wanted to talk about a conversation when I was facing a disturbing puzzle about how my life had been saved.

If Posi said it wasn't herself, it was true. Intelloids don't tell lies or make jokes.

But then – who?

I went on sitting, staring at the pendant in my hand, my mind whirling. I even began to toy with the idea that the Mansion had the tractor-beam technology, and Bartraselda had galloped to my rescue with it, to preserve me as a likely heir-provider. But then Seliki broke in on those thoughts.

"Why are you troubled, Del Curb?" she asked.

"Posi – my ship," I muttered. "Says she didn't rescue me. But it had to be . . ."

The awful thought then struck me that Posi might have suffered a malfunction, a glitch affecting data storage. So that she had rescued me but had then wiped the memory. I cringed inwardly at the thought of what a check-up and overhaul would cost me . . .

Seliki interrupted again. "But I told you who rescued you. The Allness."

I gave her an indulgent half-smile. "Yes, I know. And I really do appreciate it. I just can't work out . . . um . . . how it was actually *done*."

"It was as I have said," Seliki replied, frowning a little at what she seemed to see as my inability to understand. "The Allness reached out his will for you."

"And I'm grateful," I said, still indulgently. "But I don't see why . . ."

"Because," Seliki said softly, "the Logh-uy asked it of him. All those you met here on the ice became as one voice with me, and asked it of him."

I stared at her, suddenly thinking of a question that had been a long time, with one thing and another, surfacing in my mind. "That's a point, Seliki. What are you doing down here on the ice?"

She smiled. "I learned through the Logh-uy in the Complex that you had been captured and were being taken to the edge of the plateau. So I came down to organize our plea to the Allness – and to be with you if the Allness granted our wish."

"But I fell!" I said. "How could you get down here so fast?"

"I started down before you were thrown over," she told me. "We have a swift way, made for our enjoyment long ago, before the humans came. It is an ice-covered *slide* down from the plateau, with many twists and turns." She drew a wavy line in the air with a finger. "It follows beside a path that the Logh-uy use to return to the plateau. It is not a hard climb, for us. And on the slide, coming down – it is like flying."

"I did a little flying of my own," I muttered.

She nodded. "So you did. In the clasp of the Allness you flew down as softly as a snowflake." Suddenly she hugged me fiercely in strong little arms. "I am very glad, Del Curb, that the Allness preserved you as the Logh-uy asked."

I reached out to stroke her rich fur, feeling oddly touched. I haven't known many folk who have tried to prevail on their gods on *my* behalf.

"I'm glad, too," I said huskily. "But the thing is, I'm not a Logie, I don't know anything about the Allness, and I'm kind of puzzled about the *process* of how I was saved."

She stepped away, looking upset. "You do not believe me, I think. Why not?"

"I do believe you," I said quickly. "I'm just trying to under-stand. I mean – if you can ask the Allness to save me, why don't you ask him to save *you*, to rescue you from being almost slaves on your own world?"

She shrugged. "We have often asked that, times beyond counting. He has never responded. Yet he has done other things, now and then, that we have asked. So we believe that we are unable to perceive his plan – and must only accept when he acts or does not act." She smiled. "Perhaps, Del Curb, when he saved you, he made *you* part of his plan. Perhaps saving you is his way of starting the process of liberating the Logh-uy."

Here we go, I thought sourly. Del Curb about to be roped in again to help the downtrodden. But I'd avoided that trap before, and I could avoid it again.

"Then I hope he won't be too disappointed," I said, reaching for my clothes, "if I don't stay around to see any more of the process."

Seliki looked stricken. "What do you mean? You wish to *leave*?"

"I'd be crazy not to," I said abstractedly, trying to set my headband straight without a mirror. "I can't stay here for ever.

And up in Collopolis there are highly dangerous people who are keen on killing me."

"But what of the others?" Seliki cried, very upset. "Myron Moone and Jarli Firov? They are still captive! And the evil people are doing terrible things in the Complex! And . . ."

I put my fingers over her little mouth. "Seliki, I *know* all that. But I don't see how it would help anyone for me to get killed. The sensible thing for me is to call my ship down here to pick me up, and get away." If Posi isn't too busy gossiping, I thought wryly. "Then I can tell the FedPol the truth about everything on Colloghi, and I can bring a detachment of them back here to put an end to all the evildoing."

In fact, I knew they'd bring *me*, if they came at all. But it wasn't likely. There are a lot of planets and evildoers, and the FedPol's resources are finite. Besides, the FedPol didn't always rush to investigate charges against Famlio. Too many greasy palms, probably.

Anyway, I knew that if I went reporting things to the FedPol, they'd start asking awkward questions about my involvement, stolen stasis pod and everything. My wisest course would be just to get away from Colloghi and be glad I was in one piece. Though I did briefly wish that there was some way to take Moone along. It was maddening to think about all the kilocreds that would have come my way . . .

I said none of that to Seliki, of course. I just explained in slightly glamorized detail how wonderful the Federation's police were. But she wasn't mollified.

"*No*," she said firmly. "Your police may come, Del Curb – but even before they land on the plateau, the evil will be hidden away. Doctor Rocdril has planned for it. The Logh-uy know that he will kill all the sad ones with open brains and drop them into a deep pit that is all prepared . . . Then he will disguise the machinery and everything, and it will look as it did before, an innocent place where people are sleeping the sleep of non-death. Myron Moone and Jarli Firov will also be in the pit, and there will be no proof!"

That shook me. "Wouldn't the Logies . . ." But then I stopped myself, even as Seliki shook her head. No one would listen to supposed sub-sents. Even if anyone did, Logies couldn't testify in SenFed courts.

"You *must* stay and help, Del Curb," Seliki said beseechingly, moving close to me again. "You may have been given to us by the Allness for this purpose. The Logh-uy cannot rise up against the evildoers. We know nothing of violence or battle. But if you were to *lead* us, Del Curb, we might succeed. So you must help. You must find a way to free your two friends, and then stop the evil things."

By then she had reached out to a responsive area or two on me. And it's never easy to think straight while being fondled by an uninhibited female. Never easy – but not impossible. My pulse rate and other things may have been rising, but so was my alarm. If there had been a risk-free way to help everyone and defeat the villains, I thought to myself, I might even try. But the notion of leading unarmed Logies into righteous battle . . . I might as well go up, I thought, and jump off the plateau again.

And that led to another drawback, which I tried to put to Seliki despite her busy little hands. "I don't see . . . *uh* . . . how I can free anyone, when they're . . . *ooh* . . . up there and I'm down here. Do you expect me to climb up that Logie path?"

She frowned, her hands stopping. "No – for you do not retain air as we do. It would be a dangerous climb for you, unequipped."

I smiled. "There, you see . . ."

"But," she went on, "you said you could call your ship down here, to pick you up."

"I know I did," I said warily. "But I couldn't go and land on the plateau again, to start freeing people. I'd be spotted. I'd lose the element of surprise."

She nodded thoughtfully, then frowned again. "There is something I do not understand, Del Curb. Before, you thought your ship saved you from the fall. As if your ship could somehow grasp and lift you from a *distance*."

I was taken aback. That little display of lateral thinking was the last thing I expected from a female primitive. But I couldn't wriggle out of it – not with her bright little eyes fixed on me.

"Yes, well, it can, in a way," I admitted grudgingly. "A thing called a tractor beam . . ."

"Then that is it!" she cried triumphantly. "That *beam* can place you on the plateau!"

"The ship has to get fairly close," I told her, trying to salvage something. "I could still be seen."

"Not if it is done at night," Seliki said quickly. "And the days are short now. It will be dusk soon."

I opened my mouth, then closed it again, having no more arguments. I had been neatly sandbagged, and I knew it. Which only proves, if proof was needed, that there is no arguing with a determined woman. Of any species.

Seliki hugged me again, as fiercely as before. "You will do it, Del Curb," she said in a passionate whisper. "You will save your friends and defeat the evil. And we will help you. I will go with you, to guide you. And all of the Logh-uy will protect you however they can, die for you if they must."

I leaned back and looked down at her, frowning as I thought hard about what she'd said. It occurred to me that it sounded promising. Not the bit about Logies dying for me, since if things got to those extremes I could be in danger of dying as well. And I was aiming to avoid that, at any cost. But being set down secretly by tractor beam – and having Seliki and the Logies to *guide* me through the city and into the Complex . . . Very promising. The Logies would surely have hidden, servant routes in the Complex just as they had in the Mansion. With their help, I might be able to move around freely and unseen. With almost no risk of a confrontation.

I might even be able to get to Moone and Jarli, and get them out.

I knew that I'd have to iron out some details and weigh up the risks before setting out. But it looked possible – and tempting. And if the risks were calculated, they might be worth taking. Because if I could get Moone and Jarli away, we could set up some other means of launching Moone as the celebrity man from the past, and all those kilocreds would still come pouring in.

Why, I told myself, Jarli would even be able to use her influence to get a serious investigation started into Hiatus.

Which might put a stop to it. We might even get the SenFed to have an assessment look at the Logies, and reclassify them. So everyone would be happy. And *alive*.

Seliki was looking at me hopefully. So I gave her a thin smile and stroked her fur.

"All right, Seliki," I said. "If the Logies can help me to move around without being seen, I'm willing to go back to the plateau and . . . see what I can do."

Chapter 20

Seliki's delight was so boundless that I thought her hug would crack some of my ribs. When the hug became a further series of overheated caresses, I wondered if we were going to pass the short while to nightfall with another high-powered roll in the fur. Instead, to my surprise, she released me after a moment or two and moved away.

"If there were time, Del Curb," she said softly, "we might sip the jwryll again . . . But no."

"No?" I echoed hoarsely.

"We must be ready to leave the moment darkness falls. Who can know what may be happening to your friends in the Complex?"

So I agreed, with some grumbling, and finished pulling on my colourless coverall and boots. "There's one problem right away," I complained. "I can pick up a therm-cloak once I'm inside my ship. But I'm going to *freeze*, crossing from here to where my ship lands. And on the plateau outside the city. I could do with one of your nice big furs to wrap myself in."

"Certainly . . ." Seliki began. Then she stopped, with a big bright-eyed smile. "But I have a better idea."

She said no more, just scampered away, leaving me puzzled and a bit annoyed as I made my usual routine check on my mini-weapons. Then, with some misgivings, I took up my pendant and called Posi again.

She didn't seem at all perturbed that I'd broken the connection so abruptly before. She never is. "Hello, Del. Is everything all right?"

"Yes," I said without much warmth. "But I . . ."

She interrupted. It was becoming a habit. "I am glad to hear it. Now I can tell you about the conversation I am having. It is the most remarkable . . ."

I could hardly believe it. Not that she was having her conversation at the same time as talking to me – that was just Posi being polyfunctional. Nor that she was *still* having it, since she'll talk non-stop and for ever if anyone will let her. It was unbelievable that she still imagined I could be interested.

"Not now, Posi," I told her sharply. "I have a lot on my mind." And when she subsided, I gave her the instructions. To get a fix on me from the pendant-comm, and to come and get me when darkness had fallen on the plateau side of the mountain. And before she could start up again about her conversation, I switched off as I had before.

Then, alone, I waited for Seliki and for nightfall with absolutely nothing to do. There was no vidscreen or anything else much in that little chamber – not even a book-tape player, though normally I'm not one for reading. The leisure time of the Logies seemed about as dull as that of the moon-monks of Albacker's World. Maybe, I thought idly, they spend all their time praying to the Allness. Or in bed with each other.

I might have asked Seliki about it, later, when she bounced back into the room. But she didn't give me a chance. She was carrying a bundle of fur and looking pleased with herself. And the reason for that was that the bundle was not just an ordinary pelt but a fur *suit*. Made from Logie fur – because, I learned, dying Logies donate their own pelts to the community. The suit was fairly crude, because Seliki and some others had sewn it up quite quickly. But the stitching looked secure enough – and the whole thing seemed a terrific idea.

The suit was in fact a pullover jacket and trousers, with lots of long fur hanging down to hide the join. The jacket had a hood that came up tightly over my head. The trousers and sleeves were not open-ended, so that my hands and feet were covered. When I put it on only my face showed – and not much of it, past the furry edge of the hood.

It would never stand up against close scrutiny. But no Colloghi human was likely to scrutinize a Logie. People see what they expect, and they wouldn't expect a human inside Logie fur. So the disguise would serve, against casual glances. And it was incredibly warm, which would help outside the dome.

"You see, Del Curb," Seliki said, giggling, "just as I told you. You make a fine he Logh-uy."

I just grunted and began to pull the suit off, since it was far too hot to wear inside, over my coverall.

"Dusk is gathering now, outside," Seliki said. "When will your ship arrive?"

With the furry jacket off, I could get at my pendant to call Posi. Who turned out to be only a few minutes from landing, on a level patch just above the basin where the Logie homes were. So I pulled the jacket on again, and Seliki and I headed out, to be carried back up to the plateau.

Crossing the ice to my ship, a number of misgivings began to make themselves known, by a tightness in the belly and an openness of the pores. Of course some of my sweating was because I'd got too warm, inside, in the fur suit. I could have done with the controllable temperature of a therm-cloak, instead. But even inside the ship, when I'd removed the fur suit, I went on sweating a little. And that was the misgivings.

Still, I kept them to myself. They weren't large and clamorous enough to deflect me from the prospect of getting Moone and Jarli away and getting on with some profiting. Besides, there was no one to share misgivings with. Seliki was in a state of high excitement and enthusiasm, with not a misgiving in her entire furry being. So as she stared around the ship in fascination, I headed for the control area, curtly returning Posi's cheerful greeting.

"Everything all right?" I asked her. "Any ceptor scans as you came down?"

"Nothing like that has happened, Del," she said brightly.

"Good," I snapped. "Then take us up. Go all the way around the mountain, and set us down on the plateau – with the Magnigrip."

"Where on the plateau, Del?"

"On the spaceport, outside the dome. Where there's no one around. Keep the ship high up, near the clouds if you can, while you're setting us down. And watch for ceptor scans."

"Very well, Del." The ship had lifted while I'd been speaking, and the screens were filled with the shadowy hulk of the mountain. "Are you trying to land without being seen?"

"That's the idea."

"Then you will be glad to know that it is snowing on the plateau."

I was very glad to know that. And it was also encouraging that Posi had had no ceptor touches. Probably the people who'd tried to get into the ship hadn't bothered tracking it when she'd lifted off. So things looked good. I could even feel some of my misgivings retreating a little.

Settling in a pouch-seat, I watched the changing shadows on the screen as the ship circled the mountain. Seliki joined me, taking the other pouch-seat, looking awestruck. I was hoping for a nice quiet time of gathering my wits – but Posi had other ideas.

"Del," she said, "may I now tell you about this wonderful conversation . . ."

"Not now, Posi," I told her quickly.

"But, Del," Posi said, oddly unwilling to be silenced, "I am certain that you would be interested. I am talking with the most immense and superior mind that I have ever encountered."

I began again to shut her up – but then stopped, as warning lights went on within me. As far as I knew, there were *no* other thinking machines in the galaxy that a top-level Posi would call "immense and superior".

If there were, I wanted to know about them.

"What mind?" I asked carefully. "What's its type and classification? And where is it?"

"It is not an Intelloid, Del," Posi said, "and it has no classification. And it is located here, on this planet."

That shook me. "What is it, if it isn't an Intelloid?"

"I can define it only as pure Mind," Posi said. "The mightiest and most harmonious that I have ever known."

176

Her tone indicated that my questions were meaningless and irrelevant. Typical of Posi to carry on a conversation that probably held the galactic record for complexity and abstruseness, yet not know who or what she was talking to.

I was scowling at her terminal, trying to think of another way of finding out what was going on, when Seliki broke in. I realized that she had been staring curiously at me for some time.

"Who are you talking to?" she asked me.

A little absently, I explained about Posi and then added something about Posi's mysterious conversation. "Listen, Seliki," I said at last, "do you know anything about some kind of supermind machine on Colloghi? Maybe Rocdril has something advanced . . ."

To my surprise, Seliki laughed softly. "I do not think so. And I do not think your Posi is talking to a machine. By what she has said, I believe that she has made contact with the Allness."

I laughed as well, but sardonically. "Seliki, I don't mean to be unkind about your religion. Lots of good folk believe in things like that. But Posi is a thinking machine, operating on principles of logic and rational processes. It's *impossible* for her to believe in gods and spirits and things."

"Excuse me, Del," Posi broke in, sounding almost diffident. "What you have just said to your new friend is entirely correct. But I have just been told by *my* new friend that he *is* actually what your friend's people call the Allness."

"I knew it," Seliki said, smiling.

"It is very puzzling," Posi went on, sounding even more diffident.

"*Puzzling?*" I yelled. I'd been trying to find my voice and to keep it from being too shrill. "I don't *believe* this! Posi, just tell me where this thing *is* that you're talking to!"

"I have not pinpointed the location," Posi said, now sounding positively embarrassed. "The emanations of his mind seem to be everywhere." Seliki nodded, still smiling. "And at the moment, on our main communication link, he has gone back to enlarging on a fascinating aspect of epistemology as explored by the swarm-minds of the planet Garqu'ella . . ."

"*Stop it!*" I raged. "Posi, you can't be having a conversation with some imaginary god! If you really think you are, you're hallucinating! Which would be the biggest glitch in the history of Intelloid technology!"

And the most expensive, I moaned to myself, cringing at the thought of what it would cost to have the defect isolated and repaired. I wouldn't let myself even start to think about the cost of having Posi replaced.

"Hallucination within my functions is not possible, Del," Posi said reproachfully.

"Neither is getting religion!" I snapped.

Seliki touched my arm. "I am not sure what you are saying, Del Curb . . ."

"Don't worry about it," I said shortly. "I just think Posi has a malfunction." But *I'll* worry about it, I thought. How extensive might it be? Could I trust Posi now to take the ship into the Netlines?

Seliki was still trying to get my attention. "It may not be so," she said, "if I understand correctly."

"Understand what?"

"Your Posi. If she is talking with the Allness, it has nothing to do with gods and spirits, as you seem to think. The Logh-uy do not believe in such things. We believe only in Col-Logh, the One Being, the Allness. Though he has never spoken to us, he has sometimes heeded us when we spoke to him. As your Posi is doing."

I groaned, thinking that I didn't need outpourings of faith from a true believer. "Seliki, you can't say you don't believe in gods when your Allness *is* a god . . ."

"No, Del," Posi suddenly put in. "I have now opened a second, separate communication link with my new friend, and he has provided some remarkable data. He *is* what the Logh-uy call the Allness, and he is *not* an imaginary being. He is a very large, natural but non-organic brain. He acquired mental functions through an electro-magnetic disturbance, centuries ago, and has since developed his titanic intelligence as well as other mental powers."

I stared dazedly at the shadowy ceptor screens, with more

warning lights going on in my head. "Then what *is* he? And *where*?"

But I guessed the astonishing answer almost as I asked.

"He is Col-Logh," Seliki said quietly. "He is the Allness who is Everywhere. He is the mountain."

Chapter 21

A sentient mountain. The idea was overwhelming, but it couldn't be denied – not in the face of Seliki's and Posi's assurances. Posi then launched into a monologue about the crystals and silicon that were the mountain's main materials – and about things like electro-magnetic chains and lattices, cross-flow impulses and infra-links ... It might have been absorbing to another Intelloid since they philosophize tirelessly about the nature of intelligence, especially their own. But I paid little attention, being absorbed in my own concern about whether some advantage could be wrung for me out of this knowledge.

I was the only human on Colloghi who knew the truth about the Logies, which was proving useful. But I could see little value to me in knowing about the mountain. It was just an odd bit of fate, that I was the first person to bring to Colloghi a top-level Intelloid, Posi, whose mind was itself complex enough to communicate fully with the Allness.

Up to then, Posi was busily telling me, the Allness had been mostly isolated. He could sometimes pick up faint communications from the Logies when they all got together and "prayed" at him – but he didn't always understand the details of their tiny lives. So Posi was a revelation to him. And since they could both perform several mental functions at once, during their high-flown conversation Posi had opened her memory banks – and the Allness had acquired a galactic education in a few swift gulps.

Along the way somewhere, he had also saved my life.

Seliki and the Logies had made their plea to him on my behalf just as I was being thrown off the plateau by Pulvidon's men. But that time the Allness had more or less understood, because of what he had learned – about me and allied matters – from Posi's data stores. So he had taken action. With what seemed to be a well-developed telekinetic ability among those other functions that Posi had mentioned. He reached out, grabbed my falling body, and carefully TK'd me down to safety.

Simple. If you could believe in a thinking mountain that had TK. And a form of telepathy that he could communicate with – like a kind of non-tech version of Posi's call-beam. Posi added that he'd been able to reach out telepathically, in an undirected way, to soak up bits of data from nearby worlds. But he hadn't reached along the Netlines, since he didn't know about them. And because of his situation he hadn't understood much of what he'd picked up. Not until Posi came along to explain things.

I could imagine that, since I had long suffered from Posi's delight in meticulous and endless explaining. In fact I was growing a bit weary with her extended explanation of the Allness. Though it was good to get a few things cleared up, like my rescue. And she told me also that the heavy near-headache everyone suffered in Collopolis was caused by the gigantic, non-stop brain activity of the mountain. Creating a kind of electro-neuronic field which affected human brain cells.

But I could see no use or relevance in any of it. Not in terms of my position and needs. So I began trying to get a word in edgewise, to shut down Posi's admiring flow of talk about her new friend. Which Seliki was encouraging.

". . . and just as human brains are troubled by his mind," Posi was saying, "so he too is troubled by some outside factor, affecting the surface of his brain."

"*How* is he troubled?" Seliki asked, sounding quite upset at the thought of the Allness feeling discomfort.

"He describes it," Posi said, "as being like a human ailment that he perceived in my data banks. It is like an *itch*."

That did it. There I was sitting in my own ship, about to go out and sneak around a place full of dangerous people who had already tried to kill me, and I had to listen to a machine and an exter talking about an itchy mountain. The laughter that burst out of me was sour with tension and annoyance, but it felt good all the same.

Seliki spun around with a scandalized gasp. "You must not laugh at the Allness, Del Curb," she admonished.

"Oh, come on," I said, laughter fading. "You're talking about a great enormous chunk of *rock*. Maybe he can think with all those crystal brain cells, but I can't believe that he can feel. Or itch."

"Yet he says he does," Posi told me firmly. "And has done so for many years. It is a great trouble for him."

I snorted. "Some superior mind. You'd think a sentient mountain that also has a high-powered TK faculty could find a way to scratch an itch."

Both Posi and Seliki went quiet. At the time I thought it was from the effect of my relentless logic. So I hurried to press the advantage.

"Anyway," I went on, "let's drop the subject. Time is moving along, and we should be too. Posi, right now let's concentrate on getting Seliki and me down safely."

"If you say so, Del," she replied. "I will have the ship in position over the plateau in 2.4 minutes."

"Good," I said, turning to Seliki. "Let's go."

She still looked silent and thoughtful as we went out to the airlock. And I was thoughtful too as I pulled on my Logie suit, trying to be sure that I hadn't overlooked some possible flaw in the plan of action. But I couldn't find any. Of course, the plan was a long way from risk-free. But I'd taken risks before and survived. And it was worth a risk or two, I told myself, for a pile of creds. With Seliki and the Logies, and Posi, I felt sure that things would work out all right.

I didn't remember, then, just how much self-deception can go along with visions of prospective wealth.

A moment later, Posi plucked us out of the airlock with the Magnigrip, holding us aloft for a second while she did a final ceptor sweep of the ground below. Seliki clung to me, her face alight with a mixture of fright and excitement, staring down. But there was nothing to see in the darkness. And we were also in the middle of heavy, snow-sodden cloud cover. The ship, rumbling on planetary hover, was deafening – but I thought, or hoped, that the saturated cloud and falling snow would muffle much of the noise.

I checked with Posi via the pendant. "There are three humans in one of the buildings at the edge of the spaceport, Del," she told me, "but they are not moving around."

And probably won't, in a snowstorm, I thought. "Right," I said tensely. "Down. Put us midway between those buildings and the dome."

I never really enjoy being moved around by tractor beam. It may look like levitation, but it feels like helplessness. I always think about what would happen to me if it malfunctioned. And I'd done enough falling on that mountain for a lifetime. So I let Seliki cling to me, trembling slightly, and in turn I clung to her, face buried in the fur of her neck. Partly because my nose was cold.

I was also breathing hard, mostly because of the thin air, by the time my feet hit solidity. It was a soft enough landing, though, since the snow had deepened on the spaceport's expanse. Seliki shook herself, looked around, then stared up. So did I, feeling relieved that the ship's engines did seem muffled, with the cloud cover down fairly low that night. I thought that the people working on the spaceport would have had to listen very hard to hear my ship, especially when a mountain wind was stirring the snowflakes with a little ghostly moaning.

"That was like *flying*," Seliki whispered elatedly. "May we do it again sometime, Del Curb?"

"Why not?" I said. If we survive, I added to myself grimly, breathing hard, trying to see what lay around us through darkness and snow. And feeling the heaviness in my head growing strong again, now that we were back on the thinking mountain.

Above, the ship's diminishing rumble disappeared entirely as Posi took it up to the safety of a parking orbit. The wind's moan seemed to die a little, as if in imitation. All was quiet and peaceful, so that we might have been the only beings on the planet. It was perfect. As stealthy a landing as anyone had ever made. If the rest of the night goes like this, I thought, we . . .

I never finished the thought.

"*You!* Logies! What're you doing there?"

The sudden roar made us both jump, though I think I got twice as high as Seliki. When I recovered my balance, I whirled to stare at the bulky shadow looming out of the darkness, boots creaking on the new snow. My hands twitched, helpless, with unusable mini-weapons covered by the encumbrance of the fur.

Then Seliki grabbed my arm, pulled me down. I saw that she was going into a Logie cower, and it seemed a good move. What faint light reached us from the dome showed that the other person was a grey-uniformed city Militiaman in therm-suit and face-mask. With some kind of voice intensifier in the mask, creating a good officious bellow.

"No hit, Mast! No hit'!" Seliki was gabbling, in her shrillest pidgin. "Gov'nor send! Gov'nor!"

She was in a deeply extended cringe by then, and so was I, keeping my face turned away. But the Militiaman stopped a few metres away, looking uninterested.

"Oh – Mansion Logies," he grunted. He also didn't seem interested in *why* the Governor had sent Logies out of the city. So I never did find out what Seliki would have said if he'd asked.

"You can tell the fraggin' Governor to get a little fraggin' *bountiful* and put some fraggin' *lights* out here," he grumbled, turning away, talking more to himself than to a couple of sub-sent Logies who wouldn't understand anyway. "Then people wouldn't have to come out patrollin' in the fraggin' *snow* . . ."

His voice dwindled as he strode away, and Seliki and I straightened up, grinning at each other.

"You see, Del Curb?" she said. "You *do* make a good Logh-uy. He did not doubt you."

"We haven't tried our luck in the city yet," I said dryly. "It won't be snowing in there."

"We will follow the paths of the Logh-uy," she said. "Back streets, lanes, alleys. They are in semi-darkness – while the humans of the city, at night, travel the well-lit main streets. We should not meet any of them."

"Fine. Then let's go. I don't still want to be creeping around in Logie gear come daylight."

We sped away across the spaceport, half-crouched. If anyone looked out from the dome, they saw only two harmless Logies on some errand or other in the snow. I had a fretful moment, though, when we reached the nearest iris-door entrance to the city. But I fumbled with a sleeve and my hood, activated the ceptor in my headband, and was reassured that the street beyond the door was deserted.

Rearranging my furs, taking as deep a breath as the thin air allowed, I went through the door with Seliki as if we'd been squirted. The street was deserted indeed, and the air and warmth were delicious. Then Seliki pulled me by the hand into a narrow lane between two rows of buildings and we were on our way. On the Logie way.

As we crept along I felt a growing discomfort. Not only the tension and the return of the near-headache. Collopolis had a regulated atmosphere, while I was wearing heavy fur clothing with the hood up. I supposed that Logies had an inbuilt physiological heat regulator, for none of them had ever looked uncomfortable in the city. But I was dripping with sweat before we came to the end of that lane.

There, Seliki touched my arm and indicated a back street. "Many humans will be in the central area, where there are entertainment complexes. We must go around."

"Lead on," I muttered. I was starting to feel more worried about heat prostration than about being seen. But I stumbled along after her, sweating the strength out of myself, seeing no other living thing in the next hour or so of grubby side streets, inky-black alleys and the blank, forbidding backs of buildings.

That is, until we came to the back of one building, opening on to a fairly presentable lane. Some light from the street filtered into it, and more light poured out from a door standing open, where we saw two humans silhouetted. There was a good-sized skim parked nearby, so Seliki and I ducked into its shadow and waited.

I could see that the humans were a short tubby man in an expensive-looking suit and a short bosomy girl in a minimal skirt showing dimpled knees. He looked flushed, her tunic was unbuttoned, and their embrace at that back door indicated that they hadn't stayed late at the office to discuss Colloghian geopolitics. When the embrace ended, the girl jiggled away, adjusting her tunic, while the tubby man went in the other direction. Towards the skim where we were crouching – which turned out to be his.

He saw us as he reached for the side-panel. "Logies!" he said, his voice sharp with suspicion. "What are you doing there? *Spying?*"

We shrank back, but he had us trapped between the skim and the wall. I thought that I could flatten him, but that could cause a general alarm, a search for a rogue Logie. So we just cowered, once more, in silence.

"I said, what are you doing?" He was blustering as people do when they're irate at being caught doing something illicit. "Who sent you? Was it my wife? *Was it?*"

Seliki went on cringing silently, while I positively grovelled so that the man wouldn't see my face. But he clearly had more belly than brain, and wasn't looking closely at us.

"I'll teach you to sneak around and spy!" he ranted, red-faced. And then he attacked us, with a leather case he was carrying and with fists and feet. I imitated Seliki and twisted my grovel into a foetal position, arms round head. Seliki also subtly shifted her well-padded body into the way of many of the blows aimed at me. But it really wasn't much of an attack. The man was enjoying beating up on two servants who wouldn't strike back, but he was far from strong enough to do it well. He caught me one solid kick on the rump, by accident, but otherwise they were glancing, flabby blows that grew feebler as he ran out of breath. Eventually the attack halted as he stopped, wheezing, and reached for the skim's panel.

"Let that . . . be a lesson to you," he gasped. Then he got into the skim and whisked away while we climbed slowly to our feet.

"It would be nice to think," I said furiously, "that I might run into that fatneck again in different circumstances."

Seliki shrugged. "Do not concern yourself. There are many who find pleasure in striking Logh-uy. We feel pity for them."

Then she moved away, and I reluctantly, sweatily, tensely followed.

We went on circling the city centre, through the dingier side of Collopolis. Often I had brief glimpses of the attractive, well-lit main streets, some of which I remembered from my first drive across the city. So even without Seliki's help I knew vaguely where we were much of the time. As the night wore on I saw that we were getting closer to that outstretched passage leading from the dome to the Complex. But that also meant we were not too far from the great plaza where the Mansion stood. Which turned out to be just as well.

Almost as I realized our position, I was startled into a half-shriek and an accelerated burst of sweat by two dark figures suddenly lunging out from an alleyway. I began instinctively fumbling, with fur-covered fingers, for a weapon – until I saw that they were Logies, speaking to Seliki in their own trilling, liquid language. With some crucial news.

She translated, looking worried. "These Logh-uy have come to tell us that your two friends are no longer in the Complex. They have been taken to the *Mansion* – where they are being kept in a secure and well-guarded upper room."

It wasn't bad news, I thought, as we headed towards the Mansion while the other two Logies melted back into the darkness. I felt I'd rather invade the Mansion than the Complex if I had a choice. The Mansion wasn't a labyrinth carved deep into solid rock, full of squads of Patrolmen. And it had more than one way out, if we ran into trouble. And I had a good idea for getting Moone and Jarli away, which wouldn't have worked in the Complex.

"Seliki," I said, "when we get into the Mansion I'll need some materials to start a fire. On the floor below where the prisoners are."

"A fire?" she echoed, wide-eyed. "But it will burn the Mansion. Someone might be harmed!"

"It'll just be for smoke," I told her. "What we call a diversion-ary tactic. And it would help if you could get me a Militia uniform, or something like that."

The Logie disguise had worked well so far, but wouldn't serve inside a well-lit Mansion. Then I saw Seliki frowning doubtfully, and realized that Logie non-violence extended into a general unwillingness to hurt anyone, ever.

"Never mind the fire, then," I told her, sighing. "Just get a uniform." And I'll drop the guards with a gas grenade, I thought to myself.

Shortly after, we were slipping through some decorative shrubbery darkened by the looming shadow of the Mansion itself. A narrow path led to the building, and a narrow door – a Logie door, according to the spicy scent that hung in the air – led us inside. Into a dim passageway, where we stopped. Or anyway I did, while Seliki crept nervously away in search of some kind of uniform disguise for me.

She was barely out of sight when I did what I'd been craving to do – and dragged off that sauna of a fur suit. It was so saturated with sweat that I could have wrung litres out of it. My coverall felt as if I'd been swimming in it. But the relief was blissful. Almost overcoming the fact that I was deeply tired, increasingly headachy and murderously thirsty.

I hope Moone and Jarli will appreciate what I'm going through for them, I said bitterly to myself.

After a few moments more I began to tighten up, feeling clammy in my sodden coverall. It seemed sensible to move around. The passage I was in was probably part of the back-stairs warren that was the Logie domain in the Mansion, and I had no wish to get lost in it. But I couldn't stay still. And thirst was getting to me badly.

So I crept along a little way and found some hangings covering an opening on to a brightly lit main corridor. Civili-zation, I thought. And it was late enough that I thought no one would be about. And it could do no harm to have a quick look, to see if there was a place to get a drink.

So I pushed aside the hangings and stepped through. Sound-lessly, I crept along the broad main corridor. With infinite care, I opened the first door that I came to.

188

I had the impression of a kind of library, a high-ceilinged sweep of shelves. But I didn't look at it too closely. Instead, I was looking at the tall, robed figure of the Marshal of the Mansion, who was looking back at me with total astonishment.

But he was not overcome. Before I had a chance to get a wrist-blazer aimed, he smartly plucked a nasty-looking little scrambler gun from his sleeve and levelled it at me.

"Mister *Curb*," he said, astonishment turning to grim triumph. "I cannot *imagine* how you could possibly be here, yet here you are. It seems you are more resourceful and capable than anyone imagined."

A whole new flow of sweat, icy with fear, seeped into my coverall. "Listen, Marshal . . ." I croaked, trying to win some time.

"No," he said in a voice like a death knell. "You will not speak. I will take no chances with you."

I made a half-lunge, but hopelessly late. His finger tightened on the firing-stud. My entire nervous system seemed to burst into flame – until the flames centred themselves within my brain, and burnt it black as charcoal.

Chapter 22

I'm sick of this, I thought – when my brain had recovered enough to wake up and form a thought. I'm sick of having my nervous system mangled. It's nasty whenever it happens, but twice in two days is over the top. And this time was the worst. Even though the brain-burning is an illusion, the scrambler is more potent than the Stun-Trun by a factor of ten. You still don't stay out for long – you just wish you did. Your neurons feel all lit up, like fusitron cores on the way to meltdown. You try to open your eyes and a synaptic short-circuit makes your toes wiggle.

Though there are worse things. Such as managing, at last, to control your eyelids and open them, only to find yourself looking at the cruel profile of Pulvidon.

For once, he wasn't smiling. He probably hadn't been much amused to find me alive. In fact, I was surprised that I *was* still alive – and wondered if he was devising some new and gruesome way to finish me. That thought started me sweating again, started the Colloghi headache pressing in, started my nerves pinging and twanging all over.

The renewal of terror brought all my faculties back into something like working order. I found that I was feeling like a corpse on a slab – that is, stark naked and lying on cold stone. The gorgeous ceiling above me revealed that the stone was the floor of the Mansion's great Receiving Hall. Pulvidon was standing a short distance away from me, not looking at me but at the two people seated at the Hall's huge table – Bartraselda and her cohort in crime, Rocdril. The Marshal was hovering behind the Governor, and beyond them stood two men in the uniform of the Hiatus Patrol, armed with blazers.

Pulvidon and the two at the table were deep in discussion about mass murder.

But they weren't talking about *whether*. They were talking about *when*. That night, or later.

"...y' can't tell," I heard Bartraselda saying. "He coulda called *any*body. The FedPol could be on their way right now."

Lying there, naked and hurting, I thought vindictively that I wished I *had* called the FedPol. Not that it would have helped much, as Pulvidon made clear.

"What if they are?" he growled. "You know the plan. The bare-brains go down the pit, the Complex gets cleaned up, you act all innocent. And look sad about the tragic accident that happened to the pretty vid lady. We've got lots of time for the clean-up, between the time the ceptors pick up FedPol ships entering this system and the time they land."

"I *know* that," Bartraselda grumbled. "But things can go wrong."

"Not if we all play our parts," Rocdril said icily.

"Oh, I'll play my part, Rocky," Bartraselda snarled. "Don't worry."

"I won't," the doctor snapped. "Not when the alternative to doing what you're told is joining the brain-drains in the disposal pit."

Bartraselda's face darkened, her throat swelling froggily. "You threatenin' me, bulb-head?"

Rocdril's mouth tightened, Pulvidon glowered, the Marshal looked unnerved. It was obviously a continuation of a disagreement begun before I woke up – which was fine, since dissension among your enemies is always a good thing. I may have raised my head a little for a better view, and the movement was seen.

"He's awake!" the Marshal said, diverting Rocdril and the Governor from their mutual glaring.

"So he is," Pulvidon hissed. He stalked over to me, unclipping a blazer from his belt, and the other two joined him to stare down at me.

"*Curb*." There was an ocean of hatred in Pulvidon's voice. "I thought I knew how much of a twister you were, but it seems I underestimated you."

I looked up at him, straining my throbbing brain cells to think of some way to postpone the fate that his eyes said he was planning for me.

"I should have stripped you before," he went on. "I hadn't guessed at all the mini-weapons you carry. Though I still don't see how you used them to save yourself. I'm tempted to make you tell me."

I still said nothing, and tried to let nothing show in my eyes. So he thought I'd used the weapons in my clothes for a miraculous escape. Meaning that he didn't suspect that I'd had help from the Logies, or that I still had a few weapons on me. I couldn't see right then what use those factors could be to me – but they allowed tiny seepages of hope. Which helped me to go on coolly and silently staring back up at him.

But that tipped his hatred over into fury. "Maybe I'll make you tell me lots of things," he said savagely. "Like about any calls you might have made to the FedPol."

His face was illuminated with a terrifying hunger, as he raised his blazer and aimed it. Not at my head or body, but at my feet. He was going to make it last, char me slowly, working in from the extremities as he asked his questions. Panic swept away my mask of coolness as I fought to lever my scrambler-weakened body up from the floor, mouth opening to scream.

But there was an intervention.

"Hey, c'mon, Pulvie," the Governor said. "Not all over the floor. This plastimarble cost two months' taxes. Anyway, I want Rocky to have him 'fore y' hurt him too much. To run that fertility test, an' get an extract if he passes."

I looked up at her, awash with gratitude. She was as squat and toadlike as ever, in a short tunic and short trousers that exposed the lumpy mauve bulges of knee and calf. But in that moment, bringing my stay of execution, she looked wonderful to me.

Pulvidon lowered his blazer grudgingly. "All right. I'll inter-rogate him later. But if the FedPol show on the ceptors, Curb goes down the pit whatever his sperm count."

The Marshal looked dubious. "Is it wise to keep him alive, sir? He has escaped before . . ."

"Because of his weapons," Pulvidon snapped. "They won't help him now. But I'll put fasteners on him."

Bartraselda, staring down at me, guffawed cruelly. "It don't look like *any* of his weapons'd worry anybody much."

I kept my face expressionless, staring past her. It's in the nature of people like that to be coarse at the expense of their victims. Then Pulvidon gestured to the two Patrolmen, who marched over to me with two heavy magno-fasteners which they clamped around my wrists and ankles.

"Put him upstairs," Pulvidon told them, "with the other two."

The two men hoisted me up and carried me off. I tried to cling to my thankfulness at still being alive – and to the small gleams of hope, because of the shot or two still in my armoury, which the enemy hadn't guessed at. Yet I was still slick with icy sweat as I thought about Pulvidon's hate-filled face, and his plans for slowly barbecued Curb.

The Patrolmen carted me along a few corridors and up a lot of stairs, then finally through a door into a small, low-ceilinged room where they dumped me on a dusty carpet. Which did no good to what was left of my nerve-twanging, not to mention my brain-squeezing headache. I was untangling myself and rolling carefully on to my back when a voice from across the room said "Del!" with total astonishment.

Moone, of course, gaping at me, and Jarli looking just as startled. But also, their expressions were like those of children caught out at naughtiness. For good reason. They were sitting over against the wall on the floor, slightly apart but clearly having been a lot closer a moment before. Moone still had his makeshift loin-cloth, but didn't quite have it *on*. Jarli's cover-all was gaping open to display her smooth belly and the curve of rosy-tipped breasts. I would have turned my back on them in anger, if I'd been able to tear my gaze away from her.

"Del!" Moone said again, scrambling to his feet, not aware of leaving his loin-cloth behind. "We thought you'd been *killed!*"

"And I can see," I snarled, "how deeply you've been mourning my loss."

They both flushed red on every exposed bit of skin. Moone snatched up his loin-cloth and fumblingly rewrapped it while Jarli quickly fastened her coverall.

"No, we . . . it's just . . . I mean, we . . ." Moone was gabbling, fixed by my glare.

"Never mind, Myron," Jarli said coolly. She let her gaze travel up and down my nakedness, raising an eyebrow in a way that stopped me glaring and made me want to draw my knees up to my chest. "We need to know what's going on – how you got here, Del. Some Patrolmen were laughing about how you were thrown off the plateau . . ."

"I was," I told her, sitting slowly up.

Her sniff was derisive. "Oh, yes. I imagine you then found you had the power of flight. And probably it was so warm out there you took your clothes off."

Obviously she had resorted to a standard female tactic – if you're in the wrong, go on the attack. I had interrupted a private moment and had embarrassed her, so she responded with hostility. Which made Moone look more puzzled than normal.

"Believe what you wish," I told Jarli loftily. "The fact is that I *was* thrown from the plateau. But I . . . had some help, and survived. It's a long story. And then, you should know, I got caught again because I came back – to help *you two*."

"Oh, Del." Moone looked as if he was going to abase himself at my feet. "That's just so . . . so . . . I don't know what to say." His voice cracked with emotion, and even Jarli looked a little abashed.

"Say nothing," I replied magnanimously. "Time to stop talking and start doing." It was a line from one of my favourite splatter-films, about a gruesomely violent escape from a prison planetoid. Which seemed appropriate, as long as the grue wasn't on my side.

Jarli frowned. "Doing what? The door is reinforced and guarded, we're unarmed and – " she gestured vaguely " – everything!"

"She's right, Del," Moone put in. "Anyway, we don't need to

do anythin'. These people gotta keep us healthy to fake the show about wakin' me up."

I snorted. "Think a bit, Moone. First, *I'm* not going to be in their show, so they won't keep me healthy. Second, you and Jarli know all about them now, so you're both certain to have an *accident* after you make the show. Probably in space, with no remains."

"They wouldn't dare," Jarli said firmly. "It would attract far too much suspicion."

I laughed humourlessly. "The whole galaxy suspects Famlio of all kinds of crimes. Suspicion doesn't bother them. They don't even worry much about *proof*."

She tossed her head. "What do you suggest, then?"

"Simple. Get out of here, get to my ship, get away."

"And you're going to manage all that for us?" she said scornfully. "Naked and in fasteners?"

I was getting tired of her attitude. Especially now that her interest in Moone proved that my chances with her would be close to nil if we did get away. So I ignored her. I was going to make a move, and I thought that Moone was still impressed enough with me to follow along. Jarli could come or stay, as she wished.

Leaving her sardonic questions hanging in the air, I turned my attention to my wrist and ankle fasteners. They were standard issue plastifirm, opening with a magno-key. I had no key, but I had something just as good – the reliable little vibro-blade in my fingernail.

Jarli may have remembered the shrill whine, from the Complex. Anyway, it made them both sit up, looking curious. Its almost effortless shearing away of the fasteners made them look astonished. As I got stiffly to my feet and went to look at the door, they goggled. I paid no attention. But I suppose Jarli felt foolish about her sarcasm. So, again, in true female style, as I passed them, she counter-attacked.

"Poo!" she said, wrinkling her nose. "You smell like the locker-room of the Thotovian wrestling team!"

I still didn't let her get to me. I may have had a hot time of it that night, but it was normal human perspiration. The

Thotovian wrestlers smell as they do because their pores exude a pungent oil to make them hard to grip.

"Terribly sorry," I said acidly. "I just haven't found the time to attend to my personal fragrance."

"Hey, Jarli, come on," Moone said, still bewildered by her hostility.

And then, before anything else was said, the door suddenly slid open.

I ducked away to one side, having glimpsed the blue-and-white uniform of a Patrolman outside. But its owner hadn't glimpsed me. And to my relief it wasn't an enemy who came in, to find me free of my fasteners. It was Seliki.

She was carrying two beakers on a tray, and she was looking wide-eyed and worried. When she saw me standing there in one piece, she sagged with relief, almost spilling the drinks.

"You are not hurt, Del Curb!" she gasped. "Other Logh-uy saw you being carried here, and I feared . . ."

"It can *talk*!" Jarli burst out, astonished. "What *is* this?"

I whirled on her, my frayed temper snapping. "This is Seliki," I said angrily. "She's a full sentient, as all the Logies are, so she's not an 'it'. She's also part of the reason I'm still alive, and I'd guess she's here to help us get out. So if you *want* out, *Miz* Firov, just shut up and settle down!"

"Yeah, Jarli," Moone muttered uneasily, "let's . . . uh . . . be cool, OK?"

To my surprise, she took it. She gave Moone a swift look, swung it around to Seliki and me, then dropped her gaze and nodded. "All right," she said quietly. "Sorry."

Seliki was almost hopping up and down with impatience. "You must listen!" she burst out. "It is *urgent* that you get away!"

That seemed obvious enough not to need an answer. Instead, I grabbed the beakers on her tray and gulped thirstily. It was Oclyccical coldberry juice, which hit my throat like an icy waterfall on a desert.

"I needed that," I gasped to Seliki. "What'd you do, tell the guards the drinks were sent up by the Marshal or something?"

At her swift nod, I smiled, grateful that the enemy clearly

did want to keep Jarli and Moone healthy for a while. But Seliki was still hopping impatiently.

"We must lose no *time*, Del Curb," she said, anxiety pushing her voice up to its topmost register. "You must think of a plan for escape!"

I saw Jarli twitch at that, though she managed to hold back any derisive sniffs. "As it happens," I said soothingly, "I *have* a plan, Seliki. If you can tell me a few things."

And she could. She told me rapidly that there were two Patrolmen on guard outside, and that we were well away from occupied parts of the Mansion. She assured me that she could get us out of the Mansion, if I could get us out of the room. But that worried her, because the door – the sliding sort, separating into two halves, with a central lock – was reinforced with plastisteel.

"What will you *do*, Del Curb?" she squeaked, round-eyed. "There is so little time . . .!"

"I know," I said, trying to calm her. "I'll handle the door." That made Jarli twitch again. "One more thing – where are the guards standing? Either side of the door?"

"No," Seliki said. "They walk up and down the corridor, back and forth . . ."

"Perfect," I said. "You go out, then, and find a reason to hang around in the corridor. In a few minutes, when the two guards are *almost* coming together in front of the door, give a yell or something so I can hear. But stay well back from the door. Understand?"

She looked puzzled, but her urgency took precedence. "Yes, yes. But you must be *quick*! There is no time to spare!"

"What've you got in mind, Del?" Moone asked curiously. "Can I do somethin'?"

"Just be ready to move," I told him. Then I turned back to Seliki, who was hopping up and down again, looking more desperate with every second.

"There's no need to panic, Seliki," I said as gently as I could. "We have an hour or so of darkness yet. Once we're out of this room . . ."

"No, no, no," she interrupted. "That is not what . . ."

Then *she* was interrupted. By an unexpected sound – faint

197

and far away, but unmistakable. The bass roar of thunder. And quite a storm, I thought idly to myself, if its thunderclaps could reach us through the dome *and* inside the Mansion.

Seliki was nearly jumping out of her fur. "It has begun! Oh, hurry, hurry! There is almost no time left!"

"What?" I demanded, feeling my scalp crawl as her anxiety infected me. *"What's* begun?"

"The *Allness!*" Seliki replied in a piercing squeak. "He understood what you suggested, on your ship!" And when I still looked mystified, she grabbed me by the arms and shook me wildly. *"Hurry*, Del Curb! We are in great danger! *The Allness is going to scratch his itch!"*

Chapter 23

"What was she talking about?" Jarli asked.

Seliki had got the guards to let her out and had whisked away, probably hoping to hurry us along by example. As the door slid shut behind her with a click of the lock, I got ready to make my move.

"Tell you later," I said absently to Jarli. "It's all to do with the mountain, and I guess this storm we can hear."

As if on cue, another distant rumble of thunder reached us. It was ideal, I thought. If anyone elsewhere in the Mansion was to hear the sound I was about to make, they might confuse it with a thunderclap.

Jarli was taking a breath to ask more questions, until I silenced her – by doing something that is not considered nice in polite company. I began to pick my navel.

There aren't that many places in the human body itself where mini-armaments can be hidden. And many of those places are inconvenient, or frequently in use. But for the item I needed then, the navel is perfect. In a moment or two of fingernail-probing I had extracted what looked like a small, compacted ball of fluff. But I picked at it delicately, found an end and began to untangle it.

Jarli and Moone stared as the ball of fluff untwined and became a thread, fairly fine and a dirty off-white in colour. With all the knots and kinks out of it, it was about half a metre long.

"Whatever are you doing?" Jarli asked at last.

"Explosive," I said shortly. "Like the ordinary thermoflare, but micro-condensed."

As I spoke, I was forcing the thread into the crack that separated the halves of the sliding door. Leaving one end of the thread sticking slightly out.

"Move away," I told Moone and Jarli, "and turn your backs. It'll be bright, and might throw sparks."

I grinned merrily at them as they retreated, still staring mystifiedly. Then I turned back to the door, just in time. Out in the corridor I heard Seliki's call, piercing enough to have been a whistle. I also heard faint sounds just beyond the door, as if the two Patrolmen had stopped there, perhaps puzzled by Seliki's noise. Stay put for a second, I said silently.

Then I leaned forward, towards the end of the thread that stuck out from the crack – and spat on it.

It may have looked weird. But the folk who make my weapons have chemically structured the explosive thread to begin detonation when activated by my saliva. And by nothing else. That can be comforting, when you're carrying it in your navel.

As the moistened end started to glow, I moved away and turned my back as well, wishing that I was better protected. Even a crude loin-cloth like Moone's would have been better than nothing. I flinched as the thread detonated behind me – with a flat thump and a ferocious white-hot glare. I could hear the sizzle of metal melting, and I clenched myself in nervous anticipation of a spark assaulting my bare skin. But it didn't happen. An instant later the flare faded and we could turn around.

It had all taken about four seconds from the moment of Seliki's cry. With any luck, the guards would still be standing just on the other side of the door. Probably staring at the molten ruin of the central lock, the way that Jarli and Moone were staring.

"Moone!" I put military snap into my voice and saw his back start to stiffen. "Go!"

And I stabbed a finger at the door-release tab.

The unlocked and ruined door slid open. The guards were there, staring. Staring at us, now. And one of them was quick enough to start reaching for his gun. Which was unwise, from his point of view, for it completed what I had started, triggering Moone's hypno-reflexes.

Moone went through the open door with the speed of a Jektikijian lava-runner. A flowing stride lifted him into the air and a large flying foot bounced the quicker guard off the corridor wall, into an unmoving heap. The second Patrolman was only just getting an alarmed expression as Moone hit the floor perfectly balanced and drove a short punch that felled the man as if his bones had turned to gruel.

Seliki was further along the corridor, pressed wide-eyed against the wall. When Jarli and I followed Moone out, she began hopping up and down again.

"Hurry, now! We must run!"

I made soothing gestures and bent down to the two unconscious Patrolmen, taking their blazers, tossing one to Moone. I'd have preferred my own wrist-blazers to the full-size weapons that the Patrolmen carried, but you can't have everything. Then, though Moone and Jarli were starting away, though Seliki was hopping and squeaking, I hung back for a moment more.

Not many men are keen to go into danger with their most precious assets exposed and vulnerable. Maybe it's psychological, but it can't be helped. Even a makeshift covering like Moone's cloth is better than nothing. So I stooped again and began to pull off the outer clothing of the nearest Patrolman.

It was Seliki's fault, hurrying me with all her panicky noises – underlined by the thunderstorm, which had come much closer, bellowing above us almost non-stop. It infected Jarli and Moone, who started yelling at me to hurry. So I didn't notice until it was too late that the Patrolman whose clothes I had taken was the heavier of the two. And they were both bulky men.

So the boots were too big, and clumped. And I had to clutch at the trousers to keep them from sliding down. I might have discarded them and gone for the clothes of the other Patrolman, but by then all the panic had begun to affect me too. When a particularly huge blast of thunder seem to shake the Mansion beneath my feet, and Seliki screamed while the others yelled, I flung the equally oversize tunic aside and sprang – or clumped – to join the others.

Seliki led us to the stairs and down several flights, creeping warily but quivering with the urge to sprint. The rest of us were quivering too, and jumping every time the thunder boomed overhead.

"Del, for pity's sake," Jarli whispered at last, desperately, "tell me what all this is about!"

"The mountain," I said, trying to think of a quick and simple way to put it. "The mountain has stirred up a nice big atmospheric convulsion. It's frightening Seliki – but it'll be a great diversion for us."

Jarli thought about that, silently, as we followed Seliki along a corridor and dived with relief into one of the dim, narrow passages used by the Logies.

"How can that happen?" Jarli asked at last. "How can a mountain *do* anything?"

"I'll explain later," I said to her again. "When we're off-planet . . ."

My memory chose that moment to give a sharp nudge, like the point of a therm-knife. I nearly leaped out of my oversized trousers.

"*Off-planet!*" I said. "Seliki! I need my *pendant* to call Posi! I need my *things!*"

She looked like she would have turned pale if she could. "I do not know where they are . . ."

"Find them!" I said in a near-yell. "Ask the other Logies!"

"I cannot, Del Curb," she whimpered. "The Logh-uy have gone! They have left the Mansion, and the city . . .!"

Then I did yell, a wordless raging howl. I didn't know or care why the Logies had left. But I *had* to have that pendant, or there would be no escape.

Then it seemed that there wouldn't be anyway. The noise had been heard. Near where we stood in that passage, hangings were flung aside from a doorway. A man stepped through – and I found myself once again face to face with the astonished Marshal of the Mansion.

Once again he produced his scrambler with blinding speed, shouting for help. Once again I could only watch, frozen. Until

Moone's fist flashed past me and took the Marshal full in the face. He was flung back through the doorway, gargling through blood and broken teeth. But the damage had been done. I could hear the thud of running feet as people rushed to his summons.

Some of those thuds, though, were being made by me. I was outdistancing my companions in our first headlong dash for safety. And by combined luck and instinct, I ran the right way. Along the corridor and then down some stairs I barely saw, into a ground-floor corridor that led eventually to a narrow door. By then Seliki was running alongside me, probably helping to steer me, keeping pace as we all burst through the door. And were *outside*, on a shadowy path in the shrubbery.

As we ran off through the darkness, I heard shouts behind us. But my gaze was fixed on what I'd spotted ahead – several ground-skims, parked on a narrow drive by the Mansion. Reaching the nearest one, I tore open the side-panel and flung myself in. The ignition wasn't locked – who would steal a skim from the Mansion in that enclosed hothouse of a city? – and I got it started as the other three piled in after me.

A ground-skim is simple to drive and can hit quite reasonable speeds – if conditions are right. That is, if the roads are straight and flat. The skill factor comes when you're in a hurry over variable surfaces. Then, as the experts say, you can easily tip, skip or flip. So despite the fear clawing at my bowels, I tried to avoid setting off like a competitor in the Death Prix races of Horicus V. We swept away in a smooth, controlled curve, heading for a broad avenue across from the Mansion.

Behind us, almost as smoothly, several other skims – undoubtedly filled with armed men – stormed in pursuit.

"Faster!" Seliki shrilled, a painfully piercing sound in those confines. As Jarli turned to look back, white-faced, I saw Moone calmly examining the mechanism of the blazer I'd handed him. Then he leaned suddenly out of the other side-panel and began to fire at our pursuers. The shift of his weight nearly turned us over – but I managed instead to use it to counter-balance the centrifugal force as I swung us around a corner, the magni-energy field that supported the skim keening in protest.

"Shut up and sit *still!*" I roared, making all three of them jump and stare at me.

But then they got the message in another way, as one of the pursuing skims tried to take the corner behind us too fast. One side of it dipped too low, the edge clipped something on the road, and suddenly it was out of control, tumbling over and over like a tossed coin. Until the solid chunkicrete side of a building halted it, in a sudden bloom of magni-energized flame.

Moone started to cheer, caught my eye and subsided. There were still six skims behind us, I could see, and there might soon be others. Time to cheer if we got away from them.

And then I nearly drove into a building myself as a titanic explosion erupted above us, accompanied by an equally overwhelming blast of light. We all ducked, by reflex, deafened and blinded for an instant. The thunderstorm was directly overhead, and seeming to be just beyond the dome, its gigantic forces staging an all-out assault on the city.

That monstrous eruption of sound and fury had also affected the drivers behind us. One of them had lost control for an instant and had somehow turned turtle. His skim was sliding along foolishly upside down, until the slide was crunchingly halted by a tree.

The storm crashed and bellowed again, as if in triumph. Again we ducked – but I hung on to enough control to guide the skim around a corner, then almost at once whisked it sideways into the mouth of an alley. It was a neat manoeuvre – too neat for two of the pursuing skims. As they drifted too close to one another, their energy-fields intermingled, and overloaded. In their own mini-versions of an electrical storm, their systems blew, dropping both skims to the ground in ruins of scorched metal.

"Way to go, Del!" Moone crowed. "Just three left!"

As if the men chasing us had heard him, they responded. The top-panels of the two skims nearest us were flung open. Grim-faced Patrolmen rose out of them, firing at us with blazers. I whirled our skim around another corner in a manic curve that nearly spilled us, while blazer bolts chipped buildings all around us. The three skims kept balance and kept pace – but then the sound of blazer fire was entirely drowned.

When the storm above the city unleashed the great-grand-father of all onslaughts.

We cowered again, while the skim seemed to dance beneath us. The thunder bellowed as if it would split the world. And a jagged streak of lightning wide as a river struck down with unimaginable force.

We all cried out. But we could not hear ourselves over the scream of steel being torn apart in agony – as, directly above us, a section of the dome cracked across.

I looked up, blanched, then glanced behind. That last detonation in the sky had upset another driver among our pursuers, for one of the three remaining skims lay helplessly on its side, under-surface dark and smoking. But there were still two left, falling behind a little but coming grimly on. And as I swung the skim into another fizzing rocking turn, I knew they weren't the only lethal threat we were facing out there in the city.

I glanced at Seliki, sitting huddled and trembling next to me, silenced by the monstrosity happening in the sky. "It's the *city* that makes the Allness itch, isn't it," I said. "And he's out to destroy it."

She nodded fearfully. "He itches because of everything the humans have placed on the plateau. So he is using his own power to strengthen the storm, to smash the dome and drive the humans away." Her eyes were wide, awed. "Before it began, he *spoke* to the Logh-uy, for the first time ever. To all our minds. He told us to leave the plateau, to seek safety on the ice floes. So all the Logh-uy left – except me."

I was a little awed myself, at that. Because she was there, risking her life, disobeying the Allness, for *me*.

"It was your doing, Del Curb," she added numbly. "Your Posi explained your suggestion to the Allness, how he might use his power to scratch his itch. He had never thought of doing so."

Good for me, I thought sourly. One up on a supermind. Though I could understand that he'd need folk like me, and Posi, to explain things to him about the real universe. For a moment I could almost feel sorry for the Allness. In its own way, the sandstone-and-crystal mountain was as much a bare-brain as the poor victims inside Hiatus. All that human activity on and in his brain must have been intolerable.

These thoughts were fizzing through my mind a bit disjointedly as I drove, especially when I saw the other two skims starting to close the gap between us. We jumped and ducked a few more times as the storm hurled more electrical enormities down at the city, and I swung the skim here and there around the streets. But the other two clung to our trail like magi-glue.

"Del," Moone suddenly said, "where're we tryin' to get to?"

"Spaceport," I said tersely. "They'll have a comm-link there, so I can call Posi down to us. Once I get rid of these two behind us."

"Why not just head right on out there?" Moone asked, setting his jaw. "Let me hold these goons off while you make that call."

It seemed a terrific idea to me, though Jarli at once began trying to change his mind. But then the storm changed everything.

It was something you could *feel* rather than see or hear. Beyond the sound and movement of the skim – beyond everything. It was as if the entire sky had begun throbbing, as if the storm had paused to take a deep breath and plant its feet. Then it gathered all its power. And condensed it. And fashioned it – into one immeasurable electrical surge. A monumental, blazing spear of lightning, to be hurled down by a god.

It struck the dome directly above us. The reinforced glassteel crumpled like tissue paper. A kilotonne of it tore away – and fell, like the end of the world, all around us.

Chapter 24

In fact by some miracle our skim was only hit by small chunks that had splintered off from the main mass. But they disrupted the magni-energy, and I had to fight to keep the skim level for a second. Then it dropped to the ground and skidded to a halt, and we kicked away the crumpled side-panels and clambered out.

That was when we saw the bulk of the fallen section of dome. It lay in a huge heap of shattered, twisted glassteel – behind us. Directly on top of the two skims that had been chasing us.

But there was no time to enjoy our escape, because we hadn't escaped from every danger. The storm reared back and struck again, lightning lancing down through the great gash in the dome brought flame bursting from a tall building. From that building, as from others all around, terrified citizens began pouring into the street. They stared up wildly at the ruined dome, then screamed and cried and milled around as herd animals will do before a stampede. Many of them were as inadequately dressed as Moone and I were – and it was growing dangerously cold as a wintry snow-bearing wind slashed in through the gaping hole above us. I may even have done some milling of my own, clutching at my trousers, glaring around in hopes of finding some nearby refuge. For there was little chance that we could get to the spaceport, before the cold got us.

In the end it was Seliki again who pointed the way.

"The Complex!" she shrilled, her voice rising above the uproar. "We will be safe in the Complex!"

No one registered that a Logie had spoken properly. But they all knew that the Complex wasn't far away. So they took up the cry – "The Complex!" – and the stampede began.

The four of us were swept along in that surge, though none of the stampeders seemed to notice our appearance or weapons. We all just thundered blindly along towards the Complex, with thunder and lightning still crashing over our heads, whipping up the frenzy. Our numbers swelled as more people joined us from other parts of the panic-stricken city. Some were carrying loads of prized possessions, but soon flung them away so as to run faster. Some could not maintain the pace and fell, vanishing beneath the crowd's feet. All of them wept and howled and screamed, manic empty noises of terror. While above them the storm raged and bellowed, the lightning speared, and across the entire city we heard the crunching shriek of metal as more of the dome gave way.

Oddly, the crowd's hysteria helped me to regain control of myself. So did the reassuring knowledge that the Complex *would* offer shelter and survival. And though four fugitives would not have been able to sneak into the place, we would now go in as part of a mob, a hysterical tide of people that no Patrol would be able to stand against.

And, best of all, the Complex would surely offer what I'd been aiming for at the spaceport – a comm-link, to call Posi. Once inside the tunnels, we could easily peel off from the crowd and look for a comm, while the Patrol would be fully occupied elsewhere.

So things were working out fairly well, I thought. I could even discount the fact that I was stumbling along in the midst of a crowd of maniacs, clutching at ill-fitting trousers, where one slip would put me down under hundreds of trampling feet. Or that I was shivering with cold and my aching head felt as if my brain was being resculpted. Or that a city around me was being reduced to rubble. These things were only temporary inconveniences. I may even have been grinning as we surged along – because Jarli and Moone gave me puzzled looks while Seliki actually managed a half-smile.

By the time we reached that extension-of-the-dome tunnel leading to the Complex entrance, glassteel chunks from the dome were falling everywhere around us. Shoving and shrieking and flailing, the maddened mob hurled itself in a compact mass towards the entrance. I saw Moone swing a protective arm around Jarli, lashing out with his other fist to fend off wild-eyed hysterics. I felt Seliki's hot little hand seeking my hand, which meant that I had to hold my trousers up with the hand that also held the blazer. It was awkward, but worth it. Seliki was well balanced and very strong, and kept me upright more than once in that roiling mass.

I glimpsed the broad doors of the Complex ahead, saw a sizeable detachment of Patrolmen in front of the doors, hands raised as if to stop the mob. The stampede didn't even slow down. Suddenly neither Patrolmen nor doors were there anymore, and we poured unstoppably into the entrance foyer.

Then the pressure around me eased, as the crowd flowed forward and sideways in the suddenly larger space. Seliki instantly dragged me sideways as well, and with Jarli and Moone following we sped along passages and through doors – unchallenged – and finally into one of the cosy little preparation suites that Jarli and I had seen before.

There we simply sagged for a while and caught our breath. We could hear bass rumblings elsewhere – the storm and the crowd, I imagined, which from there sounded much the same. Now and then the floor and walls even seemed to vibrate slightly with a particularly enormous blast of thunder. But I felt safe enough. I didn't think the mountain would be bringing the storm in to scourge his own cavernous bowels.

"Come," Seliki said at last, "we should go deeper and find a place to hide."

But, surprisingly, Moone shook his head. "What *I* wanta do," he said, "is get to my pod."

I stared at him. "Don't be stupid, Moone. We have to find a comm, call Posi, then keep out of sight till the storm calms down. We can't go wandering around looking for your *pod*."

"I *need* to get to it, Del," he said stubbornly. "I been thinkin'. We're all gonna take off from this planet just as we are, right? But I don't even have any *clothes*. And the only chance I got of makin' it in this time is as a guy from the twenty-first century. But who'll believe that, the way I am now?"

I gaped at him, realizing that he was right. Probably I would have thought of it myself before long. He would seem an ordinary young man, fluent in Galac and so on. I strongly doubted if he could *fake* being a time traveller.

The others were staring too, but Jarli's expression was admiring. "Myron, you're amazing. To be able to think of that while all this is going on. But you're right. You have to try to get something from the pod . . ."

"Too bad you don't have your camera," I interrupted with bitter irony. "We could find the pod and waste a few hours staging the Awakening now."

"As a matter of fact," Jarli said coolly, "I *do* have my camera." And she reached into her belt-pouch and produced the little jewel-like mini-camera with its trailing attachments.

I was gaping again. "How . . .?"

"The guards didn't search me when we were first arrested," she said. "So when they stuck us in that clinic, while you were still unconscious, I put it . . . in a safe place."

I puzzled over that for a second, until she raised an eyebrow almost challengingly, and I understood.

"Then after I *was* searched, when Myron and I were put in that room in the Mansion, I removed it."

"Just as well," I muttered, "or Moone might have been photographed in an unusual close-up."

They both blushed a little at that, and Seliki suddenly caught on and giggled.

"But you can forget it," I said firmly. "We're not doing any filming, we're not going to the pod. We're going to concentrate on staying *alive*. We can worry about everything else when we're safely . . ."

"Hang on, Del," Moone broke in, looking mutinous. "We're not in real danger right now. The guards'll be busy for a long time, chasin' all those other people. And I think I can get us to the pod in a few minutes."

"For what?" I asked. "You think you're going to pick it up and bring it along?"

"No, 'course not. I'm gonna get somethin'," he said. "A kinda

210

survival pack. Different kinds of stuff from my century, put together to show future people where I'm from."

My mouth went suddenly dry. "You mean – artefacts?"

"Yeah, things like that. Some money, too. Stuff that my people figured wouldn't be around, intact, in the future."

I felt briefly dazed, as anyone might when they had just heard about a glorious treasure there for the taking, not too far away. "Right, then. We'd better get along to find your pod and . . . all those things."

We moved away cautiously into the maze of tunnels. Not that we had much need for caution, since the distant noises told us that something like a riot was happening elsewhere in the Complex, accompanied by the storm's undiminished fury. We didn't even bother with stealth when we reached one of the locked doors leading to the inner Complex. It was unguarded, since the Patrolmen were mostly dealing with rioters, so Moone simply blew the lock away with his blazer.

But once inside the wheel-like maze that was the Hiatus Heart, I began to feel a little nervous. All the silent tunnels with their blank, solid doors seemed to look alike. Still, Moone had wandered the Heart for some time, and seemed to have an excellent sense of direction. And Seliki also had a fair idea of where we were most of the time. So we moved with a certain amount of confidence – and eventually came to a door that looked like all the others but turned out to have a damaged lock. Damaged by me. Moone pushed it open, and there lay the pod with all its attachments, looking like it was waiting for its occupant.

Moone knelt down, reached underneath the pod, felt around, then smiled at the faint click. A small section of the underside slid open, revealing a small, flat metal box. Moone removed it, reached deeper in to pull out a tight roll of cloth, and stood up grinning.

"That's it?" I asked. "The box? Or the other thing?"

"The box," he said. "Plenty of stuff in it."

"And you can keep your sticky fingers away from it," Jarli said to me sharply.

I tried to look injured and innocent, but I suppose she'd seen the flare in my eyes. Part of that had been fury, though – to know that so much wealth had been there from the outset. If I'd known, I would never have had to waken Moone at all – and so much unpleasantness could have been avoided . . . But hindsight is a famous torturer, and I tried to stop thinking about it.

Meanwhile Moone had unrolled the cloth, which turned out to be a kind of uniform – a plain shirt and trousers of poor cloth in a dull brown colour, and sturdy boots. The markings on the sleeves, he said, spelled the acronym NAFF and showed his rank – Astro-leader j.g., whatever that meant.

"Why didn't you get your uniform out before, on my ship?" I asked him.

He shrugged. "Didn't really need it. I kinda liked that robe you lent me."

I held my head, barely resisting the temptation to shoot the big gas-head out of sheer raging frustration. Meanwhile, oblivious to my pain, Moone flung his loin-cloth aside and got dressed, watched with keen interest by Jarli and Seliki. Seeing him comfortably clothed made me wish there had been another uniform for me. But I improved things for myself by tearing a strip from Moone's discarded cloth and using it as a belt to bind my borrowed trousers tightly around my waist. When I jammed my borrowed blazer into that belt – at the *back*, for safety's sake – I thankfully had both hands free at last.

Moone did the same with his blazer, partly because he had stuffed the metal box into the front of his shirt, making an unsightly bulge at his waistline. Then we crept back out into the tunnel. And ran head-on into trouble.

A scattering of people from the city had somehow found their way into that corridor – no doubt through the door Moone had blasted. I imagined that the mob had been spreading out everywhere, like a flood, getting away from the riot that had probably been focused on the entrance foyer. The trouble was that they were all trespassers – especially in the inner Complex. As we were. And we didn't want to be around when the Patrol came storming through the Complex to gather them up.

By then most of the people had recovered from their mob

hysteria, and tended to stare at Moone and goggle at Jarli. But they looked away quickly when I glared at them, since after all I was wearing *part* of a Patrol uniform. So our progress wasn't impeded – except by the fact that none of us had any real idea where to find a comm facility.

I was pondering that problem, following Moone's lead – we were heading inwards, in the Heart, for want of a better idea – when I nearly jumped out of my over-large boots as a voice crackled along the tunnel.

"You there! Stop!"

We all spun around, with Moone's and my hands straying back towards our guns. But it wasn't the Patrol. It was a short, tubby individual who looked vaguely familiar, standing next to a shorter and tubbier woman who would have made Bartraselda look svelte. They were wearing ill-matched clothes that they'd obviously thrown on in a hurry, but they were still trying to give off an air of importance.

"Patrolman," the man said to me, "I am Commerce Commissioner Mandus Enkator. This is an intolerable situation for my wife and I, and all the Logie servants seem to be hiding from the storm. So it is necessary for me to commandeer yours. If you please."

It was an order not a request, made with an imperious gesture of his pudgy hand. I had no idea what his title meant in Collopolis, but he seemed to think it meant power. And arrogance. Then I saw Seliki's eyes narrow and her mouth tighten. And her reaction jogged my memory.

The first time I'd seen this pompous fatneck, he'd been kicking two Logies around in an alley. And one of them had been me.

"Forget it," I growled at him. "On your way."

He looked shocked by the disobedience. "Patrolman, I gave you an order!"

All the anger and frustration that had been swirling around within me over two days suddenly found that it had an outlet, and boiled over. I stepped towards the fat man and his lady, yanking my blazer out. The effect was slightly spoiled when the action dislodged my makeshift belt, so that I had to clutch hurriedly at my trousers. But the Commissioner didn't notice

– because I had rammed the muzzle of my blazer up under his nose.

"Don't *order* me, lardhead," I said in a vicious snarl. "I know you. You like hitting Logies who can't hit back. It makes you feel good. How good will you feel if I burn off your nose?"

"I . . . you . . . no . . ." he squealed. He had turned stark white, eyes bulging, fat hands waving feebly. He was too helpless even to torment enjoyably. So I stepped away, sneering.

"You'll get no Logie from me or anything else," I said. "Now take off. And as you go, you can explain to your wife about that ripe little romper who keeps you company when you work late at the office."

He managed to turn even paler at that, as his immense wife grabbed his arm. "Mandus?" she shrilled. "What does he mean? *Mandus!*"

I grinned nastily, seeing that I'd hit on the best possible revenge. But I didn't savour it for long. Because a squad of six Patrolmen chose that moment to come marching around the corner of the tunnel behind us.

And that would have been the end of everything – if I hadn't been wearing those trousers and boots.

"Good work, Patrolman!" barked the squad leader. "Netted a few more, eh?"

I flinched for only an instant, then caught myself and fell into the role. "Sir!" I said, lowering my gun respectfully.

His gaze fixed on me with a frown. "What happened to your tunic, lad?"

"I . . . ah . . ." My mind raced. "Gave it to an injured child, to keep her warm. Sir."

"Well done," the leader said, nodding. "But get a replacement soon as you can. Doesn't do to be out of uniform."

"Officer!" the Commissioner's lady shrilled, stepping up to the squad leader. "That man *threatened* my husband, who is Commerce Commissioner . . ."

It was the kind of diversion that I might have prayed for. It took the squad leader's attention entirely away from me, before he could think of any more awkward questions.

"I don't care who he is," the leader told the fat lady coldly.

"Orders are to round up all intruders. You're intruders. Talk to the commandant in the morning."

His men promptly aimed their weapons at the two fat people, which deflated them enough to silence them. The leader glanced with minimal interest at Moone and Jarli – ignoring Seliki, of course. And I felt deeply grateful that Moone's blazer was well out of sight, tucked into the back of his belt.

"Bring those two along, Patrolman," the leader said casually.

My mind had gone into overdrive, and I went with my luck before my nerve gave way. "Sorry, sir," I said, "but I'm ordered to take them to . . . to the comm facility. Doctor Rocdril wants them there."

The leader frowned at me, then at them – until the frown cleared when he realized who Jarli was. "I get it. She's what's-her-name, the vid kid, right? I heard something about her. Take 'em away, then, lad."

I turned away, pretending to aim my gun at Jarli and Moone, feeling crushed with disappointment that I hadn't provoked the leader into saying where the comm was located. But then he called after me.

"You better get that tunic first, Patrolman," he said. "Comm-link's in the central chamber, y'know. I hear the chamber's all sealed off – and Patrol guards there are shooting on sight, anything that looks like an intruder."

215

Chapter 25

"Maybe we oughta split up, Del," Moone suggested, "Jarli and me one way, you and Seliki another. *One* of us might get to the comm . . ."

I shook my head mournfully. It would have been the most sensible thing in the galaxy to let action-man Moone take on that near-impossible task. But it was pointless.

"Posi responds to my voice only," I said. "No one else can call her down."

"Is there some back way in to the central chamber?" Jarli asked, looking at Seliki hopefully. "Like the servants' routes in the Mansion?"

Seliki looked thoughtful. "There are small service tunnels around the inmost chamber. But they may be guarded too."

I sighed heavily. "It doesn't much matter. This is a simple equation. The centre of the Heart is heavily guarded – but we have to get into it, or try to." I looked at Moone and Jarli. "At least *I* have to try. With Seliki, so she can show me the way. They won't be likely to shoot a Logie. You two, though, had better wait here."

Moone seemed to choke up. He reached over to grip my shoulder wordlessly, in the way that some men do when in the throes of inexpressibly manly emotion. Even Jarli was wearing a peculiar expression.

"I . . . I think I've misjudged you, Del," she said softly.

It all startled me for a moment. Then I realized their mistake. They thought my suggestion that they stay behind was *heroic* – me volunteering to go on alone, unflinching against terrible odds, so that they might be spared. I suppose it happens that way on the vid often enough, but not in real life. Not in *my* real life, anyway. I didn't want to go on at all.

But, as I'd said, there was no choice. It had to be me who got to the comm-link. And I felt I had a chance, if I could make the partial uniform work for me again. But I'd have *no* chance trying to get into that inmost chamber in company with a beautiful vid-star and a young man in a weird uniform who had both been Rocdril's prisoners.

All the same, they insisted on coming along. Moone expressed several antiquated ideas about the dishonour of deserting a friend, while Jarli expressed a determination to stay with Moone. I saw there was no point in arguing, so didn't try – planning privately to ditch them in the tunnels if I could. I wish people could understand that if everyone was more realistic and self-serving, life would run a lot more smoothly.

By then Seliki looked like she wanted to hop up and down again, because we'd been hanging around at that one spot for too long. So we set off, heading deeper into the Hiatus Heart. Again Seliki and Moone led the way, with only brief hesitations at the nodes and crossings among the tunnels. Now and then we still saw other people, refugees from the city, wandering along looking lost and bewildered. But we avoided them fairly easily and pressed on.

By then I was fairly sure that the Patrol would be getting a grip on the riot. Which meant that more Patrolmen could soon come sweeping through the Complex to round up refugee stragglers. So we needed to hurry. And there was also a second reason for speed.

The storm in the distance sounded like its fury was still building. And I slowly came to realize as we moved along that the storm sounded louder because it was getting *closer*. So I'd been wrong about the Allness. He did want to scratch his itch inside as well as out. I got the idea that he was using his TK power to drag the storm down into the ruined city – and to hurl its lightnings, like shaped charges, directly against the Complex.

That assault, I realized, would drive people – including the

Patrol – deeper into the Complex, and faster. We might have another mob on our heels any moment.

And that was when we felt the first tremor.

It wasn't much more than the slight vibration that we sometimes felt with a particularly huge blast of thunder. Except that this time it happened between thunderclaps – like an eerie ripple of the ceramisteel floor. And Seliki looked at me with frightened eyes.

"Col-Logh extends his strength," she whispered. "He is shaking the solid rock of his own being."

Then another tremor followed, a bit stronger than the first. It brought a series of snaps and pops as the wall began to crack. And in the distance, behind us, we heard human voices faintly wailing and screaming.

So we stopped hesitating at intersections, and simply ran.

We were lucky, though perhaps it was also instinct and memory in Seliki. Just before I completely ran out of breath in that wild dash, she squeaked with relief and stopped in front of a low, narrow door. It didn't look as if it led anywhere I wanted to be – even when Seliki opened it to reveal a dusty little tunnel where two people my size might have walked abreast but two like Moone couldn't. Then Seliki pointed up, and in the dim light I saw a clutter of ducts and tubes and cables overhead. So we were in one of the service tunnels she'd mentioned, containing the conduits of power and air-conditioning and the rest.

As we crept into the tunnel, which curved away silent and empty ahead of us, I felt a new growth of hope. I couldn't believe that anyone would post guards in that grubby little passage. All we need now, I thought, is to find a door into the central . . .

My thought snapped like rotten string. Seliki, ahead of the rest of us around the curve, leaped backwards as if on elastic.

"A guard ahead!" she whispered. "By the first door that leads to the central chamber!"

The uprooting of my new hope left me crushed. But Moone stirred his shoulders, reaching for his gun.

"Gotta get rid of him," he muttered. "I'll just . . ."

Seliki made a sharp gesture. "He is armed and watchful, Myron Moone."

"And remember what that Patrolman said, Myron," Jarli added urgently. "They're shooting on sight. He might even shoot Del before he noticed the uniform trousers." He won't get the chance, I thought to myself firmly. But Jarli was going on. "*You* could get close to him," she said thoughtfully to Seliki.

Seliki took a step back, shaking her head in desperate negatives.

"She can't," I said hoarsely. "Logies have a thing about it. They don't do violence."

"Then it'll have to be me," Jarli said flatly.

"But he'll *shoot* . . .!" Moone began.

"No, he won't," Jarli said, her voice still flat. Then she startled us all.

In a few swift and graceful movements she kicked off her boots, unfastened her coverall and slipped out of it. Even in that desperate situation I was struck by her smooth shapeliness, by the effect of the tiny g-string around her hips which was more appealing somehow than total nudity.

"He won't shoot," she repeated. "He'll just gape, like Del is." I closed my mouth with a click, but didn't stop looking. "And when I get close, he'll want to grope."

"Jarli . . ." Moone started to protest.

"It's all right." She gave him an edgy smile. "Women have their own built-in reflexes in such situations. Just wait here."

She moved away, her slow stumbling walk imitating that of a dazed refugee from the city. As she started around the curve, the storm seemed to applaud her with a mighty roar of thunder, rolling through the tunnels, accompanied by another tremor underfoot that made her lurch authentically. Then she went out of our sight.

I heard a sudden rustle and a metallic click, as if someone was turning and aiming a heavy blazer. After a long moment of silence, I heard an ugly, throaty chuckle.

"Well, now," I heard a man's voice say. "Just lookit this."

"I . . . I'm lost," I heard Jarli say. She was a skilled performer, her voice sounding clogged with fright and bewilderment. "Can you . . . help me?"

219

"Sure I can, chicky," I heard the man say. "Just you jiggle them pretties along over here . . ."

There was another silence, which seemed to last for a month or two. Moone started to tense and I put a hand on his arm to keep him from leaping to the rescue. Then we all heard a new series of sounds. A stifled gasp, as if someone was sneezing with mouth and nose held tightly shut. Followed by a smack of flesh on flesh, and a cut-off cry like the croak of a Fonomerish ice-duck. And finally the unmistakable sound of a body hitting the floor.

"All clear," Jarli called softly. At once Moone sprang around the corner, with Seliki and me right behind him.

A Patrolman lay on the floor, doubled up next to his dropped blazer, with Jarli standing over him serenely. "He started getting busy with his hands, as I expected," she said. "So I brought my knee up, then got him with my elbow in the throat."

She began to pull on her clothes, which Moone had brought to her, but for once I wasn't watching. I'd crouched by the Patrolman, whose hands were clutching his groin and whose face had turned an unappetising purple. He looked dead, but moving closer I could hear the breath rasping past his mangled larynx. I stood up, trying to manage a nod of approval for Jarli, trying not to remember that not too long before, *I* had been trying to "get busy with my hands" on her person. It's the kind of thing that can put a man off.

Seliki stepped up to the door that the man had been guarding, which once again offered a small glassteel viewpanel. I joined her, peering through the panel with some nervousness. But our luck was holding. The door was situated behind some nice large cabinets and banks of equipment, yet there were spaces enough between the cabinets to give us a fairly good view of the whole central chamber. Where things looked even more horrible than before.

It was the fault of the storm, of course. All that unrestrained lightning and everything, crashing around, along with the mountain's own immense neuronic activity pulsing through the crystalline rock around us. Even the technology was affected, so that we could see plenty of flickering and wavering on the display screens of the consoles that were visible to us. Now and then the light from the huge Tropica-Lens above the central area did some flickering of its own. But far more than that, it seemed that *living* circuits were being badly troubled.

My own permanent Colloghi headache had been thumping away worse than ever since the storm began, even through the moments of tension and terror. The view through that window panel showed far worse effects being felt by those naked brains with their sprouting electrodes.

All of the wretched victims were sweating and trembling, moaning and whimpering, like tormented beasts. Some had lost motor functions, and were sitting or lying in contorted postures, twitching. Those who could still move were staggering or crawling here and there, as erratic as insects on a hot plate, seeking some escape from their torture.

I saw a few Patrolmen standing around looking alert and edgy, but not many. Probably most of the ones from inside the core chamber had been posted at its doors, like the man Jarli had felled, to fend off wandering refugees from the city. I also saw several of Rocdril's medics rushing around trying to do something for the victims, but mostly looking helpless and panicky.

Then Seliki touched my arm and pointed, towards a spot some way around the curving outside wall from where our door stood. And I felt suddenly breathless as if I'd been kicked in the stomach.

Seliki was pointing at some unmistakable hardware – a brand-new Linefinder comm-link facility. It was set slightly apart from the main scenes of activity, with plenty of big consoles and things around it to provide cover for anyone trying to sneak up to it.

But we didn't dare to try. What Seliki had really been pointing at was the two people standing at the comm. I'd hoped they would still be at the Mansion, but my luck didn't seem to have reached that far. One of them was Rocdril, looking fierce and a bit frantic as he surveyed the open central area of the chamber where the tormented bare-brains were mostly gathered.

And with him, fiddling with the comm, a blazer at his hip and cold fury in his eyes, was Pulvidon.

Chapter 26

It didn't take much thought to work out that Pulvidon was probably making a call to Famlio, maybe to get some help to clean up the mess. He would have realized that the destruction of Collopolis, and probably of the outer Complex, would require at least a temporary close-down of Hiatus. Maybe its removal to another planet, while everything was being rebuilt. And I was aware that I shouldn't be around when a clean-up squad arrived from Famlio. Because one of the things they would want to clean up would be me.

Yet my – our – only route to safety lay through a comm-link call to Posi. And Pulvidon was in the way. In fact it looked as if he was having trouble with the comm. His fingers kept stabbing at the controls, his eyes growing more livid with rage. I could imagine the kind of interference that the mountain was producing.

Moone and Jarli had also had a look through the panel, and were looking at me hopefully as if waiting for a brilliant idea.

"I could go in and distract them, draw them away from there," Moone suggested.

"And get yourself killed," Jarli snapped. "No chance."

In fact I thought it was a great idea. A nice soldierly diversion by Moone. He was probably skilled enough even to stay alive until I'd made my call. But Jarli wasn't going to let her hero go – and beyond that I had no ideas at all.

Until the screaming started.

It followed a frighteningly powerful blast of thunder, and

presumably lightning, back in the outer Complex. Along with a good strong tremor in the rock that made us stagger. But the phenomena made far worse things happen beyond our door.

The screaming burst out in the open central area, among a knot of twitching bare-brains. I also saw smoke pouring from some of the machines where their connections had shorted or fused. So had the connections in the bare-brains.

Many more collapsed in crumpled heaps, threshing uncontrollably. But others were driven into frenzied action – and the frenzy rapidly spread. Some attacked the brain-drain machines, lashing out with fists and feet that were soon torn and bleeding. Others reeled wildly around, flailing and screaming, attacking each other, biting and clawing with terrible strength in their mania. If medics or Patrolmen tried to intervene, the maddened creatures would attack them just as wildly. The scene was rapidly becoming a nightmare, splashed with blood and echoing with screams. Around us the storm seemed to bellow louder than ever, the rock heaved and quaked more furiously, which just made things worse.

Except for me – because it gave me all the diversion I needed. I saw Rocdril stare at the chaos with something like desperation, then stride away from the comm to help get things under control. Pulvidon stayed, but he seemed to have made the link, for he was talking fast, his eyes fixed on the screen in front of him.

It was the best chance I'd have. I touched the gun at my back for luck, patted Seliki's bottom for more luck. "Right," I said. "Time to go in. See you in a while."

"I'm comin' with you," Moone said manfully.

"We're all coming," Jarli said, sounding the way Seliki looked – scared but determined. "You're our only chance to get out of here, Del. We can't let you go alone."

I wanted to scream and throw things. The storm raging around us was overshadowed by the rage that filled me. I had to go in to the comm-link, which would be terrifying – but it would be far worse going in leading a parade. They would get in my way, they would give me away. They would . . .

I stopped, as a bright light went on in my mind, an idea that

I knew they would accept because it was Moone who had first thought of it.

"Right," I said tersely, "we'll all go. But we split up. I'm going around the perimeter to the comm *this* way – " I pointed left " – so Moone, you take the others around *that* way. If there's anyone at the comm when you reach it – anyone *aside* from me – do what you have to do."

By which I meant pick them off from hiding. Moone would probably challenge them to single combat, though, I thought.

"We can handle it, Del," Moone said sturdily.

Seliki moved close to me. "I go with you, Del Curb. Do not send me away."

I nodded, thinking of how she had promised that Logies would die for me if they had to, and gave her a thin smile. She smiled back, and patted *my* bottom.

Then we pushed open the door and slipped silently into the madhouse.

The noise around us was unbelievable. Screaming and howling and moaning, the yells of Patrolmen and medics struggling with crazed bare-brains, the crackle and fizz of short-circuiting machinery. Along with the extra dimension of the much closer eruptions of the storm, and the bass throbbing of the quaking rock. We had crept in on hands and knees, ducking behind some cabinets near our door. But I felt that we could have marched in with a Macilectinal drum-and-fireflash band, and no one would have noticed.

I nodded quickly at the others, evaded Moone's attempt at some more manly shoulder-gripping, and moved away to the left. I kept safely behind the banks of equipment which stood around that part of the perimeter, crouching low or crawling on hands and knees, waiting and peering around and double-checking before whisking across any exposed gaps between consoles. Only a short distance away, in the open centre, the bare-brains went on going uninhibitedly insane and no one noticed me for an instant.

Glancing behind, I saw that Seliki was staring around with amazement and some fright, but coming along steadily in my wake in a compact little crouch. The other two had vanished, to follow their own wider circle around the perimeter in the other direction. Fervently hoping that Moone wouldn't shoot me if I got to the comm first, I kept grimly on.

Around us, the different kinds of storms kept on worsening. At one point I glanced through a narrow gap between cabinets and saw a human female bare-brain, wild-eyed and shrieking, who had unslung the metal case that she had carried, and had ripped the electrodes from her brain. With blood streaming from the top of her head, she was clutching the electrodes and swinging the case like a flail – lashing out at a Patrolman, with a medic already flattened at her feet. Until something – blood loss, or a bursting in her brain – halted her, and she stiffened and toppled backwards.

As the Patrolman moved in on her, more scenes like that one were happening all around. Meanwhile other Patrolmen and medics were being diverted to shut down sizzling, smouldering machinery that had been blown out by the power surges. But I didn't watch any longer. I crawled on, suffering my own torments from the noise, jolts of static electricity from the metal I touched, and my grinding headache.

It then was beyond doubt that the Allness was guiding the storm deeper into the Complex without diminishing its strength – probably maintaining and reinforcing it with his own electrical forces. So the storm wasn't going to die down in a natural fashion. Not until the Allness had thoroughly scratched his centuries-old itch. I began to feel anxious about how we would survive when or if we went out of the Complex to be picked up by Posi.

But one worry at a time, I told myself. And the first was Pulvidon, at the comm.

Only, when I got a chance to look, I saw that he no longer was.

Maybe he'd finished his call, and had also had enough of the riotous insanity in the central area. Anyway, he was on his feet, striding fiercely away from the comm, drawing his blazer as he went. Perhaps he was about to start wiping out bare-brains. I never found out.

Around me there was a brief and terrible pause. Not in the

shrieks of the crazies and all that, but in the storm. But it didn't come as a relief. It was like that previous, awesome gathering of power before the shattering of the dome.

And then the release. An outpouring of force like some final cataclysm. Thunder seemed to enter the chamber and stalk around like an invisible giant, with electricity crackling around it. The rock below me boomed with the effort of a monstrous rolling heave – not just a tremor this time but a full-fledged quake. The floor split and buckled, ruined machinery was flung in every direction with crashes and explosions. Above, the great Tropica-Lens jerked and leaped, growing dim for a second.

I dropped flat, arms wrapped around my head, knees drawn up, waiting for something to fall and crush me. Then the floor settled, the rock fell silent, and every bare-brain in the central area started to scream even louder than before.

And the only thing out of all that destruction that landed on me was a small piece of wire – but red-hot, searing my bare back and bringing me up with a choked yell. But only to my knees. And reaching for my blazer in case I was spotted.

But I wasn't. There was no one looking at me, no one near me. No one at all. Because where Seliki had been, I saw nothing but a pile of smashed and smoking metal.

I didn't do anything foolish, like go back and dig into the rubble to try to find her. I just turned and went on. It was what I had to do. I felt it was what she would have wanted me to do.

I was crawling again, on hands and knees, trying to ignore the pain when I crawled over a sharp edge of broken metal. I could hear someone making a steady noise like a gasping whimper, until I realized it was me, and stopped. I found that my crawling was being impeded because when I had drawn my blazer I had dislodged my flimsy belt, and my trousers were slipping down again. So I wasted a moment retying the belt and jamming the gun into it again at the back.

I also wasted other necessary moments stopping to clear chunks of ruined technology out of my way. I was paying almost no attention now to other parts of the chamber around me. The maddened bare-brains were still screaming, the storm was still erupting, but I ignored them. I had no idea where Moone and Jarli were, or Pulvidon, or anyone. I didn't even know if the comm was still in one piece. But I knew where it was, and I was unswervingly, single-mindedly going there.

As I crawled along, my hands and knees were being lacerated by shards of metal. But I wasn't feeling that pain, or the magnified throbbing in my head, or much else. Except a wild delight when I saw that the comm was unoccupied and its lights and dials undimmed. Despite the rubble of other machines around it, it was operational.

Taking a deep breath, I started jabbing buttons and pressing keys. As I did so, the light in the whole chamber faded for a moment. I peered up at the huge Tropica-Lens, shading my eyes, worrying about a possible power failure before I'd got through to Posi. And I saw that it wasn't the power lines but the Lens itself that was in trouble. The last, biggest quake had sheared away some of its supports. It was swaying slowly above the mass of figures in the central area – and it looked as if there wasn't much left to hold it up.

I felt a rush of panic. If the Lens gave way ... How could I get out of that chamber in total darkness, surrounded by homicidal maniacs, Patrolmen, storms, earthquakes, and Pulvidon? But I tried to control that anxiety as the comm made a connection – crackly, fading in and out – with Posi.

"Hello, Del." She sounded subdued, depressed, not her usual cheery self at all. But her condition was not my concern right then.

"Posi, get down to the spaceport, *fast!*" I told her, in a kind of strangled yell.

"That is not possible, Del," she said mournfully. "I had hoped that you would be safely down on the ice-floes. With the Logh-uy."

"Ice-floes?" I echoed, nerves twanging. "What are you talking about? I'm in the Heart of the Complex, with Moone and everyone. And we're heading for the spaceport *now*."

"You must not, Del. The earthquakes created by Col-Logh have broken away much of the plateau – taking the spaceport and some of the city with it. And I cannot pick you up even

227

with the Magnigrip. The power surges from the storm and Col-Logh's own electro-magnetic output could dangerously affect my own neural circuits if I ventured too close."

Panic stormed through me as I stared at the comm. But then desperation brought the germ of an idea winking into life.

"Posi, is there any way you can *stop* the mountain doing all this?"

"I wish there were, Del," she said sadly, making the reason for her gloomy tone clear to me. "I had not foreseen, when I put to him your idea of scratching his itch, that he would do it so destructively. Now I feel responsible. But he is *enjoying* himself, Del, and will not stop. It seems that scratching a long-standing itch provides the keenest pleasure."

The germ of an idea took root and blossomed. "Listen, Posi – it's not *you* that should feel responsible." It may sound silly, talking about guilt feelings to an Intelloid. But I know Posi. "It's the mountain, Posi. He's responsible – and when he calms down, he's going to feel *terrible*. Because he's *killing people*, Posi, not just smashing things. If he keeps this storm and the earthquakes going, he'll kill us *all*." There was a fervour and urgency in my voice that was one hundred per cent sincere. "Talk to him, Posi. Make him see. Tell him that if he goes on he'll be a *mass murderer*. Tell him that if he has that on his conscience, it'll be a lot worse than an itch – and he'll suffer from it forever!"

I had no idea whether a sentient mountain would have a conscience or would even understand the concept. I had no real idea if Posi had, or would. But after one of her infinitesimal pauses for consideration, her reply sounded a bit more optimistic.

"I will tell him, Del," she said. "Perhaps I can make him understand."

"I hope ..." I began. But the hope never got expressed. Around me the floor heaved and rolled as another earthquake shook it like a blanket. A new detonation of thunder erupted, and with it came another mighty burst of lightning like a thousand laser-cannon fired at once. The lightning bolt blasted in through a doorway, lancing horizontally across the central area, striking the brain-drain machines and blowing them into molecules. I was flung back and away, watching other machines around me explode into flame as if in sympathy, as their circuits overloaded. A spitting crackle and wisps of smoke came from within the comm as its interior melted. Above, over all the other noise, I heard a pitiful metallic groan from the giant Tropica-Lens as it swayed on its last support, its light flickering.

I stared around wildly. One or two more assaults like that, and it would be the end of the Complex. I had to get out – but I didn't know how or where. With minimal interest I saw that Rocdril and his people had been winning against the bare-brained crazies while I'd been busy with the comm. The open central area was now mostly clear, and a lot of the more mobile maniacs were being herded into a corner. But as I watched, a group of the frothing, bulging-eyed bare-brains broke loose from the circle of Patrolmen and medics.

In the furthest reaches of agonized frenzy, many of them snatched up shards of metal as weapons. They seemed oblivious to the gashes in their hands and feet from the sharp-edged metal, indifferent to the bursts of sparks and flames around them. In one tightly packed group, as if with one maddened intent, driven on by one savagely vengeful desire, they all sprang forward together.

At their principal tormentor. Rocdril.

He tried to turn and run, but the maniacs were on him with unnatural speed and strength. Their hands grasped, tore, twisted, flung him down. And they swarmed over him as he fell, hands rising and falling, metal shards coming up red and dripping and striking down again.

Sick and terrified, I looked away. And saw Pulvidon, some distance away from that grisly execution, blazer in hand, staring around like a hunted animal. For a moment he paused in the middle of the cleared central area, as if trying to select his safest way out.

In that same fractured moment, everything went suddenly, impossibly quiet. The storm went into a lull, the lunatic bare-brains fell silent, staring down at the scarlet mess that was all that was left of Rocdril. Even the fizzing and crackling of ruined machinery seemed to die down.

In that exact micro-instant when the silence was full and complete, as if perfectly timed for the worst possible effect, Moone stood up from behind a blackened console, and called my name.

And Jarli behind him, looking pale and a bit frantic, but with her mini-camera strapped to her forehead again.

As I looked towards them, horrified, I saw on the edge of my vision that Pulvidon was whirling around in a blur of speed. In the same movement he snapped a shot at Moone – who went tumbling backwards as if he'd been hit.

And then Pulvidon saw me.

Too late, I realized that the last quake had flung aside a lot of the machinery that had been screening me at the comm. I was almost fully exposed. As if in slow motion, Pulvidon swung his blazer around to train it on me. His savage grin seemed to fill my vision as his finger tightened on the firing stud.

Yet oddly in that final moment I was not paralysed with terror – but galvanized by a kind of weird anger. Maybe it was that carnivore grin, which I'd seen too often before. Maybe it was the sheer unfairness, that I should go down that way after struggling so painfully to escape. Whatever it was that produced it, an all-consuming rage took hold of me as if I'd run amok. I reached back to snatch out my own blazer, while starting to lunge towards the meagre shelter of a broken cabinet some paces away.

I never made it.

When I yanked my blazer free, I managed to tear away my makeshift belt. Before I could aim my gun, my trousers fell around my ankles.

As they tripped me, I toppled forward – just as Pulvidon fired.

His blazer bolt seared harmlessly over my head. Then as I struck the floor, the jolt made me hit the firing stud of my own gun. Its bolt speared almost straight up, nowhere near Pulvidon at all.

But it sliced with accidentally perfect precision through the last, straining support that held up the Tropica-Lens.

There was a grinding and a snapping, then the rush of air

that comes when an enormously heavy object falls some distance. Though I was dazed from my own fall and the near-miss, I was able to see that Pulvidon, at the last, was quick enough to look up. But not quick enough to get out of the way.

The Lens crashed down on top of him, and exploded into a billion pieces as if pretending to be a proto-particle bomb.

None of the fragments struck me, where I lay. But the force of the explosion seemed to bounce me up off the floor, then painfully down again. Or maybe that was another earthquake. As I landed, I must have struck my head heavily – for in the blackness that followed the destruction of the Lens I felt that I had slid into a blackness of my own, a numbing, blinding mist.

As I drifted away into it, I had the weird feeling that someone was wrapping me in a soft, warm blanket. Then my mist thickened, and I could no longer feel anything at all.

Chapter 27

"Del? Del? Are you awake, Del?"

I heard the question, recognized Posi's voice and even knew the answer. I was awake, though I wasn't happy about it. I had the dim idea that I was on ClustAlph, and that I'd tripped over my trousers in my cabin and hit my head. There'd probably be an image of Pulvidon on the vidscreen, I thought fuzzily, and I should get up and look. But my head was hurting too much, too many other parts of me were aching in close harmony, and my mouth tasted like an Obbigharic sulphur-fungus. I wanted some gentle medication and some more sleep. I didn't want to talk to Posi.

"*Del?*" Posi's voice was growing insistent. I knew it would just go on doing so unless I managed to silence her.

"Lemme alone," I mumbled, feeling that my tongue was enlarged by several sizes.

"I need your instructions, Del," Posi said firmly. "Are we to remain on the ice-floes, or should I return to orbit?"

"*Ice . . .?*" I grunted, half-rolling over. The movement sent sharp flares of pain through my knees as well as my head – which combined with the reference to ice to jolt sections of my brain into gear. I was in my cabin, but I definitely was *not* on ClustAlph. Memory flooded back in a tidal gush, ending with the monumental collapse of the Tropica-Lens and the thump of my head against the floor.

I sat up slowly, which made me even more aware of the after-effects of that thump. "How did I get here?"

And Posi filled me in, as crisply as she could manage. She told me that it was nearly a full bio-day since that final catastrophe in the Hiatus Heart. I surmised that after the blow to my head, all the tension and physical effort of that long night had taken a toll. I had stayed asleep, while a great many things happened.

I learned that the soft warmth that had enveloped me at the end hadn't been an illusion. It had been Seliki. The pile of metal had fallen just in front of her, cutting her off from me. When she managed to find a way round it, she'd come after me, just as my shot brought down the Lens.

By then, Posi said, Jarli and Moone had also forced their way to where I lay. Pulvidon's shot had only grazed Moone's shoulder, not seriously – so he slung me heroically over the other shoulder and still managed to flatten three Patrolmen on the way out of the chamber. Then he and Seliki got us all out of the Complex, into what was left of the city.

Meanwhile Posi had managed to get through to the Allness along the lines I'd suggested. She said defensively that he hadn't considered the effect on flesh and blood of his itch-scratching urge to wreck the city and the Complex. And that he was sorry. Posi added that despite his almost immeasurable intelligence, he has been isolated on a backwater planet for all of his existence and so is a bit impractical and innocent in some ways.

Anyway, as the four of us left the Complex the storm and earthquakes and power surges had ended. With the electrical interference over, Posi was able to spot us on her ceptors and swooped down and hauled us all in with the Magnigrip. Then she headed down to land on the ice-floes. Where we all still were, she added. And then she told me that the human survivors up on the shattered plateau had found a working comm-link in the city and had called the SenFed for help. Should we wait, Posi asked, for the authorities to arrive?

We should *not*, I told her quickly. I could imagine what would happen when the authorities had a look around the Hiatus Heart. Many questions would start to be asked. And somewhere in the Heart was a certain twenty-first century stasis pod, which would raise other awkward questions. I preferred to be elsewhere when that happened.

So I got up and tottered out to the control area – and found Seliki there. I was pleased to see her. I was even more pleased to find that she had my clothes and things, which had been brought to her by Logies who'd gone up to look for survivors in the ruins of the Mansion. I hadn't looked forward to the cost of replacing all my mini-weapons.

I felt a little awkward with her, though. Not wanting to be too abrupt, yet not wanting to linger. Typically, she saw my problem and understood.

"I have stayed to be sure you are well, Del Curb," she said gently. "Now we can say our farewells."

"Yes . . . well . . ." I muttered. "There's so much to do . . ."

"I know." She hugged me with her usual rib-straining fierceness. "Will you ever come back, when the things are done? Will you visit me?"

"If you like," I said, feeling oddly pleased.

"You will always be welcome," she told me. "The Logh-uy owe you a great deal. And I . . ." She looked at me with a fondly wicked smile. "I will always have the jwryll ready for you."

So, not too long after that, we lifted off. I suppose Posi had made her own tender farewells to the Allness. She hadn't got religion, as I had thought, but she'd got *something*. In her own Intelloid way, Posi was in love.

But she would be keeping in touch with the mountain through her call-beam. In fact, everyone seemed to be keeping in touch with everyone, except me. Moone and Jarli were in the other cabin keeping in what seemed to be permanent touch. Wound or not, the young man was inexhaustible. Even after we lifted off, for two more bio-days they didn't seem to eat or sleep – or even pause for a breather, as far as I could tell from the noises through the cabin door. I suppose you get that way if you're a young primitive who hasn't seen a woman for centuries.

So I was left alone, feeling peaceful enough as my injuries began to heal. Then Jarli untangled herself from Moone and suggested rather bossily that we head for the planet Cibiess,

234

where her network had its HQ. When we got there, she promised ominously, things would start happening.

But, on Colloghi, things were already happening. The SenFed people with the FedPol had arrived. All the poor bare-brains who were still alive were carried off to various institutions, while the surviving citizens of Collopolis were taken to refuges on other planets. Where they professed total shock and amazement at what had been going on Hiatus all the while.

Naturally, outsiders knew little about it all, at first. The authorities kept it all carefully under wraps. There were too many important people from important worlds among those mind-blasted bare-brains. It was all greatly embarrassing for officialdom, as any major crime or scandal involving the rich and powerful always is.

But then we reached Cibiess, Jarli's network swiftly and neatly edited her films into a two-hour spectacular, and blasted their rival networks off the vidscreen. The shock waves from that show are still being felt around the galaxy now, long after. Though for me they are mostly only comforting ripples.

By exposing the long-standing conspiracy of Hiatus, Jarli's film ensured that none of the surviving conspirators got anything remotely like fair trials. But only hair-splitting legal types demurred. In my view, the criminals got off lightly. Even Bartraselda, who had emerged from sheltering in the Mansion cellars just in time to be arrested. I'd hoped for a suitable punishment for her, like herding the slime-mammoths on Ilcrastafan. Instead, she was just put away for life on a prison asteroid in the Ficotarius system, where I've heard she is already a dominant force among the inmates. And her Marshal, Enni Slar, along with assorted Patrolmen and Hiatus medics, got only the comparative wrist-slap of ten years or so each on another asteroid. There really is no justice.

At least Rocdril had been properly punished. And Pulvidon too. The Tropica-Lens had not only crushed him, its fragments had shredded him like small glass bullets. The only way the FedPol was sure that it was him was by those carnivorous teeth.

Famlio itself also suffered badly, after Jarli's film was shown

– and many times repeated. It offered proof of the organization's involvement, and the FedPol wept with joy and started making arrests – backed up by the powerful and vengeful families of the bare-brain victims. It won't be the end of Famlio, since organizations like that can't be destroyed. But it'll be smaller, poorer and keeping its head down for a long time.

And that's good news for me, since when it starts an upswing again it'll have new top men who won't remember or care anything about me. So now I can enjoy myself, bask in peace and quiet and quite a lot of fame.

It's probably due to Jarli's editors, rather than the Heart-throb herself. They wanted a good story, and for a good story you need more than villains, which were plentiful on Colloghi. You need a *hero*. And I was it.

I've watched that film many times, and I always marvel at how much Jarli managed to get, and how smoothly the editors improved it. Especially that final moment, where it looks as if I deliberately dived beneath Pulvidon's shot, then with deadly accuracy blasted away the Lens support to finish everything off. Still, that's not *too* far from how it happened.

So things are going well for me now. The media attention helped when the FedPol came asking their questions, since they decided they didn't need to press me too hard about Moone's pod. And the fame is also compensating me for the loss of Moone. The network lawyers took about seven minutes to blow holes like craters in my contract with him. He's all Jarli's now, and they're doing well on the profitable celebrity-and-curiosity circuit. Moone's credentials were well established by Jarli's film – and the pod, which her network acquired from the FedPol.

Moone seemed upset about the shattering of our contract, so he gave me a sort of farewell present. Out of that metal case from the pod. It's a tiny, teardrop-shaped object that you put in your ear. Activated, it plays – endlessly – a micro-bead recording of music. Quite advanced, I suppose, for the twenty-first century – I mean the technology, not the music. The bead offers singing by a group of musicians, apparently popular then, which sounds like the unharmonized love-howl of the five-sexed Plotobial sand-weevils. It was no loss when I sold the thing for a staggering sum to a museum on SenFed Central. I've since heard that Moone has *given* some of his other artefacts to museums here and there. I'll never understand the primitive mentality.

On the subject of primitives, things are going well now also for the true owners of Colloghi, who I must remember to call the Logh-uy. By now every remnant of human existence has been cleared off the mountain, and the Logies – Logh-uy – are back living on the ice-floes, with their lives much changed. Since Jarli's film showed them – in the person of Seliki – to be a long way from beasts, the SenFed embarrassedly checked, confirmed that they are sentient and awarded them associate status in the Federation. With the promise of full membership when their cultural levels allow.

And I had a bit of fun stirring up the public servants, by giving Posi an idea which she passed on to Col-Logh, the Allness. SenFed experts are now tying themselves in knots trying to work out whether, constitutionally, a sentient mountain can apply for SenFed membership as a species in his own right.

Otherwise, the Logh-uy live at peace, serving no masters, taking what they need from the sea as they always have. And earning a bit from tourism, when folk who've seen Jarli's film come along to gawp at the world where it happened. But no one stays. The Logh-uy don't want off-worlder residents, ever again, and they have the SenFed to back them up. Besides, it's a cold and inhospitable world.

Though it had its moments, for me. In fact, since I have some free time and a healthy Fedbank account, I'm thinking of heading that way again, following up on Seliki's invitation. I keep thinking about a repeat performance of that time I spent with her, driven on to undreamed-of lengths by the aphrodisiac jwryll.

Besides, I want a word with Seliki on a related matter. I hear rumours that the Logh-uy have been picking up some nice extra income by *exporting* jwryll. In very small and exclusive quantities, at exorbitant prices. I'm impressed with their new-found marketing skills, and with the apparent size of their takings. But I'm also annoyed.

After all, as the liberator of Colloghi and the hero of Hiatus, I really feel that they ought to be cutting me in.